## The funeral is off . . .

"Saw the flowers in A. Who we got?" Odell's gaze settled on the corpse. "Great gobs o' hog lard! That's Bobby Saxon." Odell rubbed the top of his bald head and spotted the casket waiting for Bobby. "An Exquisite. Good job, Callie. I know Doofus didn't sell that."

Odell barely paused for breath before adding, "What are you doing, Callie?"

"There's something in his neck," I said and pulled on the forceps. A broken hypodermic needle slid out.

"Doofus, did you break a needle off in him?" Odell demanded from Otis.

"It's not mine. Didn't even use a hypodermic on him," Otis answered.

"I'll call the sheriff," Odell said. "Phone the florists and caterer. Everything's on hold."

# A Tisket, a Tasket, a Fancy Stolen Casket

## FRAN RIZER

BERKLEY PRIME CRIME, NEW YORK

**THE BERKLEY PUBLISHING GROUP**
Published by the Penguin Group
**Penguin Group (USA) Inc.**
**375 Hudson Street, New York, New York 10014, USA**

Penguin Group (Canada), 90 Eglinton Avenue East, Suite 700, Toronto, Ontario M4P 2Y3, Canada
(a division of Pearson Penguin Canada Inc.)
Penguin Group Ltd., 80 Strand, London WC2R 0RL, England
Penguin Group Ireland, 25 St. Stephen's Green, Dublin 2, Ireland (a division of Penguin Books Ltd.)
Penguin Group (Australia), 250 Camberwell Road, Camberwell, Victoria 3124, Australia
(a division of Pearson Australia Group Pty. Ltd.)
Penguin Books India Pvt. Ltd., 11 Community Centre, Panchsheel Park, New Delhi—110 017, India
Penguin Group (NZ), 67 Apollo Drive, Rosedale, North Shore 0745, Auckland, New Zealand
(a division of Pearson New Zealand Ltd.)
Penguin Books (South Africa) (Pty.) Ltd., 24 Sturdee Avenue, Rosebank, Johannesburg 2196,
South Africa

Penguin Books Ltd., Registered Offices: 80 Strand, London WC2R 0RL, England

This is a work of fiction. Names, characters, places, and incidents either are the product of the author's imagination or are used fictitiously, and any resemblance to actual persons, living or dead, business establishments, events, or locales is entirely coincidental. The publisher does not have any control over and does not assume any responsibility for author or third-party websites or their content.

A TISKET, A TASKET, A FANCY STOLEN CASKET

A Berkley Prime Crime Book / published by arrangement with the author

PRINTING HISTORY
Berkley Prime Crime mass-market edition / October 2007

Copyright © 2007 by Fran Rizer.
Cover art by Sawsan Chalabi.
Cover design by Rita Frangie.
Interior text design by Laura K. Corless.

ISBN: 978-0-425-21800-6

BERKLEY® PRIME CRIME
Berkley Prime Crime Books are published by The Berkley Publishing Group,
a division of Penguin Group (USA) Inc.,
375 Hudson Street, New York, New York 10014.
The name BERKLEY PRIME CRIME and the BERKLEY PRIME CRIME design are trademarks
belonging to Penguin Group (USA) Inc.

PRINTED IN THE UNITED STATES OF AMERICA

10  9  8  7  6  5  4  3  2  1

*For Granny, Grandpapa, Nathan, Adam, and Aeden*

# Acknowledgments

Special thanks to special people: Jeff Gerecke, agent; Katie Day, editor; and Gwen Hunter, mentor. I also appreciate the support, encouragement, and suggestions from "my" writers' group—Jay Gross, Leonard Jolley, Ray Wade, and Larry Walker.

# Chapter One

**E**ager to pump up my new underwear, I dashed into my apartment just as the phone rang. The machine answered with my message, "Callie here. Talk."

"This is Otis," I heard my boss say. "I know it's your day off, but Odell's in Columbia at the South Carolina Association of Undertakers meeting, and we've got a client." He cleared his throat. "Bobby Saxon drowned this morning."

I grabbed the cordless. "Bobby Saxon?"

"Yes, Bobby Saxon."

"Good grief. I need to call my brother John. Bobby was his best friend when they were teenagers. What happened?" I emptied the Victoria's Secret bag on the counter.

"Maid found him dead in the pool at the Sleep Easy Inn. Guess he got drunk again, fell in, and drowned."

"That's an unattended accidental death, so you won't need me right away. There'll be an autopsy, won't there?" I held my new bra up to my chest and carried the telephone into the bedroom so I could look at myself in the mirror. The bra wasn't impressive over the T-shirt.

"Nope, no autopsy. That idiot coroner signed Bobby Saxon's death off as an accident with no investigation at all. Sheriff Harmon's furious."

"I'll be there as soon as I change clothes," I said.

"Make it fast. The widow's on the way over here to make plans."

I pressed the phone disconnect, glanced at the mirror again, and remembered how many times I'd heard my daddy say, "The good Lord gave the men in the Parrish family all the brains and the women big knockers." When I developed, he added, "Seems like He gave Calamine some of both and not a whole lot of either."

Growing up with five older brothers, I knew lots of men love great big . . . well, Daddy calls 'em knockers and my brothers call 'em hooters. My best friend Jane calls 'em headlights. Can't quite figure that out, especially since Jane is blind and has never even *seen* a headlight.

Jane was one reason I'd been shopping. Her cups runneth over, but for mine to run over, they'd have to be demitasse cups.

No way am I going under the knife for implants and risk all those complications, so on my day off from my job as cosmetologist at Middleton's Mortuary, I drove the hour-long trip to Victoria's Secret in Charleston. Bought myself an inflatable push-up bra.

The sales clerk showed me how to operate the small, detachable pump and said, "Increase the size gradually, a little each day, to let people get used to your growth." I don't have a boyfriend since moving back to St. Mary, so I figured no one would notice if my bosom were growing. Let folks think I was developing at age thirty-two.

I put the new bra on the bed, dropped my jeans and racer-back tee on the floor, and pulled a black dress from my closet. People don't necessarily wear dark colors to funerals anymore, but the Middleton twins make black dresses a requirement of my job. No pants. Not even skirts. Black dresses.

Otis had sounded nervous. Probably pacing while he waited for me. I tried, I promise I tried to resist, but I couldn't keep myself from taking the time to inflate the new bra a tiny bit with its cute little pump. I fastened the garment on, turned sideways toward the mirror to admire my slight chest increase, pulled on the black dress, then sleeked my strawberry blonde hair into a bun. I ran out, jumped in my '66 Mustang, and sped toward Middleton's.

When I arrived, I found Otis standing in the open doorway staring out between the big white columns. Wooden rocking chairs and clay pots of seasonal flowers create an old-fashioned feeling of southern tradition on the veranda, which wraps around the front and both sides of the building. Those rockers and flowers always gave me a warm, fuzzy feeling until I heard an out-of-towner say the rocking chairs reminded her of waiting for service at the Cracker Barrel. Kinda stole some of my pleasure.

Originally, the Middleton family lived on the second floor of the huge two-story clapboard house, but for the past fifteen years, the upstairs has been used for storage. Business occupies the downstairs, with kitchen, restrooms, offices, refrigeration area, preparation facilities, consulting parlors, and three slumber rooms.

No one sleeps in a slumber room. That's a euphemism for the area where a casketed body is displayed for visitation or a wake. Like folks really believe the people in those caskets are just sleeping.

When I saw Otis standing at the door, I pulled into a regular parking space at the front even though I have an assigned spot beside the loading dock near the employee entrance in the back.

Acorns from the ancient live oak trees made little plopping sounds on the rag-top roof of my Mustang. Autumn. My favorite season. St. Mary is beautiful year-round, with Spanish moss draping twisted tree limbs, but I love fall. I've lived on the South Carolina coast most of my life, but I don't like extreme heat, and I hate being sweaty.

I parked and walked toward Otis, who met me halfway on the steps. "Callie," he said, "I'm glad you're here. I tried to reach you on your cell, but, as usual, you didn't have it on. There's no reason for us to supply you with a phone if we can't use it to reach you. Bobby's wife called and said she's coming right over to make arrangements." Otis adjusted his tie, which was already perfectly aligned, and brushed a speck of invisible lint from his immaculate black suit jacket. Soft organ music played "How Great Thou Art" as we entered. At Middleton's, pressing the doorbell or opening an outside door sets off recorded hymns and gospel music.

"If Bobby Saxon drowned, why no autopsy?" I asked, ignoring the cell phone jab. When I do remember to turn it on, I misplace it and can't find it to answer calls anyway.

"No autopsy," Otis answered, "because Jed Amick thinks he'll be reelected coroner if he can campaign that he's saving money for the taxpayers."

"The body's not prepared yet, right?" "Prepared" is undertaker talk, which I call Funeralese, for "embalmed."

"No, but Odell won't be back until this afternoon, and I want you here for the planning session."

Inside, Otis stopped at the hall tree mirror and smoothed

his tinted hair implants. It looked to me like he'd been in my work makeup kit again. I think he uses a little smudge of #14 on the crow's-feet by his eyes. Could be a shade darker, though, maybe #16, since he spends so much time in the tanning bed at Bronze Bods.

After Otis admired his appearance, he continued, "Just sit in on the session. If the widow has friends or family with her, you can go to your office, but I'm not comfortable alone with Betty Saxon."

"Betty? The last time I heard, Bobby wasn't married to a Betty."

"He married Betty Cross about six months ago."

"Bouncy Betty? We went to school together. Bobby Saxon hung out with my oldest brother, John. Bobby's gotta be thirteen or fourteen years older than Betty."

"Coroner's paperwork says Bobby was forty-five. Younger wife's not so unusual these days. Especially second wives. I guess it's okay for Bobby's fifth wife to be your age. Why do you call her 'Bouncy' Betty?" He smirked.

"From kindergarten on, Bouncy Betty Cross drove the teachers nuts. She was the most hyper kid in school. Couldn't be still. If I'd had a student like her, I would've quit teaching those five-year-olds long before I did. In high school, they still called her Bouncy Betty because she bounced in other ways. You'll see what I mean."

"Oh, I've seen her," Otis mumbled.

As we walked through the front hall, I checked the dark mahogany furniture for dust. The cleaning service comes in early every morning, but I always check for dust bunnies and look to see if anything needs a quick touch-up when I know customers are coming. But it was a waste of my time and effort. Otis was steadily wiping invisible spots off the antique furnishings with his pristine white handkerchief.

"Well, hello, Calamine Parrish!" Betty yelled from the back of the hall. And here I'd thought my daddy was the only one who still called me Calamine instead of Callie. Mama passed away right after my birth, and Daddy was drunk, really drunk, when he named me. He swears he was trying to think pink, something feminine, but all he could think of was calamine lotion. Thank heaven he didn't think of Pepto-Bismol.

Betty flounced through the employee entrance and rushed to give me a big hug. Buh-leeve me, Bouncy Betty was still bouncing and as loud as ever. Her voice screamed, and so did her fire engine red outfit set off by a gigantic scarlet patent leather tote bag.

"I haven't seen you since you went off to Columbia. Your hair looks better than that old mousy brown you had. Heard you'd come back to town looking different after a divorce. Was it your second or third?" Without waiting for me to tell her I'd been married only once, Betty reached for the knob on the door labeled with a little brass "Private" sign.

Moving faster than a greased pig on the Fourth of July, Otis grabbed Betty's elbow and steered her toward the front of the building. The "Private" door, which is kept locked, leads to the preparation rooms used to embalm and make up the deceased.

In the consulting parlor, Otis motioned Betty and me to comfortable, overstuffed chairs at the round conference table. "First," he began, using his perfect, soft, controlled, comforting voice, the one they teach in Undertaking 101, "we here at Middleton's want to extend our deepest sympathy to you and the other members of your family."

Betty crossed her right leg over her left and began swinging her foot toward Otis. Her bright red miniskirt inched up her thighs, and her toeless, backless ruby-colored stiletto heel bounced away and flopped back with each flip of her foot.

"Don't bother with the sympathy stuff," Betty said. Giant silver loop earrings bobbled against her Clairol platinum blonde hair as she turned back and forth between Otis and me. "If Bobby hadn't died, I was gonna divorce him anyway. I don't want to waste a lot of time on this funeral business, but I do want to give Bobby a big send-off."

Otis removed two forms from a drawer: a planning sheet and a general price list. "Before we begin your selections, Mrs. Saxon, let me get some information from you." He quickly asked the preliminary questions for the obituary notices and wrote her answers on the paper. Betty wanted lengthy write-ups in the *State* and the *Beaufort Gazette* as well as our usual publication in *St. Mary Daily* and the memorial section of the Middleton's Mortuary web page. Didn't seem concerned about the extra charges.

When Otis asked about insurance, Betty ignored him. Otis hesitated, but she didn't respond. I knew what that meant. Before he finished, Otis would press the issue of insurance and would have her sign over part of a burial or life insurance policy. If there were no insurance, Betty would have to produce a credit card or certified check to pay.

Otis placed the price list in front of her and kept going. "Will the service be here in our chapel or at Mr. Saxon's home church?"

Betty guffawed. She pulled an ashtray close to her, dug a pack of Marlboros from her purse, and lit up. Otis and I both hate cigarette smoke, but Odell insists that ashtrays be available so smokers are less stressed during planning.

When Betty inhaled, she choked. I leaned over and patted her back. "I'm okay now," she coughed. "It cracked me up to think of Bobby in a church. We can have the funeral here, can't we?" She reversed legs and crossed left over right. Still swinging. Her other shoe flapped against her foot with its bright red toenails.

Otis gulped and subtly turned his head to the side as Betty blew smoke across the table. "Of course," he said. "Our chapel facilities are available." He tapped the price index. "You'll see all of our services and costs itemized right here."

Betty gave the form a quick look. "I'm not really interested in prices," she said. "I want to know when we can bury him."

"Mr. Saxon is our only guest at the moment, so you may set whatever time is convenient to you and your family. You might consider visitation tomorrow evening and the services Wednesday. Or, if family and friends will be coming from out of town, you may want to wait a few days for their arrival."

Betty snuffed out the cigarette and tapped her shiny crimson fingernails on the table beside her. "I meant, when will Bobby's body be available? There'll have to be an autopsy, won't there?"

Otis put on his most consoling smile. "No problem. Mr. Saxon has been released to us. Coroner Amick was at the pool when we picked up Mr. Saxon from the Sleep Easy Inn. Papers are complete. Cause of death is listed as drowning. Manner of death, accidental."

Before I came to work at Middleton's, I wouldn't have known how slack Jed Amick was. Technically, there should be an autopsy anytime there's a death that's not obviously due to natural causes.

"We can provide a minister, an organist, and a soloist if you like," Otis continued.

"All that." Betty laughed. "All that and a bag of chips." She crossed her right leg back over the left. She was swinging her leg so fast that her shoe flew off and hit the plush carpet. Otis picked it up with his thumb and forefinger. Daintily, he held it out to her. Betty slipped it on without a word. She went right back to swinging, though not quite so energetically.

"Chips?" Otis wore a puzzled frown. "Do you want a reception with chips and dip?"

"It's an expression," I said. "She means she wants the very nicest possible service."

"Yes, absolutely the best," Betty said. "I want visitation tomorrow evening, seven to nine, with refreshments. We'll plant him Wednesday."

"Afternoon service?" Otis asked as he wrote on the planning form.

"Morning. Definitely morning. No reason to ruin the whole day."

My mouth dropped open. During the entire time I'd worked for Middleton's, I'd never before seen Otis display a visible reaction to anything a mourner said. This time, one eyebrow rose a tiny bit. I closed my mouth, glad neither of them was looking at me. Burying a spouse is *expected* to ruin a whole day. Usually a lot more.

"Perhaps eleven?" Otis suggested.

"Ten. So it doesn't interfere with anyone's lunch plans," Betty answered.

Otis's other eyebrow rose. He removed another paper from a drawer and handed it to Betty. "This is a CPL," he said. "We're required by law to give you the casket price list before you make your decision." Otis stood. "Please come with us to make your selections."

"My what?" Betty looked at me. She seemed more comfortable asking me questions instead of Otis.

"Your selections," I said as I stood. "You'll need to

choose a casket and burial garments, unless you plan to bring in some of Mr. Saxon's clothes."

"Why don't I just let you plan the whole thing, Calamine?"

"We can't do that," I said.

"Why not?"

"There are laws," I answered, "to prevent unscrupulous funeral homes from being unfair to grieving families. Of course, Middleton's would never take advantage of anyone, but we must follow the regulations."

"Who's grieving? I just want it to be real nice so people can't say I skimped on Bobby's funeral to keep more of his insurance money."

"Middleton's will secure death certificates and be glad to assist you with all insurance forms," Otis said with a beaming smile.

"Bobby took out a big policy on himself and one on me when we married," Betty said. "Half million each. I can afford a big funeral." Tears welled up in her eyes. "Bobby had a drinking problem, but he limited his boozing to nights and weekends. He made good money selling cars. Top salesman at GMC Truck Corral in Beaufort." She wiped her eyes with the back of her hand. "Our marriage wasn't working, but since he bought that big policy and died before the divorce, I want to send him off in high style." Betty's attitude was swinging like a pendulum. But then, I'd never understood her.

"Yes, we understand." Otis patted her right hand with his left as he pulled out an insurance assignment form with his right. He explained to Betty that she'd need to sign the form and bring the policy to him. Betty said, "No problem-o. I've got the policy and our marriage license right here in my bag."

By the time Bouncy Betty bounced out, she'd signed the finalized plans for a Gates Exquisite bronze casket with innerspring mattress and silver handles, an Eternal vault with extended warranty, a gigantic spray of white roses, a paid preacher, a small musical ensemble, an organist, and a vocalist. Top-of-the-line in every way. Catered food for the visitation.

Lots of chips.

# Chapter Two

**S**everal years of my life were spent confined in a room with twenty to twenty-five wiggle-worms who talked, hit, bit, and screamed. Five days a week. I got enough noise to last the rest of my life while I was teaching kindergarten, and I craved quiet when I moved back to St. Mary. Working at Middleton's Mortuary is tranquil, and the people I work on don't complain, have temper tantrums, need to potty every five seconds, or get hyper and refuse to take naps.

It's quiet, but puh-leeze, there's no excitement. That's why I read Ann Rule's true crime books and so many mysteries. Good grief, I don't see how authors dream up those far-fetched things they write about, but I love them!

Eager to get back to my current novel, I faxed Bobby Saxon's obit to the newspapers and updated our web page. Posting Internet obituaries was one of the first ideas of mine that Otis and Odell adopted, and I conscientiously post notices and changes as many times as necessary each day. I finished steam-pressing the suit Betty chose from our stock for Bobby to wear and laid out the new underwear, socks, shirt, and tie she'd requested.

At last, I could read while I waited for Otis to finish preparing Bobby's body. An instrumental "Amazing Grace" over the sound system alerted me that the front door had been opened. I laid the book on my desk and headed for the entry area.

"Where's Bobby Saxon?" a male voice shouted just as I reached the hall. "I wanna see him flat on his back in a casket!"

The man's vocals stood about six feet, six inches, but he looked like a miniature hybrid between NASCAR and the Grand Ole Opry. He wore a turquoise sequined Porter Wagoner western suit and a Richard Petty cowboy hat with peacock feathers plastered to the front. A ten-gallon hat on a six-gallon head. Though it added a few inches to his height, he couldn't have been taller than me—about five feet four. Might have been even shorter if he was wearing lifts in those fancy snakeskin boots. Buh-leeve me, I like to see a man with a mustache, but the pencil-thin brown line over his skinny lips didn't add much macho. I recognized him immediately.

"Aren't you the GMC Automotive and Truck Corral cowboy in the commercials on television?" I asked.

"Sure am. Call me Cowboy. Now, whar's that sorry Bobby Saxon? Over at the car lot, they're saying he's dead. I drove right straight here from Beaufort. Wanna see that stiff for myself."

"I'm sorry, Cowboy," I said, "but Mr. Saxon won't be available for viewing until tomorrow. Would you like to sign the guest register?"

"Might as well," he said. "Been waiting for this since Saxon came to work at the Corral and started beating me out of all the top salesman awards. Danged if I can figure how ever' time I think I got the best of him, he slides in with another sale right before the competition ends. I haven't won an award, a bonus, or a trip since he showed up, but there's two more weeks before the Diamond Jubilee Rodeo contest ends, and with Saxon gone, that diamond ring will be mine."

The register stand hadn't been set up yet, so I walked back to the supply closet. Cowboy followed me, talking nonstop.

"Yep, I'm sure you've seen me in GMC Truck Corral commercials. Been doing those ads for years. I was the top salesman there, too, until Saxon showed up."

I removed a burgundy-covered guest register with attached pen from the closet and opened the book on a side table. He leaned over and signed "Cowboy" with great flourishes taking up three lines in the register, all the time talking about what a great car salesman he was.

"Tomorrow?" he asked. "You say I can see Saxon's body tomorrow? I don't want to miss a chance to pay my disrespects." He laughed. Actually had the audacity to look expectantly at me, waiting for me to laugh with him like what he'd said was funny.

"Visitation is tomorrow night from seven until nine," I said in my most teachery tone, "but you can stop by during the day if you like."

Cowboy tipped his hat and said, "I'll be back tomorrow," as he pulled the door closed behind himself. When I peeked out, I saw him drive away in a shiny red, two-door sports car with dealer tags.

Mourners behave in a lot of strange ways, but Cowboy fit into his own category of weird. I made a mental note to warn Otis and Odell that we needed to watch out for him. One of the things I like about my job is that I'm not the boss, so any real problems get passed to Otis and Odell.

Both brothers hold dual licenses as embalmers and funeral directors. They've offered to send me to Piedmont

Tech in Greenwood, South Carolina, to study mortuary science, but I don't have any interest in learning embalming and restoration. And I certainly don't want to be a funeral director and have to deal with folks like Cowboy any more than I do. I'm happy just making people look good for good-byes and final viewings by their relatives and friends.

The back door buzzer sounded before I reached my desk and book. I detoured around my office and went to see who was there. Virginia Holbrook from St. Mary Florals stood on the step with a potted yellow mum in each hand.

"Hey, Callie," she said, balancing the pots as she came inside. "I've brought the casket spray and two plants that have already been ordered. Bobby Saxon dated a lot of women in St. Mary, drank with most of the men, and sold cars to all of them when he worked at St. Mary Motors. I'm sure most of them followed him to the Corral in Beaufort when he started selling there. After all, what's a thirty-minute ride to get a Saxon deal on a truck? I expect we'll be delivering a lot of floral pieces today and tomorrow." She set the flowers by the door and paused. "I went out with him myself years ago. Did you ever date him?"

"No, but I had a crush on him when I was a teenager. He was John's best friend," I said.

"Yes, I remember your brothers hanging out with Bobby." She sighed. "We had some good old times back then." She turned toward the door. "I'll bring the casket spray in."

When the huge arrangement of gorgeous white roses was in place on the stand in Slumber Room A, Virginia asked, "When will Bobby be ready to be seen?"

"Visitation is tomorrow night from seven 'til nine," I said.

"Yeah, that's what I heard."

"But you can stop by any time tomorrow," I added, thinking she might want a private moment.

"I probably will. I liked old Bobby. It's such a shame he never grew up and got beyond partying." She stepped out, waved at me, and called, "I'll be back later."

**The empty Exquisite** casket rested on our best mahogany bier against the wall of my workroom, waiting for Mr. Robert Saxon. Bobby himself lay on a stainless steel gurney with a sheet pulled over his shoulders up to his chin.

We view our jobs much as people in the medical field do, and I wouldn't be offended by a nude corpse, but I knew Bobby was already wearing his new underwear. Otis and Odell are very particular that bodies be treated respectfully at all times. All male bodies are wearing their boxers or Skivvies before I begin my work.

I looked at the face, eyes, and lips carefully positioned with embalming devices and sealed shut with mortician's glue. I hadn't seen Bobby since I returned to St. Mary, and he was hardly the man I remembered from my younger years. I thought he was such a hunk when I first noticed not all boys were my brothers. My heart would just about pound out of my chest when he came in with my oldest sibling and threw me a "Hi, kiddo. Whatcha been up to?"

Waterproof smock already over my dress, I pulled on surgical gloves. While shaving Bobby, I remembered that he used to wear a beard and mustache, but he'd been clean-shaven in the photograph Betty had given us. Otis or Odell, whoever does the embalming, always cleans the body and shampoos the hair before I begin. I styled Bobby's hair to match the picture except I pulled a bit more forward from around the rubber block headrest. Odell taught me this trick. Most folks' hair looks different when they're flat on their backs. Placing some from the rear of the head toward the front produces a fuller, more natural look when a body is casketed with a pillow.

After carefully spraying his hair, I gave Bobby a manicure. Nothing fancy. Just cleaned his nails, clipped, and buffed them. As I finished, Otis peeked in and said, "Let me know when you're ready to dress him. I'll give you a hand."

"Be a few minutes," I said and opened my case. Cosmetics are applied before clothing. Sometimes airbrushing and sealers are used, but all I needed for Bobby was mortuary makeup. Once dry, this makeup won't smudge. Unless it's scrubbed off with removal chemicals, it stays in place until the skin disintegrates. I sponged a natural-looking color onto his hands, neck, and face. Plucked a few wiry wild hairs from his brows. Ears were hairless, so no tweezing there, but I did pull a few from his nose. On a face that was alive and moving, hairs wouldn't be noticeable. Buh-leeve me, with Bobby totally motionless in the casket, they'd look terrible.

I glanced down at the slight rise on my chest. Would I really have the nerve to increase my blow-up bra until I'd made mountains out of molehills? As I looked up, my gaze caught a small spot right below Bobby's left ear. My first thought was "Gnat!" with an exclamation point. Flying insects aren't welcome in funeral homes. I lifted Bobby's head slightly off the headrest for a better look. The small spot seemed to have a metallic shine. I tried to wipe it off. When the sponge snagged on it, I realized that the object was imbedded in the skin. Probably something Otis had used.

After touching up Bobby's lips and features, I called Otis in to help me dress the body and position it in the casket. We had Bobby in his suit and his tie knotted when I thought to ask Otis if the thing on Bobby's neck was embalming paraphernalia.

"Show me."

We lifted Bobby's head, and Otis ran a gloved finger over the spot.

"Did you put it there?" I asked.

"No, this has nothing to do with our preparation."

I retrieved the forceps from my case and locked them on the tiny round object. Otis and I both jumped when the door opened.

"I'm back." Odell boomed as he stepped in. He's always loud and raspy. Even louder than Betty. Odell wore a midnight blue suit. When the brothers were younger and hard to tell apart, they established a pattern. Otis wore only black suits, and Odell always wore dark blue. Now everyone could tell them apart, but they still dressed like they had since they began helping their dad with the mortuary.

"Saw the flowers in A. Who we got?" Odell's gaze settled on the corpse. "Great gobs o' hog lard! That's Bobby Saxon." Odell rubbed the top of his bald head and spotted the casket waiting for Bobby. "An Exquisite. Good job, Callie. I know Doofus didn't sell that."

Odell barely paused for breath before adding, "What are you doing, Callie?"

"There's something in his neck," I said and pulled on the forceps. A broken hypodermic needle slid out.

"Doofus, did you break a needle off in him?" Odell demanded from Otis.

"It's not mine. Didn't even use a hypodermic on him," Otis answered.

"I'll call the sheriff," Odell said. "Phone the florists and caterer. Everything's on hold."

Now, my belief about female intuition is pretty much the same as my thoughts about boobs. The good Lord shorted me.

But I had a bad feeling, a really bad feeling.

# Chapter Three

"**W**hen will the people of Jade County understand that the coroner should not be elected on popularity and how many babies he slobbers on at picnics? We need a medical examiner." Sheriff Harmon was ranting, but then, he usually does when talking about Coroner Jed Amick. Like most law enforcement officials and medical examiners, Harmon believes that every unusual death deserves an autopsy.

The needle I'd removed from the corpse's neck was now in a ziplock plastic bag. Bobby still lay on the gurney, not in his expensive Exquisite casket. As a matter of fact, Otis and I would soon remove Bobby's new suit and finery to avoid wrinkling them in the body bag he'd wear to MUSC, the Medical University of South Carolina, in Charleston, for the autopsy.

"Can you believe that fool Amick asked me if this could mean Bobby Saxon was a diabetic?" Harmon raved on. "Since when do diabetics shoot up in the sides of their necks?"

"Tell you what," Odell said, "let's you and me get outta the way and let Doofus and Callie get this body bagged."

"I need to go talk to the widow," the sheriff said. "His most recent wife was Betty Cross."

"Yeah," Odell said. "I'd heard that Bobby married her." He scratched his head again. I wondered if Odell was using a different product on his head. When the twins' hair began falling out, Otis got hair implants and Odell shaved his head. After a few months of shaving, he recommended Nair to me for my legs, said it gives a shinier, smoother effect than shaving. I'd noticed Odell's head was quite a bit shinier, but I'm not about to touch it to feel if it's smoother.

Otis and Odell are genetically identical twins, but you can't see it anymore. Otis is a strict vegetarian while Odell pigs out at every barbecue in the county. The man could live off pulled pork—with red sauce, mustard sauce, or even North Carolina pepper and vinegar. I had no doubt he'd emptied some buffet in Columbia while at the undertakers' meeting. Odell carries about forty pounds more stomach than Otis, as well as what I secretly think of as Odell's "hog jowls."

As we returned Bobby's new suit and shirt to clothes hangers, Otis commented, "I doubt that those roses will hold up until the funeral. Mrs. Saxon will have to postpone the arrangements, and roses don't last well even in air conditioning. At least she has enough insurance to pay for another spray."

"When will Bobby be back?" I asked.

"No telling. We'll take the body to Charleston now, and the medical examiner may get to it in the morning, but it's not likely. He doesn't like to autopsy fully embalmed bodies, so he'll put it off or assign it to someone else. What they find during Bobby's postmortem will determine when we get the body back. I have to give the pathologists samples of the embalming fluids I used on Bobby for chemical controls on the toxicology studies, and that will delay the process, too. There's no way we'll have the body back in time for tomorrow night. I don't want to be the one who has to tell Mrs. Saxon she has to change her plans."

Otis fastened the clothes bag shut, raised Bobby slightly with the body lift, and began sliding a body bag under the corpse.

"Lots of people don't want their loved ones autopsied," I said, "but Betty seemed to expect it. She acted surprised that Amick hadn't ordered a postmortem. She'll understand."

Otis grinned. "Not your typical grieving widow, is she?" He pulled up the sides of the body bag and zipped it shut.

"Do you want me to call Betty?" I asked.

"Give it some time. Sheriff Harmon went to talk to her. She'll probably call us after he leaves." Otis chuckled. "Wait until I'm on the way to Charleston with the body, so you or Odell can deal with her."

**Ex-cuuze me. There** would be no choice whether Odell or I would talk to Bouncy Betty. Otis should have known Odell would ride with him. I knew why. There's a great barbecue house on Highway 17, right outside of Charleston. Odell would have no qualms telling Otis to eat just coleslaw and plain rice while he devoured pork, beef, and chicken.

State law requires someone to be on the premises when there's a corpse in the funeral home, but with no bodies, I could call forward the telephone to my house at eight when I left for the night. I went back to my book. Janet Evanovich had my stomach tied in knots with fear for Stephanie Plum when the telephone rang.

"Middleton's Mortuary. Callie Parrish. May I help you?"

"Little Sister, this is John." Like I wouldn't know my oldest brother's voice. "I just heard that Bobby Saxon died this morning. I'll be coming from Atlanta for the services. Have plans been made?"

"Hey, John. I planned to call you after I got home. Bobby's plans were made, but they're on hold now. We found a needle in his neck and they're going to do a post-mortem exam. By the way, I'm doing fine."

"If you weren't fine, Frank would have called. He keeps me posted on our sis. What kind of needle are you talking about? I know you and those mysteries you read. What did you do? Find a knitting needle in his neck?"

"Hypodermic. Broken off. I wouldn't have noticed it except I looked down to . . . well, never mind that. Do you want me to call when we have definite plans?"

"Yes, do that, and Callie . . ."

"Uh-huh?"

"Stay out of it. You're not a detective, and you don't get paid to solve murders or mysteries."

"John, I have no intention of sticking my nose where it doesn't belong."

"And Callie . . ."

"Uh-huh?"

"I love you, Little Sister."

Having grown up in a house full of older brothers and my redneck father, I didn't hear "I love you" much as a kid. John had begun saying it after he married into a wealthy, loving, demonstrative family, who, unfortunately, have no eligible sons for him to introduce to me. The endearment still brings tears to my eyes every time John says it.

"Love you, too," I answered. "I'll call you tomorrow."

When I checked the Saxon folder to be sure everything was in order, I noticed that Bobby's real name was Robert Edward Saxon. I admit it—I'm sensitive about my name and curious sometimes about other people's real monikers. Well, actually, I'm really nosy all of the time.

Betty had signed everything simply "Betty Saxon." I pulled out the insurance policy to see if Betty was a nickname and if she had some horrible middle name. I was surprised that the policy didn't show her name. The beneficiary on Bobby's policy was named as "my legal wife." Bet Betty was glad they'd married and weren't just significant others.

I filed the folder and reached for my book, eager to see if Stephanie Plum's car would be bombed again, but before I'd read a word, I heard a loud pounding on the front door.

When we have a guest, which is Otis and Odell's preferred word for corpse, the door usually remains unlocked until eight, but I'd locked the doors early when I moved the Mustang around to my space in back.

I didn't have to peek. I recognized Bouncy Betty's voice. "Open up and let me in right now!" I unlocked the door, and the soft music chimed in sharp contrast to Betty's angry yelling. "Just a Closer Walk with Thee" didn't stand a chance against Betty's screeching. Otis had already slid the printed name "Mr. Robert E. Saxon" in the slot on the sign by Slumber Room A, and I'd set up a register stand with the guest book Cowboy had signed. Betty dashed past me into the salon. She stopped when she saw the casket wasn't there.

"Where is he?" she screeched. "Where's my Bobby?"

I put my arm around her, and she collapsed onto my shoulder, sobbing. The smell of cigarette smoke oozed from her hot pink spaghetti strap minidress.

"Didn't Sheriff Harmon come talk to you?" I asked. Betty had made a hundred-and-eighty-degree turn from how she'd acted before. From flip to flustered. Did I say flustered? More like frantic.

With wrenching tears flowing through smudged black mascara, Betty nodded and wailed, "I want to see Bobby before you ship him off. I want to see my Bobby." Did Betty know more about Bobby's death than she'd let on? How much had Sheriff Harmon told her? Maybe this was all an act so she could look to see if the needle was still in his neck. No time to think about it now. I had to do my job.

One of the first things I learned working at the mortuary is that when a mourner grabs me and sobs, I'm to pat the person on the back while saying, "Now, now." The second thing is to offer tissues from the nearest box, which is never far out of reach because we keep Kleenex on every table. Otis insists on the kind with aloe or vitamin E embedded in the fibers to keep the grief-stricken from leaving with chapped noses.

Betty made these consolation efforts impossible for me by pulling herself away and flopping onto a hunter green velvet wingback chair. She beat her fists against her thighs, then lifted her hands to her platinum blonde hair. She yanked hard on her curls, but her face spasmed with pain after only a few moments, and she put her hands down. She lapsed into soft sobs as I patted her shoulder and said something I never dreamed I'd ever tell anyone: "Why don't we go to a consultation room so you can have a cigarette?"

The sobs turned to snuffles, then Betty stood and said, "I need a drink, too."

"Come on into a sitting room. The ashtrays are in there and I'll get you a Coke, or I can brew coffee if you like."

"That isn't exactly what I meant."

"I don't have anything stronger. How about some green tea? I'll have a cup with you."

Over hot tea sweetened with honey, I told Betty, "Otis and Odell are already on the way to Charleston with Bobby. You can see him as soon as he's back."

"What about the visitation?" she asked through a cloud of cigarette smoke as she crossed her legs and started swinging. I noticed that her fingernails and toenails no longer shone crimson. They flashed fuchsia.

"Since you'd planned an open casket, we'll need to know when Bobby will be back before setting that. He definitely won't be here in time for seven tomorrow night." I sipped my tea and added, "We can't guarantee he'll even be back in time for services on Wednesday."

Betty set the fragile Wedgwood cup on its saucer on the table beside her. Since all that leg swinging was jostling Betty's hand, I was glad she'd put the delicate piece down. If it were up to me, I'd use the same mugs out here that we use in our private offices, but Otis is adamant that real china be used up front. Heaven forbid we even think about foam.

"Can we have the visitation without Bobby?" Betty asked.

"If you like."

She lit a Marlboro, inhaled, and blew out a long stream of smoke. "I called lots of people and told them to come tomorrow at seven."

"The obituary in the newspapers will announce it, too, but we could have them print a retraction and change the web page if you want open casket. . . ." I hesitated, wondering how much I should say. "Sometimes when there's a postmortem in Charleston, they keep the person several days. As I said, we can't even guarantee a Wednesday morning funeral unless you want it to be a memorial service with interment at a later date."

"Holy moley, Calamine. I have no idea what you're talking about. What's a postmortem?" Betty stubbed out her Marlboro.

"Autopsy. You want more tea?"

"Yes, it's actually good." Bouncy Betty raised her eyebrows, surprised, before she uncrossed her legs, recrossed them, and resumed swinging. Anybody else, I'd think that leg business was flirting, but I knew Betty wasn't flirting with me. Buh-leeve me, we're both extremely heterosexual. I know I am, and the whole high school knew Betty was since ninth grade. It was that old hyperactivity.

"Explain the rest of it," she said. "What's the difference between a funeral and a service?"

"Both words mean a ceremony honoring the dead." I slipped into my schoolteacher mode. "A memorial service is usually held if the body is to be cremated. Normally a funeral service is followed by interment." She looked puzzled. I continued, "You told Otis that Bobby has a plot beside his mother in the St. Mary Celestial Gardens. When we leave the chapel and go over to the cemetery for burial, that's the interment part of the funeral."

"Can I have a funeral without internment?" Once again, Betty had shifted. From flip to frantic to functional.

I didn't bother to correct her pronunciation. "You can have a memorial service without burial. Then have the interment later."

"One more question. What's a wake? Someone asked me if there's going to be a wake. Should I have one of those, too?"

"A wake is about the same thing as visitation. You don't need both."

"Thanks, Calamine." She lit another cigarette. She hadn't calmed down as much as I thought. Her hands were shaking so much that it took several tries before she got the flame to the end of the cigarette. "I was so upset when Sheriff Harmon left that I couldn't think. Now I know what I want. Keep everything the same except the internment. Visitation tomorrow, seven to nine, and I want a memorial service in the chapel Wednesday morning."

She uncrossed her legs and began jittering them. It was a wonder I couldn't hear her knees knocking together. "Another thing. I want that fancy casket I'm buying sitting in the room where Bobby's name is on the door. Shut the coffin until he's back. Put the flowers on top. If anyone asks, don't tell them Bobby isn't in there."

An empty closed casket for visitation was a first for me, but I didn't see why not, so I agreed.

Betty leaned back in her chair and began rubbing her hands together, almost wringing them. Ashes from the cigarette she held in her right hand fell on the table. Nicotine had stained her fingers yellowish brown between the knuckles of her index and middle fingers. I thought it was amazing she didn't cut her fingers with those long fingernails, and I wondered if they were real.

"Calamine, did you see Bobby before they took him to Charleston?"

"Yes, Betty, I even combed his hair before he left."

"How did he look?"

The first word that popped in my head was "dead," but even my flippant side knew better than to say that. "He looked peaceful, Betty." I didn't bother to tell her that once the embalmer seals the eyes and mouth shut, most corpses do look serene.

She began to sniffle again, and I offered more tissues. "We argued Sunday night," she whispered and leaned over toward me, holding her left hand up to shield the sound from going anywhere except to my ear. "I wanted him to stay home, but he insisted he had to go out." I could barely hear her and wondered who Betty thought might be listening. Perhaps she thought ghosts inhabited the building. I knew better. If we had any spirits at Middleton's, I would have already encountered one of them.

"He'd been drinking all day," Betty continued softly, "and I offered to drive him, but he refused." Sniffles became sobs. "I feel so guilty."

Arm around the shoulder again. "Bobby didn't have a car wreck, Betty. Your not driving didn't kill him. Married people have disagreements." Good grief, do I ever know about that! "It's unfortunate that Bobby died before you two made up, but it happens. You're planning to send him off in style."

"I told him I was gonna divorce him."

"Don't take a guilt trip, Betty." I spouted Funeralese. "It's okay to cry. It's good to grieve. You're giving him a beautiful funeral. You don't need to feel guilty."

"I guess you're right. You always were smart, Calamine. I'm going home and get some rest. Tomorrow morning I'll buy dresses for the visitation and the memorial service. I don't own anything in dark colors." Somehow that didn't surprise me.

"I'll call you when we hear from Charleston," I assured her.

"But you'll put his casket and flowers where people can see them?"

"Before I leave tonight."

I walked Betty to the door and watched her behind sway as she wiggled to her car. I'd practiced trying to walk that way when I was a teenager, but I gave up when my brothers made fun of me. It looked natural for Betty.

Since Bobby's Exquisite casket was already on a wheeled bier in my workroom, I closed the lid and pushed it down the hall to Slumber Room A. Most folks probably think a casket locks when the top is closed, but there's just

a latch there. The Exquisite wouldn't be locked—fully
locked—until the gasket seal was tightened nine or ten
turns with a special crank key. The last thing I wanted was
for some nosy or grief-stricken mourner to open the casket
before we had a body in it, so I turned the crank key in the
slot at the foot. I only twisted it twice, just enough to keep
anyone from lifting the lid.

I centered the spray of roses on top of the casket and
went to my office. I dropped the Exquisite crank key into
my desk drawer, picked up my purse, dug out my Sponge-
Bob SquarePants key ring, and headed for the back door.
Flipped the lights off, stepped out onto the porch, locked
the dead bolt, and turned to go to my car.

A heavy hand touched my shoulder.

# Chapter Four

**Heaven.** I'd died and gone to heaven.

That's what I thought when I opened one eye and saw the magnificent head of sandy brown hair, aquiline nose, and blue eyes leaning over my face. However, when I squinted through both eyes and looked beyond the hunk leaning over me, I knew I wasn't in heaven. Bright lights bounced off Odell's shiny head where he stood at the foot of the bed, and cannonballs bounced around inside my skull. I closed my eyes.

"Ah, Mrs. Parrish, you're awake," said a smooth masculine voice coming from right below the chiseled nose.

"Miss," I mumbled. "I'm single." I opened one eye. A tiny slit.

The lips curved into a handsome smile. "I stand corrected. *Miss* Parrish, can you open both eyes so I can look into them?"

I tried, I promise I tried, but the pain screamed with both eyes exposed, so I opened only one. Smooth Voice leaned closer and looked through an instrument into it.

Mmmmm. He smelled as good as he looked. When he finished, I closed the eye. "Now the other one," he said. I opened it and caught a glimpse of the man's white coat before he leaned over and blocked my sight. When he stood straight, I squeezed both eyes shut.

"How is she, Doctor?" Odell asked a few decibels below his usual volume.

"I'm sure she'll be fine, but ER was correct to admit her. I want to keep her overnight. She was knocked unconscious, and the scan shows a small, subdural hematoma. Not too serious, but enough to keep her for observation 'til morning."

Nausea washed over me. I felt kind of tingly, too. My hands and my feet. Through the discomfort, I tried to listen to Odell and the doctor.

"I only had to put three stitches in the side of her head, but—"

Both eyes flew open, along with my mouth. If I could have, I would have sat up. "Stitches in my head? Did you shave my hair?"

"No, Miss Parrish, we didn't even cut your hair. We do have a bandage over the stitches, though."

"What happened to me?"

"Do you want to tell her?" Smooth Voice asked Odell.

That wonderful sound changed to Odell's raspy drawl. He moved up to my side and leaned over me. "Doofus and I found you out behind the funeral home when we got back from Charleston. You were unconscious, and your head was bleeding. I'm glad you didn't have a neck or back injury, because I was so upset, I lifted you into the funeral coach and headed straight here to the Beaufort ER."

"Yes," said Smooth Voice, "you'll forever be known as the girl who came to the ER by hearse."

"Girl? I'm a grown woman."

Just then he put a stethoscope on my chest, and I realized I was wearing one of those little cotton hospital thingies instead of my black dress. My new bra was gone. No wonder he'd called me a girl.

"Do you remember anything?" Odell asked.

"I closed the Exquisite and put it in A with the spray on top. Then I locked up and started to leave. The last thing I remember is someone tapping me on the shoulder."

"Why did you . . . ," Odell began, but the doctor cut him off.

"Tomorrow. You can talk then. I want Miss Parrish to rest now."

I closed my eyes.


**The morning nurse** assured me several times that no pocketbook had been brought in with me. I finally quit asking for it. No purse meant no comb. No makeup. She showed me a plastic bag with my belongings: my black dress, new bra, panty hose, and low-heeled black leather pumps. "Hand me that," I said. "I'm getting dressed."

"Not until your doctor comes."

Thoughts of seeing Smooth Voice with the blue eyes and the great nose calmed me. I tried using my fingers to comb my hair, but the bandage on my head thwarted me.

A lady brought in a breakfast tray. It didn't look, smell, or taste great, but I'd only had a few cups of hot tea since yesterday's lunch, so I ate everything. My tummy got so full, I patted it, and when I did, I burped. That little gas eruption coincided with the arrival of the doctor. I was embarrassed but not mortified. After all, I'd grown up with brothers—it could've been a lot worse than a burp.

Smooth Voice was just as handsome today as he'd been

the night before. A mousy nurse walked beside him. I was glad she was plain. If I had to be caught burping while sitting in bed, braless, wearing a cotton shirt and wild hair, I didn't want the object of my interest to be with a pretty nurse.

"Miss Parrish, how do you feel?" the doctor asked.

"What's your name?" I answered.

His laughter was as pleasing to the ears as his speech. "Guess we overlooked the formalities. I'm Donald Walters, the doctor who saw you last night."

Donald? Not another Donald. At least he didn't say Donnie. My ex-husband's name was Donnie.

"I feel fine, Dr. Walters. When may I go home?"

He pulled on a pair of gloves and gently removed the bandage, tugging my hair along with it. I yelped.

"Sorry," he apologized, "I thought you'd rather deal with the bandage than have a shaved spot on your head."

"Thank you."

"The stitches look fine. You can leave the bandage off. Your vitals were great all night. I'll sign your dismissal papers, but call us if there are any changes." He turned to the nurse. "There's still blood in Miss Parrish's hair. Let's take care of that before she leaves. Give her the pamphlet on concussion and written instructions on keeping the stitches clean. She'll need to have them removed in ten days." He stepped toward the door.

"Do I come back for you to take out the stitches?" I asked.

"You can have your regular doctor remove them. If you don't have a primary care physician, stop by ER and someone will do it for you."

The most gorgeous man I'd ever seen walked out the door, out of my life.

\* \* \*

**My brother John** arrived just as I reached for the telephone to find someone to come pick me up from the hospital. Most people would call their best friend, but Jane is blind and doesn't drive. "What are you doing here?" I asked John.

"Odell called me last night. I drove straight over. How do you feel?"

"I'm good. Head hurts a little, but the doctor says I can leave."

"I'm taking you home and staying with you a few days."

"What about Miriam and the kids?" Originally I'd rented a two-bedroom apartment. Now I live in a one-bedroom and one-junk-room apartment. Not enough space for John's family.

"Didn't bring anyone with me. Gonna take care of Little Sister and stay for Bobby's funeral."

I gasped. "I've got to call the funeral home. Otis and Odell don't know that Bobby's wife decided she still wants the visitation tonight, with the casket closed, and a memorial service tomorrow."

"It won't be the casket she picked out," John said. "Odell said it was stolen, apparently by whoever hit you."

"Stole the casket? For what? It was empty."

"Who knows?"

Odell answered when I called Middleton's. After I promised him I'd be okay, he told me he would take care of the arrangements. Call the caterer and florists and set everything up again. Just to be on the safe side, he'd already sent one of the part-time drivers to get another Exquisite from a Beaufort funeral home.

"Don't worry," Odell rasped. "You take a few days off if you need them. Come back whenever you feel ready."

"What about the stolen casket?" I asked.

"What about it?" he answered my question with a question.

"We know when it was stolen. Who? Why?" Me again.

"The sheriff's looking into it. He told me and Otis not to talk to anyone about it, but you know I'll tell you when we hear anything. Haven't heard from Charleston yet. Our responsibility now is to make beautiful memories for Betty and Bobby's friends with or without the body." He sounded like he was quoting from a brochure. Then he coughed nervously. "By the way, do you have extra keys to your car? We can't find your purse."

"I had my keys in one hand and my handbag in the other when I came out. Maybe they fell off the porch."

"We've searched everywhere. No purse. No keys. Do you have another key to your car?"

I laughed. "Donnie just about died when he had to give up the Mustang. He only handed me one set of keys. I keep meaning to have a spare made."

"Whoever hit you has your keys. They must have been driving something big enough to carry the casket. The loading dock door was up and one of the industrial moving dollies is missing. Otis and I are concerned that if they have your keys, they might come back for the Mustang. I could hot-wire it and bring it to your apartment, but it makes more sense to get the locksmith to rekey it when he comes over to change the locks on our building. Want me to do that and just take it out of your salary?"

"Take it out of my salary?" I protested. "Only if you're planning to pay me overtime for lying there bleeding by the door."

Odell laughed the way he always does when he's embarrassed. "Good point, Callie. I'll take care of it and get your car back to you."

I mentally gave thanks that I'd taped an extra key to my apartment on the bottom of my mailbox.

\* \* \*

**It went right** up my leg. I felt it. I leaned over to examine my thigh as John drove us toward my apartment. As I bent, I hit my head on the dash of his Mercedes.

"Dalmatian!"

"What did you say?" John asked.

"Dalmatian!"

"What does that mean?"

"It's kindergarten cussing."

"What's kindergarten cussing?"

"The kind kindergarten teachers use."

"What do you say if you're really angry? Shih tzu?"

I laughed. "No, when I'm really mad, I say one hundred and one dalmatians."

John didn't laugh. He rolled his eyes at me in the same exaggerated way he did when I was a kid.

"Little Sister, what's got you cussing?"

"A run in my stocking. I felt it."

"Want me to stop at the drugstore so you can pick up another pair?"

"No, thanks. I paid good money for these at Victoria's Secret."

"Victoria's Secret? Little Sister shops Victoria's Secret?"

I almost told him about my marvelous bra, but there are some things a girl doesn't share, even with her favorite brother.

**John fastened my** pearls and checked to be sure hair covered my stitches. He'd purchased hardware and changed the locks on my doors while I napped before dressing to go to Bobby Saxon's visitation. I thought how nice it would be to have a boyfriend who was as thoughtful as my oldest brother. But then, John had acted exactly like the rest of them until he married Miriam. My other four brothers are just like Daddy. Redneck. Chauvinistic. Oh, I love 'em all, but they're an obnoxious bunch.

"When did Odell bring the Mustang back?" I asked John as we came out of the apartment.

"Two of the part-time drivers brought it during your nap," John said. "Do you want to take it instead of my car?"

No way. John likes to drive my vehicle, but I *love* to ride in his Mercedes.

When we arrived at five minutes before seven, Middleton's parking lot was already full. Cars, pickups, and SUVs lined both sides of the road. John pulled around behind the mortuary and found the space with my name on it was empty, so we parked there. John and I entered the funeral home through the employee door in back.

The last time Middleton's had this many people for a visitation was when the town doctor passed away a couple of years ago. I was still kind of new at my job, and the doctor's wife just about drove me crazy. She had this photo of him that must have been taken in 1950, and she wanted me to make him look just like that even though he was wrinkled and bald before he died. That's when Odell taught me how to use hairpieces and weaves on heads.

Slumber Room A was wall-to-wall people, and they were spilling into the halls, empty slumber rooms, everywhere except our prep rooms, which were locked as usual. The caterer had set up the reception in Slumber Room B. This was definitely more of a wake than a visitation.

Nick Rivers leaned against the wall by the refreshment table. At six feet six inches tall, he was the star basketball player and my secret unrequited love all through high school. He seemed slimmer, more lanky, actually skinny now. I confess, I'd wondered about Nick Rivers when I decided to move back to St. Mary after my divorce, but this was the first time I'd seen him since my return.

I moved toward Nick, hoping to speak to him. Perhaps he'd notice me now that we were grown. I wished I'd pumped a little more air into my bra. Just as I reached him, a fellow came up and asked Nick, "Where's Bobby?"

"He's over yonder in the other room," Nick answered, "but the casket's closed. Must've let him float in the pool too long to fix him up."

Ex-cuuze me. My hackles rose on that one. Bobby had looked mighty fine when we put him in the body bag.

The man standing beside Nick laughed. "I expected to see him propped up beside a jukebox. You know how he loved that song."

If Bouncy Betty had asked for it, we would have put a jukebox in for the reception. Middleton's is like Burger King. The customer can always "have it your way." That is, "Have it your way if you pay for it our way." But then, a jukebox would have been tacky, and Betty wanted this to be classy.

Just as I thought about Betty, she pushed through the crowd, threw her arms around me, and hugged really tight. She was wearing a high-dollar black dress that I wondered if she'd like to sell at a big discount after the services. "I called here to talk to you this morning," she said, "but they told me you fell and hurt your head. How are you?"

Puh-leeze. Betty and I hardly spoke to each other all through school, and now she acted like I was her best friend. Why wouldn't Nick Rivers do that? I glanced back where he'd been standing, but Cowboy now leaned against the wall beside Nick and the other guy. I had no desire to join them. Cowboy had been adamant that he wanted to *see* Bobby's body, and I didn't want to deal with questions from him. Besides, I was afraid I wouldn't be able to restrain myself from replying to Nick's comment about Bobby being in the water too long for Otis and me to fix him up.

I turned back to Betty. So the word was that I'd fallen. I could go along with that. "I'm fine now. How about you? Is everything the way you wanted?"

"Oh, yes. Look at all the flowers. Bobby was just a car salesman, but the people in St. Mary loved him, and there's arrangements from Beaufort, too." She was right. Every florist in town must have sold out. Bobby's old drinking buddies, girlfriends, and customers had reacted to his death by sending floral displays. Meanwhile, Betty's reaction to her husband's death was still swinging from one extreme to another. Compared to the night before, she was on a high.

"I really like your dress," I said. "Where did—"

*Whap!* The hand slapped my face so hard I saw stars. If not stars, they were little colored spots in front of my eyes. My natural response was the same as it had always been when one of my brothers picked on me. I swung back. My fist didn't connect because John grabbed my arm and was dragging me in the opposite direction while I kicked and struggled to escape from him and jump on my attacker.

Odell pulled away my assailant. She smelled like White Diamonds perfume, but she looked like Halloween. All she needed was a broomstick. Orange hair and a black dress just like the one I was wearing. She was spewing more profanity than I'd ever heard, all directed at me. It wasn't kindergarten cussing, either. I thought she was overreacting to our having matching dresses, then I realized what she was saying.

"You killed my Bobby. You killed him," the witch screamed.

Assuming she thought I stuck that needle in his neck, I yelled, "He was dead before I touched him."

The crowd reacted like a bunch of schoolkids. Some folks rushed straight for the exits. Others backed off, forming a circle around us, like students at a fight. I almost expected someone to begin yelling, urging us on, but all I heard were gasps. A group of men joined Odell in tugging the aggressor across the room away from me. I was jerking my arms and legs, still trying to get free and hit her back. Buh-leeve me. I didn't see it coming the night before, but enough was enough. Nobody was gonna slap me at my workplace and get away with it unless they knocked me unconscious.

My eyes focused. The men pulling Odell and the witch away were Daddy and three of my brothers, all dressed up in suits. Otis scurried over to them and said to the woman, "Not her. She works here. The widow is the woman she was talking to."

"What did you do, Doofus? Did you sic her on Callie?" Odell bellowed.

"No, she asked who was Bobby's wife, and I pointed to where Callie and Betty were standing."

Odell still held the struggling, screaming orange-haired woman, but he let loose with a stream of cussing and hollering at Otis right then. Usually he only does that when no customers are around.

John nudged me out the back door. I hoped Odell kept control of the witch while fussing at Otis because Daddy, Bill, Mike, and Frank abandoned her to Odell and joined John and me on the steps.

"What was that?" I gasped.

"Bobby Saxon's first wife," John said. "She apparently thought you were his latest one."

"Eileen always was a hot-tempered gal," Daddy added.

The Parrish men talked a few minutes and decided to drop me off at home. "Then we'll go over to June Bug's and drink a beer in memory of old Bobby," Bill said.

"Oh, no," I argued. "I've heard about June Bug's as long as I can remember, and you would never let me go. I'm grown now. I'm going, too."

Daddy said no, but John told him someone should probably watch me since I'd had a concussion the night before and another head whack tonight. The men in my family decided they wanted to go to June Bug's more than they didn't want me there.

If I'd known what I'd have to do in June Bug's, I wouldn't have been so happy to get my own way.

# Chapter Five

**J**une Bug's, a pool hall and bar fifteen miles out of St. Mary, sat in the opposite direction from Beaufort. I'd never been inside, but it's necessary to pass the bar to get to the abandoned Halsey farm. All of the Halsey family died or moved away years ago, and no one had lived there for as long as I can remember. My first real boyfriend and I used to park at the Halsey place. We spent many afternoons there talking about growing up, getting married, and living happily ever after.

A couple of times, my boyfriend offered to take me to June Bug's. I'd heard about it for years, but Daddy and all five of my brothers forbade me to go, so I stayed away even during my wildest high school days. Buh-leeve me, back then I didn't want to meet one of my brothers face-to-face in a den of iniquity. I'd never have dreamed I'd wear a black funeral dress on my first trip to June Bug's nor be with Daddy and four of my brothers.

The building was unpainted concrete block. (Concrete blocks are the same thing in the South as cinder blocks in the North.) A sloppy "June Bug's Club" sign was posted by the door. I'd have thought the biggest nights were weekends, but here it was Tuesday evening and the parking lot was packed with pickup trucks. Bob Seger's "Old-Time Rock 'n' Roll" blasted through the walls. I recognized the song because my brothers played tapes constantly when I was a little girl.

Daddy, Bill, Mike, and Frank jumped out of Daddy's Ford F-350 diesel and came running to John's car window before we even got our seat belts unlatched. "Be sure to tell Callie she has to dance at least once with June Bug or we'll all be barred," Bill told John.

Guess my other brothers think I pay more attention to whatever John tells me than to what they say. Mike and Frank backed him up, nodding their heads and adding, "Definitely."

The men paid a dollar apiece at the door. No charge for women. My first glimpse inside June Bug's was disappointing. I'm not quite sure what I expected all those years, but I never pictured an unpainted block interior with concrete floors. A long bar lined the right side of the wall. Big jars sat there filled with red hot sausages, purple pickled eggs, big green pickles, and pink pig's feet. They probably accounted for the slightly vinegary smell beneath the strong odor of beer and cigarette smoke.

Several good ole boys were shooting pool at two tables across from the bar. Old-fashioned illuminated beer signs hung on the walls with extension cords snaking down to overloaded receptacle expanders. Some of those signs would bring a fortune at a flea market. I'd pay a pretty penny myself for the one with the three-dimensional Budweiser Clydesdale horses.

Daddy and John stopped at the bar for our drinks. I called out, "Make mine Michelob." Bill, Frank, and Mike led me to the rear area of plastic-covered, unmatched booths in different colors near a bright neon jukebox and small wooden dance floor. That's when I saw the man jiggling an old-time mountain of flesh to some old-time rock and roll while a sweet young thing shook her booty just in front of him.

The man was big. No, he was humongous. I'd say five hundred pounds since I'm partial to hyperbole. But I'd bet next week's salary he weighed over three fifty. Wispy white hair hung to his shoulders, and his beard was about the length of the Santa's at the mall in Beaufort every year, but much scragglier. He wore overalls. Not coveralls with sleeves. Overalls. The straps hung over his pudgy bare shoulders with his Doughboy arms swinging in rhythm to the music while he snapped his sausage fingers. No shirt. No T-shirt. No shoes. For all I know, that pair of overalls may have been all he was wearing. Puhleeze. That wasn't a pretty thought.

Bill, Mike, and Frank grinned at me.

"June Bug?" I asked.

They nodded, smirked, and restated that I had to dance with him because he owned the place. I consoled myself that the girl shaking with him on the dance floor wasn't even standing near him. The song ended. Slaps of cue sticks and pool balls banging each other merged with loud voices. June Bug reached our booth at the same time John and Daddy arrived with five draft beers and one Coke.

"Where's my Michelob?" I said when Daddy set the soft drink in front of me.

"You've got pain pills. Can't drink beer with that medication," John said.

"I haven't taken anything since early this morning."

"Give her a beer on me if she wants one," June Bug said in a drawl that was exaggerated even for South Carolina. "When you gonna introduce me to this pretty little thing?"

"This is my daughter, Calamine," said Daddy. "My only daughter. And she ain't drinking no beer while she's taking pain pills."

June Bug bowed about as low as the Pillsbury Dough-boy could and said, "Calamine, may I have the pleasure of the next dance?"

I nodded. June Bug waddled to the jukebox and pushed in a few dollars. The next song was Elton John blaring, "Saturday night's alright for fighting." I sure was glad it was Tuesday. When I stood, June Bug motioned me to sit back down. "I gotta catch my breath on this one, but the next one is ours." He looked around the table. "Where's the Michelob she wanted?"

"I told ya. She ain't getting it because she's my daugh-ter and she's taking pain pills," Daddy said firmly. Then he said, "Do you know how many men it takes to open a man's beer?" When June Bug shrugged his shoulders, Daddy delivered the punch line I'd heard over and over while growing up. "None. A woman should open it before she brings it to him."

Everybody laughed except me. I sipped my Coke. Might as well forget the beer. There I sat in June Bug's with all my brothers except Jim. He's on a navy ship in the Middle East. I looked at my family and my surroundings. Like so many other things in life, I realized, the expecta-tion was a whole lot better than the realization.

When Elton John finished his song, June Bug nodded and offered me his hand. We walked to the dance floor and arrived just as Tammy Wynette sang out, "Stand by Your Man." It's not a fast dance. It's slow. Real slow. Not only that, but I hate it because my ex-mother-in-law once tried to explain my marital responsibilities to Donnie by playing that song to me after I caught him doing what he did that made me leave him. June Bug pulled me up just as tight as he could, which was closer than I'd have thought, considering the size of his belly. If it hadn't been for my bit of inflation in the chest area, I'd have been flat against him.

From the odor coming out of his hairy armpits, I guessed June Bug had been dancing all day. From the odor of his breath and skin, I guessed he'd been drinking all day, too. I thought about begging a sudden need to go to the restroom, but when I saw the grins on my brothers' faces, I decided to show them. I snuggled right into that smelly chest and made it to the last, "Sta-a-a-nd by yore ma-an."

June Bug escorted me to the edge of the little wooden dance floor, bowed again, then yelled over the noise of the pool tables, "This next song I'm playing is for Bobby Saxon 'cause he loved it so."

"Prop Me Up Beside the Jukebox If I Die" burst from the jukebox, and the customers laughed, hooted, cat-called, and just plain yelled.

When I sat down, Frank, who's next to me in age, only two years older than I am, leaned over and whispered. "If you want that beer, I'll buy it. You earned it."

I giggled. "I sure did, but I think I'm gonna see if John will take me home. The memorial service is at ten in the morning, and my head isn't feeling its best. I might take one of those pain pills before bed after all."

"Yeah, we ought to be going," John said.

When June Bug saw us all stand, he hurried over to our booth. "Thank you for the dance, little lady. You come back anytime you want, and don't worry about bringing all these Parrish men with you. I'll watch out for you any-time you're in my place." He walked with us, bare feet on the dirty concrete floor, while he delivered this mono-logue.

Just as we reached the door, it swung open and in walked Bobby Saxon's orange-haired first wife. She was

with Nick Rivers and a whole crowd who must have
come directly from Middleton's because, like us, they
had on Sunday-go-to-meeting clothes, except Cowboy.
He wore a royal blue western outfit with silver rhinestones. Then again, that probably *was* his Sunday suit.
The first Mrs. Saxon didn't even glance at me. I wondered if she and Bouncy Betty went at it after I left.

I thought June Bug was going to walk us out the door,
but he turned to express condolences to the orange-haired
witch.

Daddy and The Boys waved good-bye and promised
to see John and me at the service the next day. I think of
my brothers as The Boys with capital letters even though
they're all older. John is thirteen years older than I am, and
then they come like steps: Bill, Mike, Jim, and Frank, with
me at the bottom. Bill, Mike, and Frank are all boomerang
boys. They move in and out of Daddy's house depending
on their employment or marital and/or girlfriend status of
the moment.

As John drove out of the parking lot, I noticed a big silver gray SUV. "Look at that Savana," I said.

"Nice one," John said. "Don't tell me you're considering trading cars." He grinned. "Or giving the Pony back
to Donnie." John's called my Mustang "the Pony" since I
took it from my ex.

"No way, no time, no how, but if my car ever can't be
fixed, I'm going to get something big like that for Jane
and me to camp in. I promised to take her to a bluegrass
festival, and that's big enough to put cots in the back."

"Little Sister, I've got a new twenty-four-foot Win-
nebago motor home, fully equipped. If you ever want to
borrow it, all you have to do is drive to Atlanta and pick it
up."

I leaned back against the headrest, enjoying the contrast between the refreshing Armor All odor in John's

Mercedes and the stale cigarette, beer, and vinegary smell of the bar. He must have thought I looked a little worn from the past couple of days because he added, "I might would even bring it over to you."

"Thanks, I wish all my brothers were like you."

My response embarrassed him, and John changed the subject.

"Well, what did you think of June Bug's?" he asked.

"You should have told me about June Bug all those times I begged to go when I was younger. It would've stopped a lot of my whining."

"If it turns out that the hypodermic you found in Bobby Saxon's neck killed him or was to make sure he drowned in the pool, June Bug could be on the suspect list."

"Why? June Bug dedicated that song to him. Sounded like Bobby Saxon was a regular customer."

"Oh, Bobby was a regular customer all right. Regular since we were about sixteen. A few years back, June Bug's granddaughter lost her virginity. Wasn't forcible rape. Consensual, but the girl was too young and she got pregnant the first time. I know it's rare, but it happened. Bobby was trying to get untangled out of a marriage to do the right thing by the girl, but before that happened, the problem solved itself. She lost the baby and hemorrhaged so much she was hospitalized. She never told who fathered that baby, but June Bug's sworn ever since to kill whoever messed with his granddaughter."

"How old was she?"

"Fourteen, maybe only thirteen."

"That's pretty low-down."

"I'm not defending Bobby, but the girl looked over twenty-one and June Bug let her hang out in the bar a lot. All I'm saying is that if June Bug *did* find out that Bobby Saxon was the man who deflowered his granddaughter, he might have fulfilled his threat. Don't you think that might make him a suspect?"

"Not a suspect, but a person of interest," I said. John just looked at me. "New terminology," I said.

"Where'd you learn that? In all those mystery books you read?"

"Nope," I answered. "Person of interest is what the news reporters now call folks who would have been considered suspects a few years back."

John drove in silence.

We had a person of interest.

Did we have a murder?

# Chapter Six

"**C**alamine killed Bobby Saxon."

That's what I heard Sheriff Wayne Harmon tell my brother John, standing on the porch at Middleton's right before Bobby Saxon's memorial service Wednesday morning. Daddy had sent me out on the veranda to ask John to come sit with him and The Boys in the chapel. The message meant, "Get yourself in here with us," but it wasn't my job to interpret, just deliver.

The sheriff and John were talking with Hank LeGrand. Hank grew up in St. Mary, but he'd moved to Charleston and was now chief of police there. When I saw the three old buddies deep in conversation, I figured they were catching up on each other's lives and families, not accusing me of murder.

"Calamine killed Bobby Saxon."

*"I did not!"*

People walking up the steps and entering the building turned to stare at me. They didn't stop, and nobody said anything. Probably remembered me from the night before and wanted no part of whatever I was into today.

I didn't mean to scream, but my actions don't always match my intentions. I shouted, "He was dead before I saw him. He was already embalmed. If he hadn't been dead before, that would have killed him."

I'd just broken two of the first funeral business rules I learned when I came to work. Never, never say anything that could hint that a body might come to the funeral home still alive. Nothing that could lead to thoughts of premature burial. The second rule was: Don't use the word "embalming." Say "preparation of the deceased."

"What are you yelling about?" John asked.

"I just heard Sheriff Harmon tell you I killed Bobby Saxon." I spoke more calmly, but I couldn't hold back the tears. I hate, just hate, to cry. Some women cry like ladies. I wind up with red, blotchy skin, bloodshot eyes, and a runny nose. I loathe to do it, especially in front of a man, even one of my brothers, but I couldn't help it.

Wayne Harmon and Hank LeGrand laughed. Definitely at me. Gave me those same looks I got when I was a little girl and they were hanging out with my older brothers. That made me sob louder. The sheriff and chief of police both thought I was ludicrous. John handed me a handkerchief.

"Callie," Sheriff Harmon said, "I didn't say 'Calamine' killed him. The toxicology reports show that Catamine killed him." He stressed the *l* in my name and the *t* in the other word.

"Who is Catamine?" I asked.

"Not who. What," said Hank. "You know . . . Special K."

"You're telling me Bobby Saxon died from too much cereal?"

Harmon laughed at me again. Just wait. When he dies,

I'm going to comb his hair wrong. Not really. I take pride in my work, but it's a nice revenge to imagine, especially since back when Wayne Harmon and Hank LeGrand ran around with my brothers, both of them always had combs in their hands.

"Callie, there are serial killers, but not the kind you mean." Harmon tried to stop laughing, but he still chuckled as he spoke. "It sounds like your name with a *t*, but it's actually spelled k-e-t-a-m-i-n-e. It's a drug called K or Special K on the streets. Medically, it was used as an anesthetic, but now it's mainly a dog tranquilizer and street drug."

I felt my face flush red. "Why would druggies use an anesthetic?" I asked.

"It has a hallucinogenic effect," Harmon said. "They take it for the same reasons they take LSD."

"I thought LSD was out of style, a drug of the past." Actually, I thought LSD was extinct.

"No, there're a lot more hallucinogenics available now, but LSD is still around."

"Then Bobby didn't drown?" I asked.

"Autopsy shows he was lifeless before he hit the water," the sheriff answered. "Dead from a massive overdose of ketamine administered through the hypodermic needle you found broken off in the left side of his neck. That's a blessing, because less ketamine would have temporarily paralyzed him without making him unconscious. Bobby would have been unable to move but totally aware of the drowning process."

"Are you sure Bobby didn't do it himself?"

"Not likely. Bobby was right-handed. The position of the needle on the left side of his neck would have been extremely difficult, if not impossible, for him to reach."

Soft music from the string quartet wafted through the

locked windows onto the porch. Like doors, windows are kept closed at funeral homes. "I have to go in," I said. "The service will start soon, but I want to know more."

"You don't know *anything*," the sheriff said. "What we've said here is completely confidential."

As we turned to enter the building, I noticed that the parking lot wasn't quite full, and there were no vehicles lining the roads as there had been the night before. I figured the crowd from visitation had either been unable to get up early enough to make it by ten o'clock or Bobby Saxon's memorial service wasn't important enough for them to take off work.

John, Sheriff Harmon, and Police Chief LeGrand sat in the chapel with Daddy and The Boys while I went to look for Otis or Odell. Technically, Odell had said I didn't have to work, but since I felt well enough to attend, I felt well enough to help if needed.

I found Otis in the family room standing beside Betty, who sat in the chair closest to the door. Her black dress was even nicer than the one from the night before, though a little tight across the bust. I never have that problem. A tasteful hat and expensive leather pumps, both in ebony, completed Betty's outfit. Classy. She would have been completely classy if she hadn't been swinging her legs, surrounded by smoke, and still puffing a cigarette. Usually our only ashtrays are kept in the consultation rooms. Apparently Odell had decided to move some into the salon we used as a family room for this service.

I didn't know most of the people in the room with Betty, but I knew Nick Rivers. I'd wanted to know him better for years. He stood against the wall, also enveloped by smoke. I wished Odell would let Otis and me get rid of those ashtrays, but Nick looked good even with a cigarette in his mouth.

"How's your head?" Otis asked when he noticed me.

"Better. Do you want me to do anything?"

"Yes," Betty answered my question before Otis had a chance. "Sit here with me until it's time to go in."

Most of the friends, relatives, whoever they were, stood around talking to one another. The chair beside Betty was vacant, so I sat down.

"I'm sorry about Bobby's ex slapping you last night," she said. "I had no idea anything like that would happen. I hope none of his other ex-wives will be here today."

"Don't worry," Otis assured her. "Odell and I have instructed our personnel to be especially watchful to avoid any awkward scenes."

"Thank you. I just want this to be nice for Bobby." She leaned over toward me, held her hand up to cup the sound from her mouth to my ear, and whispered, "Do you know yet when we can intern him?"

The twinkle in Otis's eyes showed that he heard her whisper and caught the added *n*. I wondered if I should have corrected her before, but certainly not now. Not just before the memorial service.

Otis bent to Betty and said softly, "We may be able to pick him up this evening or tomorrow, but you don't want to set arrangements for the burial until he's actually here."

"Can I see him when he comes back?" Betty asked.

"Of course." Otis looked at his watch and straightened up. "It's time," he said.

I stepped aside and watched Otis escort Bouncy Betty and her people to the reserved rows of the chapel. They sat directly in front of the empty, replacement Exquisite topped with white roses and surrounded by the most pretentious of the floral pieces. I took a seat on the back row.

The string ensemble played softly until exactly ten. Reverend Cauble, who doesn't preach at any local church but frequently is hired by Otis for deceased persons who have no pastor, stepped to the mahogany podium. He intoned, "May we bow our heads in prayer." "Intoned" isn't a word I'd normally use, but it's perfect for how Reverend Cauble spoke. The prayer lasted so long I was glad Cauble wasn't one of those pastors of the Roman collar persuasion. They make people stand for every prayer.

"Amen," the mourners echoed. The preacher sat down, and Lisa Owen, who sings in a nightclub over in Beaufort, came forward and did a great job with "Just as I Am." Cauble returned and intoned some more. I admit that since I now knew this was not going to be one of those services where I'd have to jump up and down for prayers and responsive readings, I let my mind wander to thoughts of a drug called Special K.

Who could have killed Bobby Saxon? In books I read, the most obvious suspect or person of interest is usually the spouse. Had Betty killed him instead of divorcing him? Was the money from the insurance her motive? Had June Bug discovered Bobby's secret and killed him in revenge?

Cauble used funerals as an opportunity to reach sinners who didn't usually hear any preaching, which was probably why he was willing to hire out cheap for services of strangers. He talked so long that my mind drifted from drugs and murder to more pleasant thoughts about a certain doctor. That smooth voice was telling me all kinds of sweet nothings when I realized that everyone else was standing.

Bouncy Betty sobbed loudly as the pallbearers pushed the bier with its empty casket down the center aisle, probably all the way back to my workroom. The people from the reserved section followed the casket out. Nick Rivers actually glanced my way. I smiled without thinking whether or not it was appropriate under the circumstances. At least I didn't grin.

The audience remained standing while Lisa Owen sang

"God's Other World," which is performed frequently at Middleton's because it's Otis's favorite funeral song, so he always suggests it. Cauble invited everyone to join Mrs. Saxon for coffee in the adjacent salon. Good grief! More food. Would they have a picnic at the graveyard for the burial, too?

Betty and her people stood right inside the salon door, and guests stopped to express sympathy before heading to the buffet. Nick Rivers wasn't in the receiving line. He stood near the refreshments like the night before, though I hadn't seen him with any food. I headed that way, hoping to get a chance to talk to him. Besides, I was curious to see if we were serving last night's leftovers, but the trays were filled with new, different delicacies. Before I could reach Nick, Daddy called me over.

"Calamine! Come here," he yelled. "You're gonna like this!"

Eyes bored into me as I walked across the room. I'd been the center of attention the night before, and now my dad had made everyone look at me again.

My father grabbed a hefty fellow in a brown suit and black shoes by the arm and pulled him toward me. When we reached each other, Daddy said, "Calamine, this is Happy Jack Wilburn. He's got some exciting news."

The man's expression exuded pure puzzlement. "You mean about the campground?" he asked Daddy before turning to me and shaking my hand. "I'm building a campground over on Surcie Island. Do you camp?"

"Not really," I said.

"She's not interested in camping," Daddy said. "She's a banjer player—a good one, too. You said you're gonna have a bluegrass festival next spring. You oughta book her to play at it."

Happy Jack politely said, "We're mainly booking big names, but what's your band called?"

My face flushed. I've always been able to feel when I blush. "I don't play with a band."

His turn to look embarrassed. Maybe more puzzled than embarrassed. "You're a solo banjo act?"

"No, no," I said. "I don't perform professionally, but I'll plan on being part of the audience. Maybe do a little parking lot picking after the show."

"Yeah, should be good. I've booked Second Time Around already." He kept looking around as we talked. Obviously distracted or searching for something.

"I'm impressed," I commented. "Second Time Around's been hitting the top of the charts. They're really good."

Happy Jack Wilburn looked over my shoulder, nodded and smiled as though he'd found what he wanted, and said, "I'll look forward to seeing you there. Tell your friends about it, too. We'll be advertising on WXYW radio." He headed straight for the food table with Daddy following, pelting him with questions about the campground and festival.

Dalmatian! Even with my pump-up bra, that man had found sandwiches and chicken drumettes more enticing than me.

A hand touched my shoulder.

I admit, I came close to swinging. The last time someone touched me there unexpectedly, I woke up in pain at the hospital.

"How's your head?" a voice whispered. *His* voice. A sound as smooth as the one I'd daydreamed about during the service. His lips even brushed my ear, and he smelled just as delicious as he had at the hospital.

I turned, gazed into those blue eyes, and blurted, "What are *you* doing here?"

Dr. Donald Walters laughed. "Well, I didn't come to pronounce Bobby dead. I came to pay my respects."

"You know Bobby?"

"I knew Bobby." He nodded. "But Bobby's gone. I'd like to know more about you. You're Miss Parrish, right?"

"Yes, Callie Parrish."

"But it's definitely 'Miss,' not 'Mrs.'" He laughed. "I remember that."

"Are you married?" I asked. It was tacky to be so blunt, but I know morals aren't what they used to be, and I believe in fidelity. Besides, my motto is, "If he'll cheat *with* me, he'll cheat *on* me."

"No, I'm not married. Why don't we go have some coffee? Better yet, I'll buy you lunch."

"We can get coffee and fancy little sandwiches right over there." I motioned toward the silver coffee urn. "Lunch is free."

"I meant I'd take you out. An impromptu date."

"I can't do that. I came with my brother. He's from Atlanta and drove over for the service. I work here, too, so my bosses might have something for me to do after this."

"You work here? So that's why you came to the ER in a hearse."

My turn to laugh.

"I'm off Sunday night," he continued. "Are you? Give me your number and we'll make plans for then."

"Sunday night?" Buh-leeve me. This doctor was a real hunk, but I hate missing *Six Feet Under* even more than missing *SpongeBob SquarePants*. The people on *Six Feet Under* are so messed up they make Odell, Otis, me, and all the Middleton's part-timers seem like normal folks. Maybe I could videotape the program if I could find the instruction booklet for my VCR.

I couldn't believe that I was standing there talking to this good-looking, single doctor, who had just asked me for a date, but my mind had wandered to last week's episode of *Six Feet Under*.

"Callie?" Dr. Walters's expression turned to concern. "Are you all right?"

"Yes, I'm sorry. Dinner Sunday night will be fine, so long as we can be back to my apartment by eight." I added directions to my place. He grinned and said he'd pick me up at six.

An hour after Dr. Donald Walters left, I realized that I hadn't told him why I wanted to be home by eight. No wonder he'd grinned.

Bet he would be expecting something more than my favorite television show.

# Chapter Seven

**J**ohn seemed serious as he drove wordlessly from Middleton's toward my apartment after the memorial service. Finally, he said, "Callie, my old friend Bobby was murdered. I'm not sure it's a good idea for you to work at the funeral home. Whoever knocked you out and stole the casket thinking Bobby's body was in it must have been Bobby's killer."

"Probably, but I like this job better than anything else I've ever done."

"I'm not saying quit for good. Just suggesting you might take a leave of absence until everything's cleared up."

"I promise you I won't get myself in trouble," I said, "but I'm not going to give Otis and Odell a chance to replace me, even temporarily." I didn't plan to try to solve Bobby Saxon's murder, but I confess that I wanted to look around a bit. I had a personal vested interest in catching the murderer if the opportunity presented itself. After all, John was right—it must have been the killer who hit me on the head.

* * *

**John headed back** to Atlanta early that evening. Since Otis had said not to return to work until tomorrow, I changed into jeans and my T-shirt that has "Virgin" emblazoned across the front in silver glittered letters. (By the way, it's an old shirt.) Jumped into the Mustang and cruised over to Jane's.

I don't know why Jane and I bonded so quickly when Jane's mom took her out of a special residential school for the blind and brought her home to St. Mary. The first time the teacher led Jane into class in ninth grade, I liked her. The friendship grew quickly, especially when Jane learned I had no mother and I found out Jane's father abandoned her mom right after learning his newborn daughter was blind. Jane was an only child, and she liked all the noise and males at my house. I liked the calm and quiet of her home.

While teaching five-year-olds to use computers in kindergarten, I often thought how much easier classroom computers would have made school for Jane. She'd mainstreamed through high school using a portable Braille machine to take notes and an electronic typewriter to prepare work for teachers.

It's a miracle Jane has survived to her thirties, because she knows no fear. Her blindness hasn't slowed her down—and she's not just "legally blind." Jane has no sight at all, doesn't even see shadows or bright lights. She was born with no optic nerves. Her mom died right after we finished high school, and Jane has lived alone most of the time since then. She does her own cooking, cleaning, and laundry.

Jane and I tried rooming together for a while when I came back after my divorce, but Jane says I'm too sloppy. Ex-cuuze me. I'm not sloppy, just totally non-anal, whatever the proper word is for that. I don't always put things where they belong. After Jane put garlic powder on her cinnamon toast and had some other Callie-induced fiascoes, I rented my own place. Probably saved our friendship.

In her younger years, Jane got into drugs and was caught shoplifting at the Kmart in Beaufort. Imagine a blind person shoplifting! The store rent-a-cop could've been standing right beside her and she wouldn't have known it. The worst part is she had no regret. She was furious when they arrested her because she'd had sticky fingers for years without being caught. The judge let her off because of her "visual handicap."

Jane also claims she went through a promiscuous period while I was away at college. I'm not sure if it really happened or she just told me all those things for shock value, but she swears she's settled down now. She's the one person who accepts me exactly as I am, no matter how I act at the moment. She's also the only person who really understood why I divorced Donnie.

I called Jane on my cell phone just before reaching her apartment. "Hey, Jane. I'm headed over. Turn on the lights."

Jane lives in a one-room efficiency over Mrs. Pearl White's garage. Mrs. White has been a widow for years, but she wants to be called Mrs. and she wants it pronounced "Miz-uzz," in two syllables. Her maiden name was Gray, so she was Pearl Gray before she became Pearl White. I'm not kidding. Every time I see her, those names make me think about teeth-whitening ads.

Mrs. White works for the Commission for the Blind, and she's been trying to reform Jane for years. She tells Jane to remember that she represents all visually handicapped people, and some of her behaviors aren't good for the image. Jane declares she's no stereotype for blind people, or for women, or for red-haired folks, or for southerners.

The porch light flicked on just as I pulled into Jane's drive. The steps up to her apartment are steep. She's never fallen on them, but I have. And I wasn't even drinking. Jane stood in the open door at the top of the flight, wearing one of her hippie dresses, her long red hair hanging down her back. Some women pay big money for vintage dresses from the sixties, but Jane inherited hers from her mother.

"Hey, where've you been? I haven't seen you in days." She turned to go in just as my foot hit the top step. She recognizes her friends' cars by sound, and she can always tell where I am if she's near.

I gave Jane a hug, reached around her, and flipped on the light switch. If it weren't for me and other sighted friends, she wouldn't even bother to have bulbs in the fixtures. Jane's apartment is a big square room with one corner walled off around the bathroom. The other three corners hold a kitchen area; a loveseat, television, and recliner in another; and her bed in the fourth. The room is just barely big enough for everything. The foot of her bed touches the little kitchen table, and there's hardly any space in the middle of the room.

The fragrance of caramel-flavored coffee filled the apartment. Jane loves to experiment with coffees. I never know what the *café du jour* will be. I sat on the couch and watched Jane take mugs from the kitchen cabinet, fill them with steaming coffee, and add the cream and three spoons of sugar I like in mine. "Here you go, Candy Donkey," she teased as she handed me my cup. She used to call me something else, but I've been teaching her kindergarten cussing, so now she uses the word "donkey" instead of its three-letter synonym.

"Have you ever used Special K?" I asked Jane as she sat in the recliner and sipped her black, unsweetened brew.

"Nope. Don't like it. Way too healthy for me. I like Froot Loops and Lucky Charms."

"I'm not talking about breakfast cereal. Special K is a drug. Do you know anything about it?"

"Calamine Lotion Parrish! Don't tell me you're considering getting high. You're too old, too smart to start that foolishness."

"Look who's talking." When Jane and I first became friends, I cringed with embarrassment every time I used a sight word like "look" or "see" around her. Finally, she convinced me not to worry. She's always saying "See you later" when I leave.

"I'll have you know I haven't done any drugs lately," Jane said.

"Then what do I smell just under the scent of caramel?"

"You smell gardenia incense from this afternoon, but I didn't use it to cover up anything. I'm clean, really."

"Stay that way. Now tell me about Special K."

"First, I've never done it, but I know someone who has. In fact, that's why I looked it up on the Internet." The Commission for the Blind supplies Jane with all this software that enables her to send and receive e-mail as well as surf the Net.

"What did you find out?"

"Anesthesiologists first used it to induce a type of paralysis during surgery, but doctors stopped using it with humans. Vets have it, and now it's on the street. It causes muscle paralysis and hallucinations. It's scary because the dopers can't move while they hallucinate, and there's only a very fine line between a recreational dose and a fatal shot."

I finished my coffee. Jane reached for my mug and stepped over to the kitchen area to refill it. I'll never understand how she does that. She always knows when a guest's cup or glass is empty.

"Fatal shot?" I asked. "A little drink like a shot of bourbon?"

"No, shot like a needle in the arm."

I told Jane about the hypodermic in Bobby Saxon's neck. She remembered Bouncy Betty from school and wished she'd been there when Bobby's first wife slapped me. No doubt Jane would've gotten into a catfight with her. When I described my trip to June Bug's, Jane howled with laughter. "Do you know the story of that bar?" she asked.

"No, I just know I always wanted to go."

"Did you see the farmhouse right down the hill from the club?"

"Didn't notice."

"Callie, you've got two eyes that work and you don't use them. The house is where June Bug and his family live. June Bug used to go to clubs, get poopy-faced." She laughed. "Kindergarten cussing. Aren't you proud of me?" I giggled, too. "Anyway," she continued, "he'd try to drive. Deputies would stop him and take him home.

"June Bug drove drunk so many times that the officers were totally disgusted with him. Finally the sheriff told all his deputies that instead of driving June Bug home next time, just haul him off to jail. Sure enough, the very next time June Bug got pulled over for DUI, the smart-aleck deputy mouthed that he was taking him to the pokey, and June Bug went nuts."

"How bad nuts?"

"Nuttier than a pecan roll at Stuckey's. The deputy had to radio for the sheriff to send reinforcements. It took six men to get the handcuffs on June Bug. When they tried to put him in the deputy's car, he got loose, charged at the sheriff's new cruiser, and butted his head into the driver's side door. Left a big dent. Sheriff told June Bug next time he got a DUI, he'd shoot him. June Bug believed him, and when June Bug got out of jail, he built his club. He's been drinking and dancing there ever since without driving."

"The sheriff threatened to shoot him?" I asked. Like me, Jane is inclined to exaggerate at times.

"Not Wayne Harmon. Douglas Cooper, the sheriff before Harmon. Sheriff Cooper left town right before the town could fire him. This happened over twenty years ago. Before I even moved here from the home for the blind. Who knows? Maybe that sheriff *would* have shot June Bug."

"Interesting story. How do you know all that if it happened before you came?"

"Listen, just because I'm going through a quiet phase doesn't mean I haven't been around."

"Then you've been to June Bug's?" I asked.

"Yep. More times than I can count. By the way, if you know the right people who hang out in June Bug's, you can buy drugs."

"Special K?"

"I don't know. You can buy pot and other dope, though, if you know who to see. Callie, listen—just keep out of June Bug's and stay away from investigating Bobby Saxon's murder. You're not streetwise and you could get hurt."

Jane's clock beeped nine, and I put my empty cup in the sink. Jane said, "You don't have to go, Callie. Stay and watch me work." Now, there's no watching Jane work. There's *listening* to Jane work. I generally leave when it's time for her to start. "I'll let you talk," she teased. "Who knows? You might find yourself a boyfriend. I get some calls with very familiar voices. I think some of them might be local men."

"Buh-leeve me, I'm not interested in finding a boyfriend *that* way. You haven't been giving out personal information about yourself, have you? Don't warn me I might get hurt checking out Bobby Saxon's murder if you're seeing men you meet on that 900 line."

"Do I have 'stupid' written all over me? What I do on that phone is work only."

"Good! Besides," I said, "I've seen someone I might be interested in. Actually seen two."

"Miss Monogamy is looking at two men?"

"Looking at one, got a date with the other."

"Do I know either of them?"

"Yes, you remember Nick Rivers from school, don't you?"

"Nick Rivers? Crazy Nick Rivers, who stole the Beaufort High School mascot and rode all over town with it on the seat beside him? Dumber than dumb Nick Rivers, who passed his classes only because he was such a whiz on the basketball court?"

"Jane, I don't think Nick was crazy or dumb. I think he did all those stunts because he had a great sense of humor. Why study when he was guaranteed B's so he'd be eligible to play b-ball?"

"Yeah, B's for b-ball. Not like blind students who had to work for them."

"Or sighted girls named Callie who had to work, too."

"You just can't see beyond that guy's good looks, can you?"

I didn't say that if Jane could see him, she might have the same reaction. I kept my mouth shut and she continued, "Did he ask you out?"

"No, the doctor I met while I was in the hospital asked me out for Sunday night."

"Fall in love with him quick and leave Nick Rivers alone."

The phone rang when I opened my mouth to continue defending Nick. Jane cooed, "Hello-o-o-o, this is Roxanne. I'm so-o-o-o glad you called me. Can you hold just a minute while I change into something sexy? Then I'll describe what I'm wearing, and I'm sure you'll love it." I jumped up and headed for the door. Jane held her hand over the receiver and asked me to come for supper the following night. As I pulled from the drive, I saw the lights go out.

**I had lots** to think about. John said June Bug might have reason to kill Bobby Saxon. Harmon said Bobby Saxon was murdered, and Jane told me that the source of the Special K might be found at June Bug's. I'd bet Bouncy Betty was a regular at June Bug's, too. And what about Cowboy?

Sometimes driving helps me think, so I drove around for a while. To tell the truth, I took the Mustang from Donnie out of pure spite. Just to take what was most important to him. He had kept the Mustang covered and only drove it to car shows, but that baby handles like a dream. Donnie thinks it's a sacrilege that I sold my Jeep and use the Mustang daily, but I like to drive it for pleasure. Top up if it's raining. Top down when the weather's nice. This was a top-down night.

About the time the coffee did its number on me, I wound up near Middleton's. A locksmith had rekeyed the doors to the building when he rekeyed my car, but Odell had left me new keys to everything when he brought the Mustang over to my place. I pulled into my parking space in the back. The lot was empty. Kind of surprised that no one else was there. On the porch, I did what teachers call the tee-tee dance while I unlocked the door. Then dashed for the bathroom in the back.

*Splash.* A hundred and one dalmatians! I thought I'd sat in my last toilet with the seat up when I stopped living with Daddy and The Boys. It happened every now and then when Donnie and I lived together, but this was a first for work. The water was a cold, uncomfortable surprise, but it didn't delay anything. Feeling much relieved, though I'd had to dry off with paper towels, I went to my office and checked my desk. No notes, just the day's unopened mail. I read everything that's not marked personal. I only leave it on Otis's or Odell's desk if it's something I can't handle.

The letter from the South Carolina Association of Undertakers in Columbia was addressed to Odell Middleton, but I opened it as usual. I expected to find some note about the Monday morning meeting, but not this:

*Dear Mr. Middleton:*

*We regret that you were unable to attend the meeting of the South Carolina Association of Undertakers on Monday. Enclosed you will find a copy of the minutes for Monday's meeting.*

The letter was signed by some secretary named Sandra.

I dropped the paper on my desk. Had Odell lied about where he was Monday? I stuffed the papers back into the envelope and dropped it on his desk before I left. Odell *said* he went to that meeting.

What kind of deal was this?

# Chapter Eight

**O**ne sandwich short of a picnic. A brick shy of a load. Elevator doesn't go all the way to the top. Not the sharpest knife in the drawer. I sat behind my desk and tried to focus on the Tamar Myers book I was reading about a murder at Magdalena's Pennsylvania Dutch full-board inn, but my mind kept straying to the terms folks had used in high school to describe that tall drink of water, Nick Rivers. Not quite bright didn't fit my concept of Nick at all. Jane might be right, but I always thought it was an act he put on. Never could figure out why.

"No calls?" Odell's voice blasted right into Magdalena's life, and I dropped the book, losing my place. He glowered at me as though I could wave my hand and dead bodies would magically be lined up awaiting our services.

"Nothing all morning." I tried to unobtrusively slip the paperback mystery into my desk drawer. Otis and Odell know I read when business is slow, but there's no point in rubbing their noses in it.

"I'm going out for a while. Beep me immediately if we have an intake call." An intake call is notification for us to pick up a body. Odell's frown changed to a pleasant smile. He's usually very nice to everyone but Otis. Probably hadn't even realized what a scowl he'd given me. "How's your head?" he asked.

"Hardly hurts at all. Do you know yet when we can pick up Bobby Saxon?"

"Haven't heard. Hope it's soon. Betty wants to view him."

Modern embalming is not like Egyptian mummification. Those pharaohs wanted to last forever. When we embalm people now, we're creating a beautiful memory picture to last just a few days. Even though Bobby Saxon's body had been embalmed and would be refrigerated in Charleston, the longer they kept it, the harder it would be to re-create that image for Bouncy Betty.

I didn't mention the S.C. Association of Undertakers meeting to Odell. With business so slow, the time definitely didn't seem right to stick my nose where it didn't belong. After all, Odell is my boss. When the door closed behind him, I retrieved my book and tried to find the place I was reading when he'd startled me.

Barely half a page later, Otis popped his head in the door, and, sure enough, I dropped the book again. "Hey, Callie, do you know where Odell is?"

"I saw him a few minutes ago. He said he was going out, but I can beep him for you."

"Nothing important. No calls?"

"No calls."

"I'll be out for a while, too," Otis said. "Beep me if we have an intake."

The heroine of my book didn't even have time to *say* "horizontal hootchie cootchie," much less *do* it, before the front door sounded "The Old Rugged Cross." It's terrible to admit that I hoped someone was dead, but everyone at Middleton's was feeling a little let down. The only body we'd had in three weeks was Bobby Saxon. Slumps happen in the business, but this was ridiculous.

I stepped into the main hall to see who had come in and immediately jumped back. The fragrance of White Diamonds filled the room.

"No, no," the carrot-haired witch said. "I came to apologize." She wore tailored brown slacks and a tan-colored sweater, better with her coloring than black, but she still had the big bright orange hair. Jane is a natural redhead, but this woman's hair looked like she used orange Easter egg dye on it.

"If you slap me again, I'll lay a hurting on you this time," I threatened and gave her my meanest schoolteacher look.

"I said I came to apologize to you. The other night, I thought I was slapping that bimbo Bobby married, but even hitting *her* would've been wrong."

"Do you need to make plans for a loved one or did you just come to apologize?" Otis would be so proud of me. He always tells me to assume that anyone who comes through the door is a potential customer.

"Could we talk for a few minutes?"

Though I doubted she'd come because of a death other than Bobby's, I led her to a consulting room and invited her to sit, but she remained on her feet. I sat in a chair across the table from where she had begun pacing back and forth like a soldier on sentry duty.

"I'm Callie Parrish," I said.

"I know. You're John and Bill and all those other Parrish boys' little sister." She raised her hand to her face and I noticed her short, frayed nails. She slipped her forefinger into her mouth and tore off a hangnail. It had to hurt, but she didn't flinch. I offered her a tissue and she dabbed at the spot of blood on her finger.

"If you knew that, why'd you hit me?"

"I didn't know it then. I'm Eileen Saxon. Yes, Saxon. I've kept the name." She nibbled at another finger and paced round and round the table, occasionally bumping into a chair leg.

"That's my claim to fame. Bobby Saxon's first wife. We married in high school, separated twenty-three months and fourteen days later. All these years I waited for Bobby to get through sowing his wild oats, and when he finally did, he's dead."

"No offense, Ms. Saxon, but are you sure he'd finished planting all those oats? After all, he married Betty not long ago, and he'd been drinking last weekend."

"He was not!" She stopped still. Put her hands on her hips. Her green eyes flashed with anger. "Bobby married Bimbo Betty Boobs when he was drinking six months ago, but he's been in AA almost three months now. Dry as a chip. Not drinking at all. That's why him drowning in a pool doesn't make sense. Bobby was an excellent swimmer, and he'd been sober for months. Why'd he drown?"

"Ms. Saxon, are you telling me you don't know how Bobby died?" I asked the question before realizing that the sheriff hadn't made any kind of announcement, so she wouldn't know about the needle and the autopsy.

"I understand he drowned. Fell into the motel pool and floated right out of this world." She paused. Tears glistened, and I handed her another tissue. She dabbed at her eyes. "I want to know why the casket was closed at visitation. Why didn't that bimbo let anyone see him? I want to know why there was a funeral service yesterday morning, but when I went over to the cemetery a while ago to put flowers there, Bobby's grave beside his mother was still empty. Hasn't even been dug. I left right after the preacher finished yesterday because I was ashamed of what I did at the visitation and I didn't care about being polite to Bimbo Betty Boobs. I didn't stay to express my condolences, but I want to know what she's done. Did she have my Bobby cremated or something?"

"He hasn't been cremated, but if you want me to answer questions, you need to tell me a few things. Quid pro quo." She looked at me like I was speaking Latin. Which I was.

"What does that mean?" she said.

"You didn't see *Silence of the Lambs*?" I asked.

"Sure I saw it, but I don't remember that," Eileen replied.

"It means if you want me to answer your questions, you have to answer mine."

Eileen put her hand to her mouth and tore at her ragged thumbnail with her teeth. "Okay," she said. "Ask me what you want to know."

I thought carefully about how to word what I wondered. "When you thought I was Betty, you accused me of killing him. What'd you mean by that?"

Eileen sat down on the edge of a chair across the table from me, still chewing at the thumbnail. "I thought Bobby drowned or even hit his head when he fell because Betty got him back to drinking, but I found out Bobby attended an AA meeting early Sunday night and he was sober. Explain that."

"I don't have the answers. I've got more questions than answers. Why are you bringing this to me?"

"Since our incident at the visitation, and I apologize again for that, I've been told you're honest and a straight shooter. I figure you'll tell me more than Otis or Odell will." More tears. More tissues. Ragged nails on every finger. The thumbnail and two others bled. She stood and paced back and forth, stirring the scent of White Diamonds in the air.

"Like I said, I just came from the cemetery. Bobby's grave hasn't been dug. If Betty didn't have him cremated, where's she hidden him? I thought if the body is still here, you might let me see him. I came to the visitation to see Bobby one last time. I hoped I could slip something into the casket, but the casket was closed. Will you let me put something in with him if he's still here?"

"Ms. Saxon, I'd have to ask permission to let you, but I can't anyway."

"Can't or won't?" she asked.

"Can't."

Sheriff Harmon told me to act as though I knew nothing, but I hadn't sworn secrecy to him or anyone else. Maybe Eileen Saxon had important information. The first and last wives couldn't both be right. Betty claimed Bobby drank all day Sunday. Eileen said he'd been as dry as a dehydrated martini at an AA meeting that night. I made my decision to share what I knew with the first wife. Quid pro quo.

"Eileen"—I bent toward her and realized my inflated bra was touching the table. Nothing on my chest had ever done that before—"the reason the grave hasn't been dug is that Bobby's body had to be sent to Charleston for an autopsy."

"Then she didn't cremate him." Her eyes fired up again. "She murdered him, didn't she?"

"I don't know about that, but if I share what I know, will you tell me what you know?"

"Of course."

"I'm willing to talk to you, but I really wish you'd sit down."

She sank into an overstuffed chair and sighed. "Everything," she said.

I explained about the sheriff telling us Bobby had died from an overdose of ketamine. She assured me that Bobby's drug of choice had always been alcohol and though they hadn't lived together for over twenty years, they'd kept in touch. She didn't believe Bobby had ever been into street drugs.

"Eileen, will you tell me who said Bobby was at an AA meeting?"

"I can't. Anonymity is part of the AA program."

"Could you ask that person to contact me or Sheriff Harmon about where Bobby was Sunday night?"

"I will. Can you ask the sheriff to have them check Bobby's blood for alcohol?"

"Well, they can't exactly check his blood for alcohol," I said. After all, I thought, Otis drained as much blood as possible out of Bobby Saxon before we knew there'd be an autopsy, so he didn't save any. "But I think they screen for alcohol in eye fluid or tissues or something like that anytime there's a postmortem. Sheriff Harmon already knows they found the drug, and he may already know Bobby wasn't drinking. I'll tell him what Betty says about Bobby boozing all day Sunday may not be the truth."

"*May* not be!" She jumped from the chair and resumed pacing. "I told you Bobby was sober Sunday night." She gnawed her right thumbnail again. "Can I see Bobby when you get the body back?"

"I'll do what I can."

"Can I put something in the casket with him? It's something he'd want buried with him."

"What is it?" We've had people want all kinds of strange things buried with their loved ones, and there are caskets with built-in memento drawers, but we didn't stock those yet.

"Something small and personal. I'd rather not talk about it."

"I'll do my best."

Eileen Saxon thrust her damp right hand out to me to shake. Otis and Odell insist on courtesy, so I had no choice but to shake that hand she'd had up to her mouth almost the whole time we talked. We parted with promises to get back together and share information.

"Dalmatian! Somebody's lying," I said before Eileen's car was out of the parking lot. Was it Betty or Eileen? Odell was lying, too. I wondered who would be next. I don't lie for anyone. I hardly ever even tell people they look nice unless it's the truth.

I went into my workroom and scrubbed my hands with disinfectant soap. My self-righteous attitude deflated a little as I looked down at my inflated chest. What about implied lies? Thank heaven the phone rang and I didn't have to delve into the rights and wrongs of boob enhancement. I hurried to my desk.

I picked up the receiver in one hand and a pencil in the other. Ready to write an order. The tone was low and broken, masculine, but distorted as though filtered through some electronic device.

"Mind your own business, Calamine Parrish."

*Click.*

I heard the disconnect, but sat motionless holding the receiver to my ear. What was this? If someone thought it was funny, he was wrong. When I hung up, the telephone rang again immediately. The ringing shrilled over and over until I gathered enough courage to answer, fully expecting that strange automated voice to threaten me again.

"Middleton's Mortuary. Callie Parrish speaking. May I help you?"

"Is this that pretty little filly over at the funeral home?" No distortion and no doubt who was talking. He didn't pause for an answer. "This is Cowboy. Why was Bobby Saxon's casket closed at the visitation and the memorial service? I told you I wanted to see him laid out. I been looking forward to seeing him dead."

"I'm sorry, sir, but we're not allowed to give out that information." SOP still working even as upset as I felt. Otis and Odell taught me to never discuss suicides, murders, or "whys" with anyone other than next of kin.

"Well, this had better be on the up-and-up and not some danged publicity stunt for him to come back and sell more cars."

"I can't tell you anything about the closed casket, but I can assure you that it's not a publicity stunt," I said to a dial tone. Cowboy had hung up on me.

The phone rang again immediately. I answered, assuming Cowboy had been disconnected instead of hanging up.

This time, Sheriff Harmon was on the line.

# Chapter Nine

My hands shook on the steering wheel. I blinked my eyes and bit my lower lip to keep the tears away. Really, I didn't understand why I couldn't stop crying. I wasn't upset about driving the hearse. Ex-cuuze me, the funeral coach. I'd driven it before. Besides, having driven Daddy's combine like I did on the farm, I'm not scared to drive anything.

I wasn't afraid of seeing a dead body. Corpses are my business. And no one had better dare try to blame my emotional condition on hormones. It is my opinion that testosterone dictates men's actions a whole lot more than estrogen does women's anyway. Jane thinks the same thing, but she says it a lot less politely.

The call from Sheriff Harmon, a pickup and deliver to Charleston for a postmortem exam, surprised me. It's a safe bet those folks in Charleston would be shocked to receive two autopsies from St. Mary in a week. They hardly ever had any business from us.

I bit my lip a little harder and tried to remember Odell's

directions. When he'd returned my page, he told me he was near the location and to bring him the hearse. I mean funeral coach. I have the hardest time remembering my Funeralese.

The form on the seat beside me was filled in to pick up a James L. Corley. I hadn't known the victim was June Bug until Odell started giving me directions, then asked, "Don't you know how to get to June Bug's place? I thought everybody did." Even though I'd been to the bar on Tuesday night, I hadn't paid much attention to how we went. If I'd been thinking clearly, I would've realized that June Bug's was on the way to the old Halsey place. Because I remembered how to get to Halsey's, I could go to June Bug's, but I didn't seem able to think at all, much less think straight.

Until then, I'd been lucky. Most of the folks we bury in St. Mary die of old age or long illnesses. And none of my relatives had passed on since I came to work for the mortuary. Though I hadn't known June Bug well, perhaps the fact I'd danced with him only a few nights before bothered me subconsciously. Or maybe I was frightened. The strange, threatening phone call might not have been a prank like I'd been trying to tell myself.

When I turned off the paved road onto hardscrabble, I saw the Corley home. Right where Jane had said it was, at the bottom of the incline with the parking lot between the house and the club at the top of the hill. The yellow crime scene tape shone brightly in the sun, fencing off part of the bar's parking lot. A Beaufort EMS ambulance, forensics van, fire truck, Jade County Sheriff's Department cruisers, Coroner Jed Amick's SUV, and Odell's car surrounded the yellow secured area. I parked beside Odell's Buick and walked over to the huddle of men, all looking down at the ground.

When I reached them, I saw why.

June Bug's body lay on its back in the dirt.

Two women, one very thin, one very heavy, were tugging at an older, birdlike woman just outside the tape. She was thin to the point of anorexia and had a little beaklike nose. The younger women were trying to pull her away. She struggled to escape their grasps though she looked so puny and so upset that I thought she'd collapse if they released her. Her fuzzy yellow bathrobe matched the crime scene tape except for the dark red smudges on the cloth. She had pink sponge rollers in her gray hair. She shook. She moaned and wailed, "Jimmy, Jimmy, Jimmy," in a high, chirping voice.

The larger woman tugged on the yellow chenille sleeve and said, "Come on, Mama. There's nothing we can do here for Daddy. Let's go back to the house and let them do their work."

The metallic smell of blood punctured the air. A blessing. June Bug had obviously been lying dead in the dirt for a while. Buh-leeve me, the odor of blood is less offensive than some smells given off by dead bodies. The deep crimson puddles, which had gushed from a massive chest wound, appeared to have partially dried on June Bug's overalls and skin. His open eyes and slack-jawed mouth showed an expression of surprise and horror. The inevitable flies buzzed around him. Iridescent wings reflected in the Carolina sunlight. Not a pretty picture. Especially for his wife and children.

Odell came over to me and we exchanged keys. I'd be driving his Buick back to the mortuary. "Did you bring extra-large-sized bags?" he asked softly.

"I brought everything you said you wanted. What in the world happened?"

"June Bug didn't come home last night. Mrs. Corley assumed he'd passed out in the club. He's done it before. She woke up this morning, put the coffee on, and came up the hill to check on him. Found him here. Two of her daughters are visiting and came running when they heard their mama screaming. One of them called the sheriff."

"Was he stabbed or what?"

"Gunshot. Something big from the looks of the wound. Harmon said that when he arrived, Mrs. Corley was leaning over June Bug, trying to give him mouth-to-mouth resuscitation, but he'd already been dead for hours." He glanced toward Mrs. Corley and added, "Speak to her and see if you can help her daughters get her back inside her home. After that, if one of the girls is up to it, set a time to make arrangements tomorrow or Saturday. 'Course, we won't be able to set times until we know when we'll get 'im back from Charleston." I didn't bother to point out that both of those "girls" were older than I was.

Dealing with severely distraught survivors is the worst part of my job. Making corpses look good for their loved ones is pleasant work, but some of my other responsibilities aren't so pleasant. I like working at Middleton's much better than teaching kindergarten. As I boast frequently, I take pride in my position and enjoy knowing I've done my best. Sometimes the bad comes with the good. This one was bad, but I couldn't help being thankful that the shot was in June Bug's chest, not his face.

Mrs. Corley peered up at me when I touched her shoulder. "Are you from Middleton's Mortuary?" she asked.

"Yes, ma'am," I answered. My black dress pegs me every time.

"The sheriff said they'll have to take Jimmy to Charleston for an autopsy. If he's gotta go, I want Otis or Odell to do it. Their daddy always handled anything to do with death in our family."

"Yes, ma'am. Odell is here, and he'll see that everything is just the way his father would have done it," I said.

She stopped crying and wailing, so I continued. "I'm Callie Parrish," I said. "Mr. Corley needs to be taken care of, but they can't do that until your family goes back to the house." A lie. I hate to lie, but the forensics techs weren't going to wait for Mrs. Corley to leave, and I didn't want this old lady standing there when they shoved a thermometer into her dead husband's liver. I didn't want to see that, either, but from the books I read, I understood that was one of the procedures.

I almost told this frail woman that she didn't need to watch, but I suddenly felt that anyone who'd managed to stay married to June Bug was probably stronger than she looked. She might have dealt with that thermometer better than I would have.

"Mrs. Corley, your daughters don't need to see this. Come get in the car and let me drive the three of you down," I said. Mrs. Corley rubbed her red, swollen eyes. Her daughters released their hold on her, and Mrs. Corley allowed me to walk her to Odell's Buick. The skinny daughter mouthed *Thank you* to me.

The Corley home was immaculate inside. A country house, neither big nor fancy, but . . . well, I can't seem to think of the right word. Maybe "precise." It had those starched, crocheted doilies with the stand-up ruffles on almost every surface in the living room. Perfectly aligned family photographs perched on the mantel.

The fat sister led us to the kitchen. Everything there seemed too precise also, maybe "persnickety" is the word I want. Shiny brass-bottomed pots hung suspended from a black wrought-iron rack over the stove, arranged from largest to smallest. They had that "just for show" look. I'd bet the pots they used for cooking were hidden behind closed cabinet doors. Mrs. Corley moved the napkin holder a bit to the left so that it was perfectly centered and told each of us where to sit around the Formica-topped oak table.

The sisters introduced themselves. Patsy and Penny. They both lived in Charleston and just happened to be spending a few days with their parents. I had to fight an urge to laugh. When I taught kindergarten, I used mnemonic methods to help me learn students' names, and associative thoughts still popped into my head when I met someone new. Skinny Penny and Fatsy Patsy.

Skinny Penny poured each of us a cup of coffee, pointedly ignoring the mug already set out on the counter. Her mother told her to put it in the cabinet. "There's no need to leave that out cluttering up everything," she added. The cup wasn't really cluttering anything, but I was positive June Bug wouldn't be needing his "World's Greatest Grandpa" mug again.

"We need to call your brothers and sisters," Mrs. Corley said.

"Yes, ma'am," Fatsy Patsy replied. "I'll go call them on the bedroom phone."

"Is there anything I can do for you, Mrs. Corley?" I asked.

"Just do what Middleton's always does," she answered. "Bring that white wreath for the door, the one with the silk magnolias. We'll need a lot of those folding chairs and that huge silver coffee urn Odell's daddy lent us when Papa died. We have a big family."

"Yes, ma'am," I said. "Someone will bring all of that as well as registers for food and guests."

"I don't want *someone* to bring them. I want you or one of the Middleton boys." The firmness of her words was hard to reconcile with the high, chirping pitch of her voice.

"Yes, ma'am. I'll bring two wreaths, one for the house and one for the club."

"Don't need one for Jimmy's playhouse up on that hill," Mrs. Corley said in the strongest voice I'd heard her use yet. Not only deeper, but louder, too. "When my boys get here, we're going to smash that evil building block by block."

Skinny Penny must have seen that I didn't know what to say. "Yes, Mama, if that's what you want, we'll do it," she said to her mother, then turned to me. "When will be convenient for us to make arrangements?"

"Middleton's is at your service to make arrangements at whatever time is agreeable to the family, though we don't know what day Mr. Corley will return from Charleston, " I answered, sounding just like Otis. After all, I thought, business wasn't exactly booming.

"How about tomorrow at ten? My brothers and sisters should all be here by tonight, and I'd like for them to be there."

"That's fine," I said. "I'll be back in an hour or so with everything."

Mrs. Corley pointed her finger at me and shook it like I was a puppy who wet the carpet. "Be sure all the chairs are alike."

"Yes, ma'am. All our folding chairs are beige, and will the mahogany guest register stand be satisfactory?" I asked that question out of courtesy. Nobody ever cares. Mrs. Corley, however, was not a nobody.

"Oak! My furniture is oak. Don't you have one that will match?" That chirping voice now had a demanding tone.

"Yes, ma'am."

I fled before Mrs. Corley thought to specify what color covers she wanted on the registers. I'd used the last burgundy one for Bobby Saxon, so we had only ivory until our next order arrived.

*  *  *

**By the time** I reached Jane's apartment for dinner that night, I'd had about as much of Mrs. Corley as I could take in one day. I felt sorry for the lady, but I could understand why a day married to that woman would drive a man to drink at night. Maybe even before noon. Everything had to be exactly the way she wanted it. Exactly!

I'd had to rearrange the folding chairs in her living room over and over. She'd changed her mind repeatedly about where to put the guest register stand. She wasn't happy that the oak was a shade lighter than her furniture. I wanted to tell her that her furniture was old and darkened with age, but Otis and Odell insist I must always be mannerly. I definitely wasn't looking forward to meeting with the family the next day to make arrangements.

When I have dinner with Jane, she likes for me to call her when I turn in to her drive so that she can take up the food. I scrambled around in my purse looking for my cell phone to let Jane know I was there, but no phone. Then I remembered leaving it on my desk at work. When I knocked on the door, Jane demanded, "Why didn't you call and let me know you're here? Lost your cell phone again?"

The smell of lasagna improved my mood before I even reached around Jane in the doorway to flip on the lights. "It's not lost," I said. "I forgot and left it at work."

"Callie, you've gotta get yourself organized. Hang your keys the same place every day and assign your cell phone a special spot."

"I did leave my cell somewhere special—on my desk."

"It needs to be on *you*. Sit down while I take up dinner."

I sat on the loveseat while Jane put serving bowls on the table. "Where would you suggest I keep the phone?" I asked. "You know Otis and Odell aren't going to let me carry it in a fanny pack or on a belt like a biker's keys."

"Put it in your bra," Jane said and turned to open a bottle of wine.

"In my bra? That's going to be great . . . bells or music coming from my chest while I'm escorting someone to see the body of a loved one."

"Set the phone on vibrate." She giggled. "It'll be a tit-illating experience."

"Did you say the word I thought you said?" I asked with surprise. Jane knows how I feel about the *t* word.

"I didn't say what you think," Jane responded. "I said, 'titillating.' It means interesting, exciting." Like I needed vocabulary lessons.

She placed two wineglasses at our places and said, "Come to the table. I was just saying that if you kept your phone in your bra, you'd know where it was, and"—she grinned—"the vibe might make your headlights shine."

The slight inflation in my new bra made me feel like my headlights had already developed a bit of a glow, but I didn't mention it.

As we served our plates, Jane asked, "Who croaked?"

"How do you know someone died?"

"Didn't hear from you all day. I figured either you got a fresh body or they sent Bobby Saxon back."

"Both. Somebody shot June Bug Corley, probably in the wee hours of the morning."

"Actually, I'd already heard about June Bug getting killed," Jane said. "I just asked you that because you hate the term 'croaked.' Does the sheriff think Bobby and June Bug's deaths are related?"

I'm always amazed how Jane knows what's going on even though she hardly ever leaves her apartment. She must spend a lot of time on the phone during the day as well as at night.

"I do hate for you to ask who croaked. Makes it sound like I work on frogs and reminds me of those dissections we did in tenth-grade biology," I said. "So far as I know, they don't have a suspect for either murder yet, and the only way the two deaths are tied together is that they both took place in St. Mary." I inhaled the scrumptious scent of Jane's lasagna before adding, "And Bobby Saxon's body *is* back. When Odell took June Bug to Charleston, they let him pick up Bobby. Otis is working on him now."

"Thought you finished Bobby before they decided to send him to Charleston for the autopsy," Jane said.

"Yeah, but most of my work has to be done over."

"Why?"

"The medical examiner scrubs the body and uses chemicals that remove the cosmetics. About the only thing I did that won't have to be redone is his fingernails."

"Why remove the makeup?"

"Don't want to miss a bruise or contusion that might be under it. You know they examine the outside of a body before they cut it open."

Jane mimed a gag and said, "You do that on purpose. You know I don't want to hear about it."

She was right. Sometimes I talk about postmortems and my work just to upset Jane, but since I hoped she'd made cheesecake for dessert, I changed the subject.

"Otis wants me to come in early tomorrow, so I'll be finished with Bobby before the Corleys arrive to make their plans."

"Thank heaven for small favors," Jane laughed.

"Thank heaven for lasagna," I said.

Over the pasta and merlot, I caught Jane up on June Bug's death and Bobby Saxon. The sheriff told Otis, who told me, who told Jane, that Bobby's autopsy showed he was dead before he went into the pool. No telling if the ketamine killed him at the pool causing him to fall into the water or if he was thrown in by his killer after dying somewhere else. The only other significant findings were that toxicology showed no alcohol in his system and that he had cirrhosis of the liver, apparently the type caused by long-term alcohol abuse. No drugs other than the K.

"Wonder if he knew it," Jane said as she served me another square of lasagna.

"Knew what?"

"About the liver problem. It's not surprising, considering how many years he drank every night and weekend, but you said he took out a life insurance policy after he married Betty. Wouldn't doctors have found the liver disease when he took the physical?"

"I don't really know. I've never taken out that kind of insurance. Matter of fact, I kept what the school district supplied when I was teaching. Hospital and life. Just converted them over to private policies."

"Middleton's should be paying for your insurance."

"Everybody who works there is part-time except me and Otis and Odell. The group policies they've checked into would cost me more than what I pay now. By the way, do those perverts who call you pay for your insurance?"

"Thought you weren't interested in knowing anything about my clients." Jane returned the subject to murder. "I know you're nosing into everything. Who do you think killed Bobby Saxon?"

"The spouse is always the first suspect, and Betty admits they were talking divorce," I said. "With that much insurance, maybe she decided to get rid of him and is having this fancy funeral out of guilt. If ex-spouses are next in line as suspects, it's a long line for Bobby. There's also a salesman who worked with Bobby and is overjoyed about his death. He calls himself 'Cowboy.' Makes no secret about how he feels—it's a wonder he didn't throw a celebration party."

"That's the man who does commercials for the GMC Corral, isn't he?"

"How'd you know that?"

"I listen, Callie. I listen and learn." She laughed. "Don't get bent. Cowboy used to hang out at June Bug's."

My mind raced. "Seems like June Bug's was everybody's stomping grounds except mine. Makes me think June Bug's death could be related to Bobby Saxon's."

"What about MO? I thought you said that in those books you read, most killers stick to one method," Jane said. "A hypodermic needle and a gun aren't exactly the same. Could June Bug have killed Bobby Saxon and someone else murdered June Bug in retaliation?"

"Anything's possible," I said, "anything except me ever learning to make lasagna like this."

"Guess that means you want some more." My comment was a hint, but even without my saying anything, Jane always knows the moment I take my last bite.

"Just a little," I said. "Jane, your cooking is always fantastic. This might be the best you've ever made."

"What you don't eat here, you can eat later. I'm giving you a doggy bag to take home."

I expected that. Jane's tasted my cooking and knows that I'm definitely culinarily challenged. Feels sorry for me, I guess. She usually gives me leftovers.

Before nine o'clock, Jane opened a second bottle of wine. I don't know whether merlot is the correct wine to serve with Italian food or not, but Jane kept refilling her glass. I declined. It was smooth going down and I wanted more, but I didn't want to risk impairing my driving, and I certainly didn't want to drink enough to need to stay at Jane's. No way did I want to listen to Jane talk Roxanne all night.

By the time Jane's clock beeper announced time for

her to start work, I was at her door holding my disposable Glad container of leftover lasagna. Jane was a bit inebriated. She stumbled as she followed me to the door and thrust the second bottle of wine at me. Half full.

"Take it with you," she said.

I didn't really want the merlot, but I didn't think Jane needed it. I locked the bottle in the trunk of the Mustang. We have laws against open alcohol containers in cars, and I had better things to do than sit in jail. Never been to jail and have no desire to even visit there. I wanted to get home and think about Bobby Saxon and June Bug Corley, try to figure out what clues I'd overlooked.

As I pulled out of the drive, Jane yelled. Not words. Just a loud, long, "Whoooo-ee!"

I'll bet Roxanne melted her phone after I left.

At home, I brought the wine in from the car and decided another glass or two would help me sleep. Later, cozy under the covers, thoughts drifted in and out of my drowsy, wine-mellowed mind. The only thing better than snuggling with my pillows would have been if someone I loved were cuddled there with me. Would I ever date Nick Rivers? Would I fall in love with the doctor? Good grief. Forget the doctor, lawyer, and the politically correct Native American chief.

A chef who could cook like Jane would be the man for me.

# Chapter Ten

I didn't want to wake up. This day couldn't possibly hold anything good. Nothing. I turned over and realized I dreaded moving any part of my body, especially my head. I pulled the sheet over my face, but even that slight pressure on my skin was excruciating. I sighed. Exhausted and the day hadn't even begun. Each time the clock beeped, I pressed the snooze alarm.

*Oh, my head.* My skull hurt and every hair screamed agony. Where was my Aleve? The pain pills from the hospital? Was this a late reaction to my concussion? Then it hit me. This wasn't from my subdural hematoma. Nor was it my three-stitch contusion. I had a hangover. My first since college days. I crawled out of bed and managed to lurch to the bathroom medicine cabinet. Dry-swallowed a couple of tablets and told myself I'd feel better. Eventually.

Today meant working on Bobby Saxon, sitting in on the Corley planning session, and probably dealing with both Betty and Eileen Saxon before the day was over. I knew Otis would press to have Bobby's burial as soon as possible, probably in the afternoon. Saturday at the latest, though we rarely bury anyone on Saturday or Sunday. Gravediggers charge overtime for weekends. But then, Betty didn't show any worry about expenses.

Friday was once my favorite day of the week. I'd take end-of-the-week treats to my students, and before Donnie and I married, Friday was date night. Even after the wedding, we celebrated the arrival of the weekend by going out to dinner.

Since my return to St. Mary, I'd been asked out on dates, but not by anyone who interested me. I finally stopped accepting invitations unless I thought there might be a potential long-term relationship. Not necessarily second husband material, but at least a possible long-term friend. I was tired of dating the creeps to check out the crop.

Before Jane began her current job, we'd frequently go out to dinner and a movie on Friday night. Yes, Jane goes to the movies. She knows what happens, too. When I go to the snack bar and come back, Jane can tell me everything that happened while I was gone. With her new job, which paid better than telemarketing, Friday was one of her busiest nights. She started at six instead of nine o'clock like she did other nights.

I spent too many Friday evenings at home reading mystery novels or playing sad love songs on my banjo. Buh-leeve me, banjo music is supposed to blaze, not simmer. I needed to change instruments or find some happiness to sing about.

In addition to all these woes, I wanted to go back to Charleston. I'd been washing out my new bra every night and kindergarten-cussing my idiocy in buying only one of them. If I didn't have a day off soon, maybe I could stop by Victoria's Secret if Odell would only let me make the run to Charleston to pick up June Bug's body. Of course, out of respect to Mrs. Corley, I'd go to Victoria's Secret before I picked him up. I'd never be so rude as to leave June Bug lying out in the funeral coach while I shopped for underwear. On second thought, June Bug would probably have enjoyed visiting Victoria's Secret. I could just haul him in with me. Only kidding. I wouldn't do it, and besides, he was way too big for me to handle alone.

I pumped up my bra a little more. My chest was beginning to look so-o-o-o-o good. With my headlights shining brighter, and with Aleve, several cups of coffee, and a couple of slices of toast in me (since I didn't have any Moon Pies or doughnuts), I was feeling better by the time I headed out my door.

Wouldn't you know it? Rain. Not a heavy downpour. A steady, light drizzle, just enough to wet the interior of the Mustang. Someone had left the top down. Musta been me. I breathed thanks to the good Lord that Donnie wasn't around anymore. I would never have heard the end of it.

By the time I put the top up and towel-dried the inside of the car, I was late for work. Otis had asked me to come in early. Instead, I was tardy. As the saying goes, poop happens. Particularly when you're half hung over from the night before. Well, maybe more than half.

Not only is Middleton's usually a quiet place to work, my bosses—well, at least one of them—doesn't yell even when I do something wrong. I was glad Otis met me instead of Odell. My head would never have survived Odell's growl. Otis just said, "Come on and get started." Not a word about my being late.

In my workroom, I pulled on a waterproof smock and removed the sheet covering Bobby Saxon's body. He wasn't bad at all. No skin slippage. Very little discoloration. He had the usual autopsy souvenir, a raggedly stitched Y-wound on his chest extending down to the new boxers Otis had already put on him.

Sometimes I wonder if as many men wear boxers in life as they do at the mortuary. My ex-husband Donnie wore Skivvies, those white knit jockey shorts that my brother Jim in the U.S. Navy calls "whitey tighties." Come to think of it, I once read that wearing those could reduce a man's sperm count. Maybe Donnie's preference in underwear was an unknown blessing to me. That shouldn't have any bearing on what we stock at the mortuary, though. A dead man has no sperm count anyway, does he?

The sports heroes on television commercials wear fancy, bright-colored undershorts, and I've seen ads for men's bikini briefs. I have to admit that, except in photographs, I've never seen bikini briefs on a man—living or dead. I try to never think anything personal about the people I serve, but I'd bet Bobby Saxon didn't wear plain cotton boxer shorts when he was alive. I'd also wager that Otis, who makes most purchases for Middleton's, does wear them. That thought made my head hurt worse.

Checked Bobby's hands. With cosmetics, they'd be fine. I used a little sealer and airbrushed makeup on all areas that would be seen after he was dressed. His hair was more difficult than the first time because of the postmortem incisions in his head, but I managed to make him look very natural, which is Funeralese for as normal as possible for a corpse. Otis helped me dress him and with the assistance of the body lift, Bobby Saxon finally lay on the innerspring mattress of his second Exquisite.

"Put him in A," Otis said. "Call Betty and see how soon she can come to view him and then schedule the burial as soon as possible. When she leaves, arrange for the pastor, the excavators, and police escorts. Find out what music she wants, too."

"No problem," I said and smiled in my most fetching way. "Otis, may I have a favor?"

"Sorry, Callie, you can't take off any time right now." Odell would have fussed at the thought, but Otis said it kindly.

"That's not what I want. Is it okay for Eileen Saxon to see Bobby before we seal the casket?"

"What makes you think she wants to see him?"

"She asked me. Said she figured I'd be more agreeable than you or Odell." I laughed softly. "Don't think she wanted to ask Betty's permission."

Otis was silent. He looked thoughtful and rubbed his chin before he answered, "Set up everything for Betty to see him first. After that, if it's convenient to let Eileen see him before the interment, it's okay. After all, Betty originally planned an open casket service. She's never requested that other people not see him."

"Thanks, Otis." I made up my mind to be as sure Eileen saw Bobby as I would be that Cowboy didn't see him.

"Don't tell Odell." He chuckled and added, "Don't think I'd tell Betty, either."

When I called, Betty said she'd stop by at ten o'clock and specified she wanted me there, so I didn't go in with the Corleys when Otis and Odell began their planning session in our largest consultation room.

I'd almost decided Betty had changed her mind when the clock struck eleven, but just then she arrived. Her widow's weeds must have been hanging in her closet because she bounced in wearing turquoise flip-flops, orange Daisy Dukes, and an overflowing yellow halter top. Betty was abundantly bouncy. I smiled as I remembered Eileen calling her Bimbo Betty Boobs.

Otis had draped Bobby's casket.

The drape is a semitransparent lace or gauze-type cloth placed to hang over the open top half of the casket. We drape anytime we suspect we might have a hysterical survivor. It discourages the overzealous from trying to climb into the casket or pull their loved one out of it. That's the truth. I've seen folks try both.

We never know what to expect. Sometimes the most reserved person will go berserk when faced with a loved one in a coffin. Then again, normally uninhibited people will stand totally motionless and silent, just staring at the deceased. Betty was the second type. She stopped for several minutes. I was right beside her, ready with a handful of tissues. They weren't needed.

She tentatively lifted the cloth. "Betty," I cautioned.

"It's all right. I just want one last look."

She leaned over, almost nose to nose with Bobby. I put my hand on her shoulder just in case. Otis would kill me if I let her move that body. Just kidding. I've tried to drop the expression "would kill me" since I came to work at a mortuary, but I've spent so many years saying I couldn't do this or that because "Daddy would kill me" that sometimes I forget.

Betty whispered. Really soft, but I heard it. "Who's rid of who, you motherf . . ."

Ex-cuuze me. She spoke a pair of words I never used even before I took up kindergarten cussing. She kissed the body on the cheek and said, loud enough that I knew I was meant to hear it, " 'Bye, Bobby." The widow swung from one extreme to the other in her reaction to her husband's death. Now she called him a really bad name right before kissing him. Bouncy Betty was also Batty Betty.

Abruptly, Betty turned and asked, "When can we plant him? We might as well get all this done and out of the way."

"We might be able to schedule everything for late this afternoon."

"No, it's not supposed to stop raining until tonight. Tomorrow morning is better."

"Let's go sit down and talk about it," I suggested as I touched her elbow to lead her down the hall.

When we passed the closed door to the main consulting parlor, Betty asked, "Who's in there? Who died?"

"The Corley family is here making arrangements for Mr. James Corley."

"June Bug?" she screamed. "June Bug's dead?"

"Please, Betty." I tried to move her down the hall to the other consulting room. Odell opened the door, peered out, and gave me a scowl worse than any schoolteacher look I've ever given. Glad Otis wasn't the one who looked out. He would've passed out with shock at Betty's attire, or lack thereof, on the premises of the formal, classy Middleton's Mortuary. After Odell's glance settled on Betty's bouncing abundance, he hesitated and his frown reversed to a slight Mona Lisa with indigestion smile.

When I got Betty seated and closed the door behind us, she put her head on her folded arms on the conference table and moaned, "What happened to June Bug? Did he have a heart attack? I just danced with him Wednesday night at the club."

Ex-cuuze me one more time. The memorial service for Betty's husband was Wednesday morning. She'd gone dancing that night?

I told Betty I couldn't tell her how June Bug died. We're never supposed to discuss death by murder or suicide, but I let Betty assume I couldn't tell her because I didn't know. She wanted Bobby's interment at ten on Saturday morning, but even agreeing to pay overtime, I was unable to arrange to have the grave opened that early.

After I explained to Betty that graveside services are usually short, probably only fifteen or twenty minutes, and assured her that we didn't need refreshments at the cemetery, she agreed to move the time to eleven. "Would you like to see Bobby again before you leave?" I asked.

"Nope. I've said my good-byes." She walked right past the open door to Slumber Room A without even a glance. I watched her drive away before I called Eileen.

"The sooner, the better," I told her.

"I'll come right now," she said. "And thank you."

Eileen must be a quick-change artist because I doubt she normally wears black on Friday mornings. She showed up in the same outfit she'd worn the night of the visitation, the dress like mine. I sure was glad I wore a different one today. I definitely needed the tissues when I stood beside Eileen as she bid Bobby farewell. Her shoulders shook and tears streamed. She touched the veil draped over the casket and asked, "Is it okay to look under this?"

When I lifted the cloth, Eileen inquired politely, "Can I leave something in there with him?"

Unless the casket has a special memento drawer, usually anything placed in the coffin to be buried with a body is put there by the next of kin. I never wanted to have to admit I'd told Eileen okay, so I just said, "I'm not authorized to give you that permission, but, if you'll excuse me, I need to check something in my office."

I walked out of A, stepped past the door, then leaned back to watch Eileen place something very small beside the body. She tucked it down into the casket lining. "I love you," she whispered. "All those years I waited, and it ends like this." She kissed Bobby in exactly the same spot on the same cheek that Betty had kissed him, turned, and joined me in the hall.

I'd barely closed the front door behind Eileen when

Odell called me. "Callie, can you come here a minute?" His head was sticking out of the doorway to the main consulting parlor. "Mrs. Corley wants to talk to you."

He motioned me into the room and nodded toward a seat. Mrs. Corley was wearing a flowered print dress, and her gray hair curled tightly to her head. Fatsy Patsy, Skinny Penny, two more women, and two men sat around the conference table. None of them could have been in-laws. They looked alike except for sizes. Some with their daddy's build, some with their mama's. Six kids. Like my family.

Skinny Penny nodded toward me and began, "Mama wants—"

"I don't need you to talk for me," Mrs. Corley snapped in her chirpy voice. "I know this child. She was in and out of the house all day yesterday." She turned to me, and I realized I was the "child" she was talking about. "What I want is for you to find a suit for Jimmy," she said. "Odell tells me you'll take care of dressing Jimmy Lee and fixing him up to look good."

Good? I doubted it, but I said, "Yes, ma'am."

Mrs. Corley continued, "Patsy read in a magazine that clothes supplied by funeral homes aren't really clothes. She said the backs have to be open like hospital gowns so you can dress the deceased. Is that right?"

"No, ma'am, we can put Mr. Corley's regular clothes on him."

"But he doesn't have a suit. He hasn't worn one in years."

"He doesn't have to wear a suit. He can wear any clothes you select."

"That's just it. I want him to wear a gray suit and a white shirt and a light blue necktie just like when we got married. And shoes, too. With socks. Jimmy Lee don't have any of that." June Bug had been barefooted when I danced with him, but I never dreamed he didn't own socks or shoes.

"Odell says clothes are part of your job," Mrs. Corley said, "so you bring some out to the house and I'll tell you which ones I like."

My mind was racing. We do stock clothing, but I'd have bet a year's salary that we didn't have a gray suit to fit June Bug. Even if we *did* cut the back seam. And shoes? Most families supply shoes if they want their loved one to wear them in the casket. We stock very few. None that would fit.

"Mrs. Corley," I answered, "I don't want to upset you, but—"

"But," Odell took over, "it will be tomorrow before Callie can bring them over. That will be all right, won't it? After all, Mr. Corley might be in Charleston a few days."

I guess Odell knew that I was going to tell her we didn't have anything in stock that would fit June Bug. Odell smiled. "Everything's set, then. Callie will bring the clothes over tomorrow. We'll let you know as soon as Mr. Corley is back, and you can finalize your arrangements then."

He escorted the seven of them to their cars. I was headed into A when Odell came in and called me. He didn't look happy.

"No wonder the poor man drank," he said. "She's determined to ignore anything anyone suggests. I don't know why her children came with her. Every time one of them tried to say something, she cut them off. Did you notice she didn't let any of her sons-in-law or daughters-in-law come? That old lady probably sat in that house and planned her husband's funeral for years while he was out partying."

For once, Odell and I agreed, and I didn't remind him

that our policy was for families to always have funerals exactly the way they wanted them. That would have been a little too brassy. I mean, I wasn't really interested in trying to find another job.

"She didn't like any of the extra-large-sized caskets we have in stock," Odell complained. "Had to pick a mahogany custom-order from a catalog. Now I've got to see how fast I can get it. What I want you to do is get on the phone and find the nearest large-men's clothing store that sells gray suits that'll fit June Bug."

"What size?"

Odell cut loose with some cussing that definitely wasn't kindergarten. More like postgraduate.

"I guess I could call the house after the Corleys have time to get home," I suggested.

"Do that." He turned away from me in the way that I'd come to understand meant Odell was dismissing me for the moment. "Otis," he yelled and started down the hall just as "Rock of Ages" announced the opening of the front door.

Betty bounced back in. Still in halter, shorts, and flip-flops, but she'd added a purple canvas tote bag. Good grief. She and Eileen had barely missed each other.

"Hey, Calamine. Have you closed up Bobby's casket yet?"

"Not yet. Did you decide to see him again?"

"Not really, but I decided I want to bury something with him. Won't take a minute. I'll just slip it in there."

Her flip-flops flapped on the carpet as she went to her husband's coffin. She reached into the tote and pulled out something so small that I couldn't see it in her hand. Dalmatian! She reached in beside Bobby just about where Eileen had tucked her remembrance. I hoped the fifth wife didn't find whatever the first wife had left with Bobby.

"There," Betty said, patting the lining almost exactly as Eileen had. She turned toward me. "Gotta go now. See you tomorrow. Don't forget, now. I want a cop at the beginning of the car procession and one at the end."

Two escorts for a three-vehicle parade that would only travel a few blocks. I swear she would've catered in a barbecue lunch if I'd told her it would be appropriate. Odell would probably have agreed to it if the caterer was from one of his favorite barbecue houses.

It was all I could do to wait for Betty to drive away before I was beside that Exquisite, feeling around Bobby. I removed two tiny packages, each folded in white gift tissue. One contained a locket with a picture of a baby in it; the other, a plain gold wedding band. I quickly tucked both back where they'd been and tiptoed out of A. Not that I'm sneaky, but if Odell knew I'd let Eileen put something in with Bobby's body, Middleton's might have a casket to put in Slumber Room B—mine.

I'd only glanced at the two items that were hidden in Bobby Saxon's casket, but my photographic memory kicked in. That only happens when I'm into something I'm not supposed to be into or when I'm feeling guilty. The baby picture had been in color, but faded. A blond, curly-haired infant wearing a mint green jumpsuit. Couldn't tell if the baby was a boy or a girl. The wedding band was wide and plain with no engraving. Not too wide for a woman. Not too narrow for a man.

There's an old saying, Curiosity killed the cat. If I were a cat, I'd be dead now.

Which packet was from which wife?

# Chapter Eleven

"**Yo.**"

    If there'd ever be a house of mourning where a family member answered the phone "Yo," I might have known it would be June Bug's.

I asked for Fatsy Patsy. Well, duhhh. I didn't ask for *Fatsy* Patsy, I asked the man who said "Yo" if I could speak to Patsy. When Patsy said hello, I identified myself and asked her for June Bug's sizes. Of course, I called him Mr. Corley instead of June Bug. Patsy went somewhere, checked her daddy's overalls, and came back to the telephone with a numerical size, a big number. She had no idea what size shoe he would wear. Said he'd gone barefooted for years.

"I have a color photo here of Mama and Daddy when they got married," Fatsy Patsy added. "He's wearing the gray suit and blue tie like she wants. You can pick up the picture if you'll return it." I told her I'd be over in an hour or so, hung up, and began calling every big-men's shop in surrounding towns.

About an hour later, I hit pay dirt. When I did, Lady Luck smiled on me. The closest gray suit large enough for June Bug was in Charleston, and a trip to Charleston meant a visit to Victoria's Secret.

"I'll be standing on the stoop waiting for you," Jane said when I telephoned and invited her to ride along.

Being efficient, I also called the pathology department at the Charleston division of the Medical University of South Carolina to see if June Bug's postmortem had been completed. I couldn't help but wonder if June Bug's autopsy might show drugs, specifically ketamine. The MO was totally different, but two murders in less than a week in a town the size of St. Mary made me fear a connection between them. If they were related to each other, it was more likely that my threatening caller was serious, not just a prankster. Of course, the only information I could get was whether the body was ready to be released.

No, June Bug's body couldn't be picked up yet. That meant we didn't have to drive the hearse. Pardon me, the funeral coach. It also meant there was no point in trying to pump the sheriff for info about June Bug's postmortem results.

Contrary to the weatherman's prediction, the skies had cleared, so I put the top of the Mustang down. "Great day for a ride in a ragtop," Jane said when I picked her up.

Jane began sniffing like a blue tick hound before we turned off the paved highway.

"Something's burning," she said.

A moment later, I smelled smoke, too.

By the time we were on the hardscrabble road leading to June Bug's place, I saw the fire. Billowing smoke and flames licked the sky. June Bug's bar burned high. The concrete block walls stood, but the roof blazed. We pulled up to the edge of the Corley property. Surrounded by her grandchildren, her offspring, and their mates, Mrs. Corley stood near the crime scene area. Her back was turned to the yellow tape. She stared across the parking lot, watching June Bug's club go up in flames. There was a big Cheshire cat grin on her face.

Fatsy Patsy looked toward me and waved. I wheeled the Mustang into the parking lot but away from the flaming building, and Patsy walked over. The jeans she wore forecast that someday she might need the same size she'd told me June Bug wore. She reached into a pocket, pulled out an old, faded Polaroid picture, and handed it to me.

"What's going on?" I kid you not. That's what I said.

"The sheriff told Mama not to make my brothers knock the building down, so she set it on fire."

"Did you call the fire department?"

"What for? It belongs to her now. If she wants to torch it, let it burn. That thing's been a thorn in Mama's side ever since Daddy built it." She glanced at the photo in my hand and added, "That's Mama and Daddy when she was twenty pounds heavier and he was at least a hundred pounds lighter, but it will give you the shade of gray she wants for his burial suit. I figured the picture might help."

"It will. Thanks."

Patsy leaned across me and said, "Hello, Jane. How are you?"

"Fine," Jane answered. "Sorry about your dad."

"Yeah, we don't understand why anyone would murder Daddy," Patsy said. "The sheriff thought someone might have tried to rob him on his way from the club to the house, but the receipts were still in the cash drawer and nothing seemed to be missing from the club. Harmon hasn't told us much more than that. They made plaster prints of tire tracks near where Mama found Daddy, but I don't think they found anything worthwhile."

"Did you call Sheriff Harmon and tell him your mother's burning the place?" I interrupted.

"Nope. We figure he'll find out soon enough. After all, like I said, it's hers now. The sheriff's men had already searched it before he forbade her to knock it down. The only person in this family who *ever* disobeyed Mama was Daddy." She hesitated a moment, then suggested, "If you want to call the sheriff, you do it. None of us will."

My brother John, my friend Jane, and the sheriff had all told me to mind my own business. I didn't think this was my business, and besides, I didn't want to alienate Mrs. Corley. After all, I would need her approval on the clothes I planned to buy for June Bug.

**Doing seventy mph** on Highway 17, hair blowing in the wind, Jane and I didn't even try to talk. When we made a pit stop for a restroom break and to buy Cokes, I asked Jane, "How do you know Patsy? I never met her before June Bug died."

Jane laughed. "I met her in the club. All June Bug's kids worked there at one time or another. They were his bartenders, waitresses, and janitors." Jane's voice turned solemn. "Patsy was always the sweet one. She's gained a lot of weight, hasn't she?"

"How can you tell?"

"Callie Parrish, you don't use what the good Lord gives you. I can hear it in her breathing and when she talks."

"I don't know how large she was before, but you're right. She's a big girl now." I almost added, "But she has a pretty face." Didn't say it because it would have been so trite, but it was true.

We purchased sodas—Coke for me, Dr Pepper for Jane—and packs of nabs. Nowadays, folks call 'em peanut-butter cheese crackers, but Daddy always says nabs. Think-ing about Daddy, I got a package of shelled roasted peanuts, too. When we got back into the car, I handed Jane her drink and pack of crackers. I poured the peanuts into my Coke, just like Daddy used to do. Peanuts in soda sounds hokey, but it's good. Besides, Jane couldn't see me do it.

Jane popped the top on her can and said, "Callie, how well does your nose work?"

"Fine, I guess. Why?" Uh-oh. I wondered if she smelled my peanut-cola cocktail.

"Did you identify any particular smell in the smoke back at June Bug's?"

"Not especially. Why?" I breathed a sigh of relief. She was talking about the club.

"There was a definite hint of reefer in that fire. Maybe that's why none of them wanted firemen or law officers on the scene."

"I didn't smell it, but then, I'm not as used to that odor as you are."

"I told you. I'm clean as a baby's bottom."

I laughed. "Jane, you might want skin as soft as a baby's bottom, but in no way is a baby's bottom clean. Are you trying to tell me you're using again?"

"Nope, just got my metaphor mixed up. I'm clean as a baby's bottom right after a bath. Does that suit you?"

"Stay that way. I was really worried about you when you were into drugs. I was scared you'd spend your life in and out of rehab." I cranked the car but didn't take off while we talked. The Mustang idled.

"Oh, I dabbled in soft stuff, but I never did anything hard and I had enough sense to stop while I could. Some of that stuff is so surreal that I can see how folks get hooked. I'm glad to be clean." Jane frowned and sipped her soda. "Let's change the subject."

"I wonder if Mrs. Corley burned the building because she knew drugs were there," I said.

"I doubt it. Patsy said the sheriff's deputies had searched the club already. There would be no reason to think they would examine it more thoroughly later. I wonder where the stash was hidden that the deputies didn't find it." She chuckled and added, "I know what you're doing. Chew those peanuts or you'll choke on them."

We buckled our seat belts and turned onto Highway 17 again. I leaned across Jane and pulled my Charleston map from the glove compartment. I almost handed it to my friend to find our way. No kidding. Sometimes I forget she can't see.

Charleston is a city of one-way streets. After a few attempts to read the map and several stops to ask directions, we found the men's shop.

Jane insisted on staying in the car. "I've got no interest in men's clothes unless there's a man in them," she said.

The sales clerk was a big guy himself. Not fat, just big. Probably as tall as Nick Rivers, who everyone knows is six feet six inches because of the sports write-ups when he played basketball. Unlike Nick, this guy was muscled and solid looking, and, I might add, courteous and helpful.

"It's impossible to tell the exact suit size from the number on his overalls," he explained. "We can get as close as possible, but we'll have to guess sleeve length." He grinned. "I guess if there's a problem, you can slit the jacket up the back if it's too small and tuck the sleeves up if they're too long. I've heard that's what you folks do at funeral homes."

Ex-cuuze me. "No," I said firmly. "The wife of the deceased mentioned her daughter read somewhere that mortuaries do that, but I don't dress just the front. I want a suit coat that is slightly bigger than you think from his overall size. I can take it up, but I can't let it out, and I won't just cut it to make it fit."

He showed me a suit that seemed close to the shade of gray in the snapshot. The white shirt was easy, and we added a pair of black dress socks. Since Mrs. Corley wanted choices and was footing the bill, I selected three blue ties, all similar to the one June Bug wore in the picture.

The hard part was the shoes. I told the clerk, "I couldn't trace around the man's foot because he's not at the funeral home yet." Patsy had told me her daddy hadn't owned a pair of shoes in years. If Mrs. Corley hadn't specifically said she wanted him buried in shoes and socks, I would have settled for just socks. She hadn't selected a couch casket, which would have exposed his feet, but I'd bet she'd make me show her his shoes.

"Probably wouldn't have helped anyway," the big man said. "The reason the very obese stop wearing shoes is that the tops and sides of their feet become large and swollen, and unless they come to shops like this, they can't find shoes that fit. I do, however, carry a special shoe that is made for"—he grinned—"fat feet."

I learn something new every day. Shoes for fat feet. The clerk showed me black dress shoes that were not only made with extra-large uppers, but that would stretch also, though they looked like leather. I was so enthusiastic that I went ahead and bought June Bug new underwear, too. I don't know what he wore under those overalls, but he'd have on fresh Skivvies under his new suit. None of Otis's cotton boxers. I charged it all with Middleton's Visa and left the store proud of myself.

"Next stop, Victoria's Secret," I joyfully announced to Jane when I got into the driver's seat after loading all the big-man purchases into the trunk of the Mustang.

"Are we going for anything particular?" Jane asked.

Good grief! I couldn't believe I hadn't told Jane about my blow-up bra. She smiled, grinned, giggled, and belly-laughed while I described it. When she stopped guffawing, Jane said, "I want to see it."

Now wait a minute. Knowing how Jane "sees" things, I quickly folded my arms across my chest. I'm not a homophobe, but I really didn't want to be seen sitting in an open convertible on a public street in Charleston with Jane feeling my bosoms, even if they were only air.

The Charleston branch of Victoria's Secret that I frequent is in a strip mall across the road from a long row of car lots. When I see the big "Charleston Charlie's Cars" sign, I know I've arrived.

Some folks might think the hour we spent in the lingerie shop was hysterical, but it wasn't at all funny to me. I should have known Jane was up to something when she reached for her cane and perched her rose-colored sunglasses on her nose as we got out of the car. *Tap, tap, tap.* As she entered the store she touched the floor loudly with her cane every three or four inches. She knows how to use that cane discreetly and silently. Her tap, tap, tapping was to make everyone aware of her presence. And her blindness.

Though I "showed" Jane a bra like the one I'd bought, she insisted the clerk demonstrate the pump-up mechanism. While I selected several bras and some panties in different colors, the saleslady did her presentation with Jane touching, feeling, oohing, and aahing every step.

"And, of course," the saleslady continued, "you only need one pump, so additional bras are less expensive. They come in many colors and styles."

"How would I know I had both sides inflated the same amount?" Jane asked as she patted the cups of the display bra.

"The bra is designed so that the two cups inflate an equal amount at the same time," the clerk explained.

"Well, what if one breast is smaller than the other and you want to make them even?"

"Then this wouldn't be the bra for you, unless you used an insert beneath the smaller side. We have styles different from the one your friend selected, including one designed specifically for women with that situation, possibly due to mastectomies or just uneven growth."

"I haven't had a mastectomy," Jane blurted. Her offended tone echoed throughout the store. She'd been leaning over the counter, but now she straightened up.

Standing at the register to pay for my bras and panties, I grimaced. I had honestly thought Jane had given up playing the games of her youth.

The saleslady stammered, "I didn't mean that. I just meant we carry special lingerie for special needs." Across the room, I could see her face flush to bright red.

"Special?" Jane shouted. "Isn't that a word for different, for freak?" She leaned back and howled like a banshee. I flinched. The saleslady cringed.

I handed my money to the cashier, hoping she'd finish our transaction quickly, but she stood frozen, her eyes flicking back and forth between Jane and the horrified clerk. I wanted out of there. Didn't want to be anywhere near Jane.

"A freak! A freak! You called me a freak," Jane shrieked and stepped toward the saleslady. The clerk moved back, and when she did, Jane fell on the floor. Actually, I've known Jane long enough to know that she didn't fall. She threw herself on the floor and screamed, "You called me a freak and tripped me because I'm disabled! I want the manager."

The scam worked as it always had for Jane. She left the store with a large bag of garments and a gift certificate. Like others in years past, the store would rather placate her than go to court. The manager even carried Jane's belongings to the car and seated her.

As I slammed my door, I saw Nick Rivers pulling into Charleston Charlie's Cars across the street in his gray Savana SUV. He stared straight at me, but made no acknowledgment. Strange, I'd been back in St. Mary several years without running into him. Now I seemed to see him everywhere, even in Charleston.

"Let's stop for dinner," Jane suggested. "I'll treat. You probably spent all your money in there."

"Nope, I'm taking you home. You promised me you'd never do that again when I was around."

"That woman insulted me."

"Dalmatian, Jane! She didn't insult you and she didn't trip you. I've seen that little act before."

Jane grinned and started feeling through her gift bags. "Bet I got more stuff than you did," she said.

"I know you did. Don't even talk to me. I don't want to have dinner with you. I've warned you before that I don't want to be a part of your shenanigans."

"It was just a little joke, a little fun," Jane defended herself.

"No, it's not funny at all. It's illegal. It's stealing."

"Then I guess you're so mad that we really won't stop for food."

"Yes. I'm too angry to spend any longer with you than I have to. Besides, you've got to get home to work."

"Glad you reminded me. If your cell phone's off like it usually is, turn it on before six o'clock. I'm signed in to start early, and I forwarded the 900 calls to your line."

# Chapter Twelve

**H**onesty is a virtue. Modesty is a virtue. I have lots of virtues. But, buh-leeve me, good housekeeping isn't one of them. The only time I really enjoy cleaning is when I'm upset. Somehow scrubbing and vacuuming releases more endorphins in me than exercising does. Jane's actions in Charleston left me in the mood to scour my apartment. Of course, it also made me want to wring Jane's neck or at least put her out of my life, but she's my closest friend. I know from past experiences that I miss her horribly when we're not speaking.

I can describe my apartment in one sentence: It has avocado green shag carpet. A second sentence completes the picture: The kitchen appliances match the carpet. Ugh.

An old brick duplex, the other side has been vacant since I moved in, so I've always felt like I was living in a single-family dwelling with a driveway on each side. A shared concrete porch stretches across the front of the building from corner to corner, and nandina bushes grow by the steps. I love their red berries during the winter months. There's a young oak tree at the front edge of the yard, and the thin, scrubby grass requires little cutting, even in summer.

I borrowed a good idea from Middleton's—the large terra-cotta pots of seasonal plants on the mortuary veranda. I put a smaller clay container by my front door. Each time St. Mary Florals replaces the plants at work, I change mine at home. Pink azaleas in spring, bright mixed annuals in summer, and now, in autumn, I'd planted yellow chrysanthemums.

If cleanliness is next to godliness, I'm in a world of trouble. My biggest problem with cleaning is that I'd rather read mysteries. That creates my next dilemma. I read so much that I have books lying all over the floor, the couch, the windowsills, everywhere. The other day, after looking fifteen minutes for my cell phone, I found it hiding under the newest Mary Higgins Clark mystery. The problem is, when I start picking up books, I invariably see one I want to visit again. I wind up cuddled with a cozy for hours.

Most of my novels come from a secondhand bookstore here in St. Mary. They'll buy the books back or take them in trade. But, to me, a good book is like a good friend. You don't sell them or trade them in. Books and friends. Two wonderful assets, always worth keeping.

But what if your best friend persists in doing things that you know are wrong? Jane wouldn't hurt a fly, and I don't believe she'd steal from an individual. She justifies what she does by saying that Kmart, Wal-Mart, and other big stores can afford to "donate" things to her. I've tried to convince her that theft is theft, and I really thought Jane had stopped stealing when she quit drugs. I was disappointed.

By the time I finished pondering my friend's unique

personal values, I'd scrubbed the kitchen and moved to the bathroom. Note I said bathroom, singular, not plural. Buildings the age of mine only have one bathroom per apartment. I was on my knees, tush in the air, rubbing the toilet brush around inside the bowl and kindergarten-cussing Jane's morals, when the phone rang. I waited to hear who was calling, but the answering machine clicked off after my outgoing message. The caller said nothing. I stayed on my knees and cleaned the tile floor.

The sheets and blanket my brother John had used on the couch went into the clothes hamper. I carted stacks of books into the second bedroom, my improvised storage closet. John suggested I forget buying a bed for that room and just line the walls with bookcases, maybe even put in a desk. I don't think so. I enjoy having a room where I can just stuff things and close the door.

Friday night and I was cleaning my apartment. I needed to get a life. Maybe my Sunday night date with the doctor would be the start of something. Puh-leeze. Spare me my own personal pity party. My life is better than some folks'.

Back in college, I had a friend who was a worse house-keeper than I am. When company was coming, she threw all her soiled clothes in the shower and closed the curtain. Dirty dishes in the sink? No problem. She hid them in the oven. Just goes to show, no matter how sloppy you are, someone can nudge you out of first place. Following that line of thought, lots of people are worse than Jane. But I don't choose to be friends with them.

Enough cleaning. Enough thinking. I jumped into the shower and soaped all over with my favorite melon-scented body rinse. Washed my hair with peach-perfumed shampoo and realized I'd punished myself, as well as Jane, by refus-ing to have dinner with her. I was hungry. Those odors made me dream of a gigantic bowl full of fresh fruit salad.

I dried off, wrapped myself in a white, fluffy terry cloth robe, and went to the kitchen.

Still no doughnuts. Not even a Moon Pie. There are people who make jokes about Moon Pies, but I still love them. When I was a young girl, if Daddy or one of my brothers took me to the store, I always got a Moon Pie. Not the new banana-, strawberry-, or vanilla-coated ones. The original chocolate covering over marshmallow between two round graham crackers. No, I didn't have an RC Cola with my Moon Pies when I was little. Daddy insisted I drink milk.

My stomach growled, but my refrigerator was empty except for a quart of sour milk, two beers, and a chunk of blue cheese covered with green mold. The pantry yielded better results. A can of Campbell's tomato soup and some powdered Coffee-mate. I stirred them together with a bit of water in a saucepan and warmed myself a yummy concoction. It certainly wasn't gourmet, but for a gal who survived most of her college years eating tomato soup made of ketchup and boiling water, this would be delicious.

By the time my supper was bubbly hot, I was into Gwen Hunter's book *Grave Concerns*. I'd read the mystery several times. Hunter has a newer series, but Dr. Rhea-Rhea Lynch is an old literary friend of mine. I was deeply involved in Rhea-Rhea's exciting life and slurping soup when I heard the first noise. *Bump. Bump. Thump.* The sound came from next door. Strange. The landlord told me she wouldn't be renting out the other side for a while because it needed lots of repairs. Surely workmen weren't beginning renovations on a Friday night.

When the sound moved closer to my side of the duplex, I thanked the good Lord that John had changed the locks on my doors. Footsteps. Across the front porch. *Rattle. Rattle.* My doorknob moved. My heart froze. *Bam. Bam.*

*Bam.* Someone was going to break the door to get in. I stalled for time, called, "Who is it?" while searching frantically for my cell phone.

No answer. Just *BAM! BAM! BAM!*

"I've called the sheriff. He's on the way over here," I shouted. A lie. I was frantically looking for my phone. Fear has two main effects on me. It makes it hard for me to think and it makes me hurl. Duhhh. I could use my regular phone, right? I grabbed it just as I threw up. I desperately punched in 911. I won't describe the condition of the telephone at that moment.

The dispatch clerk said someone was on the way. I heard a siren while she said it. Another tremendous thud against the door. The sound of footsteps again. This time running steps. Off the porch. A screamed curse that wasn't kindergarten cussing faded into the distance.

I pushed the curtain aside and peeked through the living room window. I didn't see anyone, but my pot of chrysanthemums lay smashed with blooms spilling over the sidewalk. The sheriff's car screeched up to the curb. Harmon jumped out and ran toward the building. I opened the door before he got there.

"Callie, are you all right?" he asked.

"Someone tried to break in. He ran away."

I was feeling important that the sheriff himself responded to my call until he explained that he'd been only a few blocks away. I described everything that had happened. Sheriff Harmon made notes and called for technicians to come dust the front door for fingerprints. He took my prints for comparison before the techs arrived.

I went to my bedroom to change from my bathrobe. I thought I was okay, but fear flooded over me again. My stomach lurched. I ran for the toilet. My nice spotless, freshly scrubbed toilet. After I cleansed my face and scrubbed the commode one more time, I put on sweatpants and a black University of South Carolina sweatshirt. The night wasn't cold, but I needed the comfort of extra warmth.

When I returned to the living room, the technician was telling Sheriff Harmon that the door and lock had revealed nothing. He explained that all he'd gotten was a few partials of my prints and lots of smudges indicating the attempted intruder was wearing gloves. Didn't even get a clear print that might have been John's when he changed the locks. I went to the kitchen and washed off the telephone at the kitchen sink.

The deputy told me he thought he'd found my key ring on the lawn. The one that I'd had in my hand the night the casket was stolen and I was hit on the head. No doubt it was mine. The yellow SpongeBob SquarePants still hung from it with my Mustang, apartment, and mortuary keys. The deputy held it up in front of me suspended from a ballpoint pen. When I identified it, the sheriff stared at SpongeBob.

"My niece watches SpongeBob," he said. "Where'd you get this? I want one for her."

My diet plan is to eat only kids' meals if I gain any weight. The SpongeBob had come as a toy in one of my kids' meals. I told Harmon he could have it, but he said they'd have to keep those keys as evidence. Finding the keys that disappeared the night the casket was stolen connected tonight's attempted break-in with the perpetrator of assault and grand theft. It didn't matter to me if the sheriff's department kept the keys. All the locks those keys fit had been changed anyway.

"Did you find my purse out there?" I asked hopefully.

"Nope," the deputy said.

"Have you canceled all the credit and bank cards that were in your handbag when it was stolen?" the sheriff asked.

"John took care of that."

"Don't guess I need to remind you to replace your driver's license, too?" Harmon said it without even looking patronizing. How'd he know I hadn't done that yet?

"I'll do it tomorrow," I promised.

"Monday," Sheriff Harmon said. "They won't be open tomorrow." He checked that my windows were all locked as he spoke. "Callie, why don't you let one of us take you to your dad's for tonight?"

"No, I'll be fine," I assured him; then added, "Is there any news on the murders? We're burying Bobby Saxon tomorrow."

"I know. I'll be there."

"Figured you would. Looking to see if the perps show up."

"Callie, you read too many books and watch too many crime shows on television. Nobody says 'perps' in real life."

"What about persons of interest? Are there any good suspects?"

"You know I can't give you details. We're checking out all leads. My thoughts are that whoever killed Saxon stole the casket and attempted to break into your apartment tonight. I can't legally require you to leave here, but I wish you'd let me drive you over to your dad's or follow you there if you want to take your car."

I refused and he stood on the porch until he'd checked the dead bolt after I locked it. I thought I was okay until Sheriff Harmon and the deputies left. Five minutes later, the scared shakes grabbed me again. I called Jane. She offered her couch, actually a loveseat. Her behavior in Charleston now seemed less horrible than my fear of staying alone the rest of the night. I cautiously peeked out the door and ran to the Mustang, glad I'd put the top up.

I'd climbed in and locked the doors before I thought to look in the backseat. Lady Luck had returned. No one was in the car with me.

Jane stood in her doorway waiting. She'd already turned on the lights both inside and out. I felt safe getting out of the car and heading up the steep steps, like someone was watching out for me. Jane might not have been able to see if anyone approached me, but she'd have heard. That's for certain.

My best friend claims she never wants to be "saddled with children" because she's not "a nurturer." Her words, not mine. If I ever hitch up with the right man, I want to be a mommy like I never had. I'm glad babies didn't happen with Donnie, but I haven't given up on the white picket fence. Despite Jane's denial, she's been a real nurturer to me when I needed it, like when I went through the divorce blues. Jane also swears that she neither gives nor takes guilt trips, but I hoped my scolding on the way back from Charleston had given her a few guilt steps if not a real trip.

When I reached the top of the steep stairs, Jane hugged me. She bolted the door after we went in. The apartment was saturated with the wonderful smell of cinnamon hazelnut coffee, my favorite. She was also warming a pot of meatball stew from her freezer. Jane insisted I sit in the recliner, the most comfortable seat in her place, and tell her about what happened. As I relaxed with a mug of cinnamon hazelnut and told Jane all about the past few hours, my mind cleared enough for me to remember the weird phone call at work and the hang-up at my apartment.

"Did you tell the sheriff about that?" Jane demanded.

"No, I forgot it."

"Forgot it! Why, oh, why'd the good Lord give you a brain if you refuse to use it?" She pressed numbers on the phone keypad, more than 911, then handed the receiver to me.

"Jade County Sheriff's Department. Deputy Smoak speaking. How may I help you?"

"This is Callie Parrish," I began. "The sheriff was over at my apartment earlier tonight, and I forgot to tell him something. Can you have him call me?"

"Hold one moment, Ms. Parrish. I can connect you to him now."

"Callie? This is Sheriff Harmon." Maybe it was my state of mind, but he had a really soothing voice. I'd never noticed that before.

"I forgot to tell you about a phone call I had Thursday, right before you called about June Bug. Someone rang me at the mortuary and told me to mind my own business."

"Why didn't you tell me this before?"

"I didn't take it seriously. Until now."

"Did you recognize the voice?"

"No, it sounded like it came through some kind of machine. It was distorted." I thought for a moment. "It could have been the same person I heard outside tonight, but I'm not sure."

"Callie, you've got to think hard and tell me everything."

"I had a hang-up call at home tonight, too."

"There's a high probability that whoever hit you and stole the casket was the person on the phone and at your door tonight. Where are you now?"

"I'm at my friend Jane's house."

"Can you stay there or maybe with your dad until we catch whoever is after you?"

"If you catch him soon, I'll stay here. You couldn't pay me to go back and live with Daddy and my brothers."

Sheriff Harmon laughed. "Call me if you remember anything else."

I didn't want to remember anything, especially how I'd lost all my tomato soup. My stomach was empty and growling again. Jane ladled meatball stew into two bowls and dropped a handful of mozzarella cheese on top of each. Italian meatballs in a sauce with freshly chopped onions, celery, peppers, zucchini, and tomatoes. I love it. Jane gave me the recipe long ago, but mine never tastes as good as hers. I was into my second helping when I realized Jane's phone wasn't ringing.

"Roxanne doesn't seem too popular tonight," I said.

"I called in sick when you telephoned me. I know how much you despise my job, and I didn't want you to have to listen to Roxanne all night."

"I do hate your job, Jane, but I realize you need the money and it pays more than you've ever made before."

"Yeah, besides, I don't have to worry about transportation to and from work. It's really easy. I just tell them all the same things. You could do it if you wanted. Want to try it?"

I won't repeat my answer because I forgot to keep it on a kindergarten level.

Jane continued, "I don't see how you stand what you do. Working on dead people all the time." She stuck her finger in her mouth and mimed a barf. Considering my reaction to fear at my house, I didn't need that.

"Then we're even, because I don't see how you stand your work," I taunted. "Spending all your nights with dirty old men."

"You'd be surprised. Most of them don't sound old, and I told you, a couple of them have familiar voices." She paused. Frowned. "Let's don't go there." Jane stacked the dishes in the sink. "Is your banjo in the car?"

"No. The last thing on my mind when I left my place was bringing the banjo."

"You haven't brought it over lately. Are you getting

tired of it?" Jane has this idea that I'm fickle. Not with men. I've never cheated. She thinks I'm easily bored and fickle in general. Everybody thought I'd do hair in Mary Alice's Beauty Parlor the rest of my life when I graduated high school. After all, I got my cosmetology license through vocational ed my senior year. Ex-cuuze me. It only took six months of listening to women gossiping about who's cheating on who to convince me I was in the wrong profession.

I decided to go to the University of South Carolina in Columbia and become a teacher. Got my certification. Taught for a year. Married Donnie. Supposed to live happily ever after. Sorry. After what Donnie did, I wanted out. Left him, drew out my state retirement for those few years I'd taught, and moved back to St. Mary. I don't believe I'm fickle or restless. I've been looking for my niche, and right now, I like working at Middleton's.

"I'll bring the banjo next time, I promise."

"For more than a year you been telling me you'd take me to one of those whiney bluegrass jams and let me hear you play with the other folks. Now you don't even bring the banjo over to play for me anymore."

I mock scolded her, "And until you stop referring to bluegrass as whiney, I'm not taking you anywhere near it. We'd get there, and you'd insult someone. We both know I can't trust you to behave. You proved that again today in Victoria's Secret." I didn't even think to tell her about Daddy's friend planning a festival on Surcie Island.

"You've had a rough evening, Callie. Don't make it worse by forcing me to throw you out or call and sign in to work so you have to listen to Roxanne all night." She motioned toward her video collection, each neatly labeled in Braille. "How about a movie?"

Jane buys DVDs of old movies and has two favorites, *Forrest Gump* and Stephen King's *Stand by Me.* I've never pointed out to her that *Stand by Me* is about kids going to look for a corpse. I think Jane likes the King movie because of the music. I expected that or *Forrest Gump*, but she surprised me. *Weekend at Bernie's.*

Seems I can't get away from dead bodies.

# Chapter Thirteen

In Columbia and Charleston, I've been in tall buildings that have a twelfth floor, then a fourteenth. No thirteenth floor at all. I noticed it when I rode the elevators. Buh-leeve me, I'm not scared of dead people or graves. I don't believe in vampires or werewolves, and I'm not really superstitious. But I don't walk under ladders, and I won't take a trip on a Friday the thirteenth. Nor do I tempt the good Lord by walking through poison ivy or trying to pet a wasp, even though Auntie Sally Brown, the prophet lady in Summerville, told me my name would bring me protection. After pondering all of the above, I, Calamine Lotion Parrish, have no intention of writing a thirteenth chapter for this book.

# Chapter Fourteen

"**A**shes to ashes and dust to dust," Reverend Cauble intoned. He dropped a handful of South Carolina red clay onto Bobby Saxon's beautiful Exquisite, which would soon be lowered into the waiting Eternal vault beside his mother's grave at St. Mary Celestial Gardens. Several empty seats under the Middleton's canvas awning remained available, but Otis and I stood at the edge of the tent watching Betty, the pallbearers, the preacher, and fewer than ten friends and relatives. Plus Cowboy, who sat on the back row, all decked out in purple with silver rhinestones. I had no idea how to classify him. Friend or relative? I didn't think so.

I was surprised that Sheriff Harmon wasn't around. In the mysteries I read, law officers always go to the funerals of murder victims to watch for suspicious persons. Besides, he'd told me he would be there. I wondered if the police escorts were doing double duty. Not probable. Middleton's hires off-duty officers, and the ones for this funeral were Beaufort city policemen, who wouldn't be investigating a St. Mary death for the Jade County Sheriff's Department. Just like the locals balk when the feebs, FBI agents, show up in novels, real-life law enforcement agencies in the South take jurisdiction matters seriously. I'd almost given up on the sheriff when his cruiser arrived.

Behind him, Nick Rivers pulled up in a new GMC Envoy with a Charleston Charlie's Cars temporary license tag. The Envoy was like a shorter, smaller version of the Savana I'd seen him driving the day before in Charleston. The same body shape and the identical shade of gray, probably pewter or silver in new car talk.

Some people like to have the same color vehicle over and over. Not me. The next car I have will be yellow. Light, buttery yellow. I'd been tempted to have the Mustang painted yellow when I got it, but I knew the value would stay higher if I left it the authentic Mustang blue Donnie had custom-ordered. Then again, Cowboy's bright red Solstice, parked directly behind the family car, was eye-catching. I'd noticed it when Betty and I got out of the limousine. I wondered how the Mustang would look painted scarlet.

I'd spent the night in Jane's recliner. Never got to the loveseat. Went to sleep during *Bernie*, and Jane covered me with a sheet and let me snore. I used to get all self-righteous about Donnie's accusations that I snored until one night he taped the night sounds. The noise was neither pretty nor feminine. If I ever do replace Donnie, I'm going to have to buy some of those nose tapes to keep me from snoring, but since I sleep alone, I don't worry about it.

When I'd awakened at Jane's, I wondered if the thief had been back to my apartment while I was gone. He hadn't taken anything that I knew of last night, but I thought of him as a thief since it appeared he'd stolen

Bobby Saxon's first casket as well as my purse and keys. I'd stopped by my apartment to change into a black dress and low pumps before heading to the mortuary. I found the rooms immaculate. No burglars.

Checking out the apartment left me rushed to reach Middleton's in time to ride in the family car like Betty had requested. She seemed to have decided I was one of her best friends.

My attention returned to Reverend Cauble when he said, "Go in peace." He stepped to Betty, took her hand, and bent to speak to her. The preacher gasped and stopped midsentence when Cowboy jumped up, ran to the casket, and turned to face those who were seated. Buh-leeve me, my mind didn't drift anymore. I've always wished someone had objected when the pastor said that thing about speaking now or forever holding your peace at my wedding to Donnie, but I never imagined someone objecting at a funeral.

"I worked with Bobby Saxon at GMC Automotive and Truck Corral," Cowboy announced, "and I want you folks to open up this coffin and let me see that he's in there."

Betty leaped from her folding chair and shrieked, "Ain't nobody going to open Bobby's casket."

I expected Betty to hit Cowboy. Sheriff Harmon and Otis must have thought she would, too, because they both rushed up (as Reverend Cauble turned away and slunk off toward his pickup truck). Betty collapsed back on her chair and sobbed. I hurried to her side and began patting her shoulder, comforting her with words.

Cowboy snarled, turned, snatched the casket spray off the Exquisite, and threw it on the ground. Sheriff Harmon grabbed him as he pushed the lid of the casket, trying to open it, but, of course, Otis had fully engaged the seal back at the funeral home, so Cowboy didn't have a chance in the hot spot of getting it open.

I nudged Betty's elbow and said, "Let's go. Sheriff Harmon will take care of this."

"I don't want it opened," she cried in short, quick breaths.

"It won't be without your permission," I said as I succeeded in getting Betty to stand. By then the sheriff had Cowboy stuffed into the backseat of the county cruiser, and Cauble had scrambled from his pickup and was headed back over our way. Betty and I sat down again.

"Let us remember that the Lord works in mysterious ways," Cauble said. He leaned over to Betty and whispered, "Please accept my sympathies for the loss of your husband."

Betty stayed seated as folks lined up to give her hugs and spoke condolences that all seemed to be, "I'm so sorry." I noticed how her platinum hair glimmered and contrasted with the black outfit in the sunlight.

Nick Rivers finally glanced at me when he told Betty, "I'll call you soon." I sure wished he'd call *me* soon.

As Betty and I walked from the burial site to the limousine, Nick's eyes caught mine again. His expression was solemn, aloof. He didn't acknowledge me, and I conscientiously avoided making further eye contact with him, though my heart did flutter around some.

As soon as the driver closed the door behind us, Betty dabbed her eyes with tissue, then asked, "Callie, do you know when I'll get the insurance money?"

Good grief. That was the last thing I thought she'd say. I fully expected Betty to explode about Cowboy's behavior. She didn't mention it, just the money. I answered, "We need the death certificates before you file for the insurance." My teacher voice. The soothing one I used to use on five-year-olds who skinned their knees or wet their pants. "You've already signed the paperwork authorizing direct payment of part of the insurance to Middleton's for

Bobby's services. When the survivor does that, the check usually comes made to both Middleton's and the beneficiary. A few insurance companies will make separate checks. One to Middleton's for the services and another for the remainder made to you, but it will probably be one check requiring both endorsements."

"What?" Betty said, frowning and cocking her eyebrow. She crossed her right leg over her left and swung it. I was glad her black leather pump didn't flap on her foot like her red sling-back heels had, but her toe tapped the back of the front seat each time she swung her foot. She flipped a Marlboro from its pack and lit up. I didn't respond. I'd said all I had to say and I couldn't help wondering if her question about the insurance money was more for herself than to pay Bobby's funeral bill.

"Well, you already have the death certificates, don't you?" Betty asked.

"No, the forms Otis filled out Monday have to be redone since the autopsy."

"Oh," she said. Nothing else. Just sat smoking and swinging her leg until we reached the mortuary parking lot. She got into her car and drove away without another word to me.

**June Bug's new** shirt and suit were steamed wrinkle-free and lay across the backseat of the Mustang on padded hangers when I drove to the Corley home. The front yard was full of kids playing ball and hopscotch. I expected difficulty with a capital D from Mrs. Corley, but when I entered the house, she was catching trouble rather than pitching it. Sheriff Harmon must have gone directly to her house from the Saxon burial service. He rants and raves about the coroner, but I've never heard him as fired up as he was at the Corley home.

The six grown children and their spouses were sitting in the living room with Mrs. Corley. She seemed even more birdlike with her beady eyes and beaky nose, and the blue dress she wore made me think of a blue jay.

Sheriff Harmon looked and sounded livid. "What do you mean I didn't forbid you to burn the building?"

"You didn't say don't burn it. You told us not to knock it down. Mama wanted it burned, and she set it on fire," blurted one of the Corley sons.

"Did you try to stop her?" Sheriff Harmon asked.

"No, sir. Mama said leave her alone."

"And if Mama said jump off the roof, would you do that, too?" The sheriff's tone dripped sarcasm. I'd heard that one from Daddy and The Boys almost every day when I was little. I thought the sheriff could come up with something better. He didn't disappoint me.

"What if I haul all of you over to the jail and lock you up for interfering with an official investigation?" The family looked shocked. A tear welled up in Mrs. Corley's eye. "I'm not going to," the sheriff reassured them, "but I should. Somebody killed June—Mr. Corley. There might have been a reason to go back in the club as part of our inquiry."

The same son mumbled, "Your men should have searched it completely the first time."

Mrs. Corley jumped up from her chair, popped that grown man an open slap across his face, and chirped, "Keep it up, Walter, and you'll get more than that."

I'd been standing just inside the door holding the clothes hangers. I almost dropped my pants. Did I say that? I mean June Bug's pants. I decided I should come back at another time, but just as I stepped away, the sheriff spotted me and said, "Come on in, Callie. Are those clothes for Mr. Corley?"

"Yes, I've brought them for Mrs. Corley's approval."

I was more shocked by her reaction to the clothing than I'd been to her slapping Walter. "Look at these," Mrs. Corley said and waved her arm, gesturing to everyone in the room. "They're perfect. Jimmy Lee is gonna look positively handsome." She admired all three neckties and allowed her daughters to choose the one they liked best. The shoes thrilled the whole family, even the in-laws. The family kept saying they wished I'd shopped for Daddy while he was alive. Their approval would have made it worth my while to go to Charleston for June Bug's clothes even if I hadn't stopped by Victoria's Secret.

After thanking everyone, I got myself out of there before they could change their minds. As I pulled off, I saw Sheriff Harmon standing alone, staring at the soot-blackened concrete block walls still surrounding the burned rubbish of the club. He shook his head side to side with an expression that was hard to interpret. Disgust or disbelief.

My cell phone sang to me before I got back to the highway. I'd remembered to turn it on for a change.

"Callie, are you done for the day? Are you headed this way?" Jane asked.

"Yes, I'm done, but I'm going home. I can't stay away forever."

"Forever? It's only been one night. What if that man comes back?"

"I thought about that. I'm going by Daddy's house and pick up some protection."

"Protection? I thought your date was tomorrow night."

"That's not funny, Jane. I was thinking of a dog and maybe a gun."

"You'll blow your foot off."

"Come on, Jane, you know I hunted with Daddy and The Boys when I was growing up. I can handle a gun."

"If you tell them why you need it, your daddy will make you stay there."

"Then I won't tell them."

"I'll be working tonight. If you change your mind, come on over."

I swung by the mortuary and dropped off June Bug's clothes, then headed to the homeplace.

# Chapter Fifteen

**M**oss-laden branches arched over both sides of the dirt road to Daddy's house, met in the middle, and created a mystical scene typical of many backwoods roads in the low country. When I was a little girl, I'd dreamed of being married under a draping arch like that. Instead, I'd wed in a highfalutin ceremony in Columbia to make my future in-laws happy. Would have been nice to divorce somewhere pretty, but the end of my wedded nonbliss had taken place in a cold, sterile courtroom with Donnie sitting there looking like an idiot with a self-conscious grin and his mama sobbing. Like she'd ever thought I was good enough for him anyway.

As I wheeled the Mustang off the road onto the long driveway up to the homeplace, I noticed both sides were plowed. Dark, rich earth ready for winter planting. According to history, the farm might have grown indigo or rice hundreds of years ago, but those two crops were obsolete in St. Mary before my grandparents were born. I used to know what followed what, but my years away from the farm had weakened my knowledge of planting seasons, and I didn't know if the fields would be seeded with soybeans, wheat, or something else. Not tomatoes, though. I remembered they made a good profit but knew they were a red, juicy ripe *summer* delight.

At the end of the drive sat the ugliest house in St. Mary. Originally clapboard until Daddy got tired of painting it and covered it with asbestos shingles. There was a discount price for dark gray at the Beaufort Home Supply because no one would buy them, so the Parrish house has gray shingles, a tar-colored roof, and jet-black shutters. The old house would have been a perfect backdrop for *The Munsters*. It's a miracle we weren't all institutionalized for depression. If I'm ever rich, I'll have white vinyl siding installed.

The only redeeming feature about the Parrish homeplace is the black painted porch on the front with three, count 'em—one, two, three—porch swings. Daddy had started with one, then added the others as The Boys and I outgrew sitting side by side, six little bottoms crowded into the swing, to listen to Daddy play his guitar every evening.

Daddy taught each of my brothers to pick guitar, and everybody sings, but for my fifth birthday, he gave me a banjo. The finest times of my childhood were spent accompanying ourselves and harmonizing on the front porch of that dark, ugly house we called home.

I parked and climbed the stairs. "Callie's here!" my brother Frank yelled when I knocked and he opened the door. There's always a celebration when I go home. Anyone would think I lived in China and only visited every two or three years.

Daddy jumped up from his chair in front of the television. "What ya knocking for, Calamine? This house will always be your home. You just walk right in."

The Parrish men clean up pretty good, and Daddy had looked fine in his suit at Bobby Saxon's visitation and memorial service. Today, he was back to normal. At home, my father bears a strong resemblance to a sixty-five-year-old version of a television star. One on Comedy Central. That cable guy. Paunchy stomach, baggy jeans, and a plaid shirt with sleeves cut off at the shoulders. More than that, he sounds like him, especially when he says, "Get 'er done," which is fairly frequently.

"Come on in and set a spell, Calamine." Daddy motioned toward the couch. He turned to Frank. "Get your sister a Coke or some sweet iced tea."

Just to test them, I said, "I'll take a brew." They were both drinking Coors.

"We don't have another beer right now," Daddy sputtered. "I've got the last one right here in my hand." *Liar, liar, pants on fire.* I thought it, but I didn't say it. I knew perfectly well that Daddy's refusal for me to have a Michelob at June Bug's hadn't been due to pain pills, but because in his mind, I'll always be his little girl. The refrigerator in that house stays full of beer and leftover carryout food. Daddy just won't acknowledge that I'm old enough to drink alcohol. And me grown, married, and a divorced woman already. In all probability, Daddy thinks I'm still entitled to wear white at my next wedding.

"Where are Mike and Bill?" I asked.

"Fishing," Frank said and handed me a canned Coke. I popped the top and drank about half of it in one long gulp. I hadn't realized how thirsty I was.

Frank went back to the kitchen, and I explained to Daddy that I wanted to borrow a gun and a dog.

"You going hunting, Calamine?" Daddy said. "You don't need to take one of the hounds to your place. Just pick it up on your way to the field."

I didn't want to lie, but I couldn't tell him the truth,

either. If Daddy knew someone was threatening me, I'd never get out of his house.

What to say? Saved by my brothers. Mike and Bill pushed the door open and shouted, "Callie!"

"We saw the Pony parked out front," Mike said. "You're just in time. We've got a stringer full of crappie just waiting to be cleaned."

"Crappie" are panfish, pronounced to rhyme with "copy" in some places but rhyming with "cappy" in the Carolinas. Like the word "deer," there's no *s* added to make the plural. A fellow might catch one crappie or ten crappie, not ten crappies. It doesn't matter what you call 'em, they're delicious.

I suddenly realized that I was as hungry as I'd been thirsty, and yes, I'd like to stay to eat.

"I'm not cleaning them," I told Mike.

"Why not?"

"You two boys get out there and get those fish cleaned and fire up the cooker." No mistaking who's the boss when Daddy talks. "Now get 'er done." He turned to me. "Did you bring your banjer?"

"No, I didn't."

He grinned at me. "You never bring it anymore. You don't hardly ever come over, then you don't bring your banjer, so I got a surprise for you." He walked into his bedroom, came right back out carrying a banjo case, and handed it to me. I opened it and squealed.

A pristine prewar Gibson Mastertone.

I grabbed Daddy around the neck and blabbered out my appreciation.

"Don't thank me," he said. "It ain't yours."

"What? Nobody else here plays banjo," I protested.

"It's mine. Belongs to me, but I'm gonna *let* you play it when you're here. Maybe you'll come see your old pa more often."

By the time I had picks on my fingers, Daddy had brought out his Martin D-18 guitar and looped the strap around his neck. "Let's go out on the porch," he said.

I would've protested that I wasn't staying, just wanted a gun and dog, but I couldn't resist playing that good old Mastertone. When we opened the door, I smelled fish frying from the gas cooker out back, and I knew I'd made the right decision to stay for a while.

Daddy and I were doing "Wildwood Flower" when Frank came out of the house with his guitar in one hand and a mixing bowl in the other. "Let me take this hush puppy batter to Mike and Bill, then I'll join you," he said.

"Did you make tartar sauce?" I asked him. My brother Frank makes the best in the world. He won't let anyone watch, but I think it's mayonnaise, pickles, onion juice, and sugar. I used to make sandwiches out of it. Tartar sauce sandwiches. Loved 'em.

"Made the sauce, and the grits are simmering while we waste time talking instead of playing music."

When I moved to Columbia, I learned that some folks eat fried potatoes, even baked potatoes, with fish. Down home, we eat grits with fish. Add a few hush puppies, and it's a meal, unless real company's coming. In that case, add some coleslaw and baked beans for a fancy fish fry.

Daddy and I were picking "Little White-Washed Chimney" when Frank came back. "Come on," he said. "Bill's got the table set up and there's fish ready."

We went in the backyard to the gas cooker out by the shed, where my brothers had put a red-and-white-checkered plastic cloth over one of the picnic tables and topped it with a big bowl of tartar sauce and a pot of grits. A slab of real butter on a saucer let me know Daddy wasn't paying any more attention to his cholesterol than he ever did. Crusty fried fish and hush puppies drained grease onto folded brown paper bags on a tray. Paper plates, plastic forks, and a roll of paper towels lay by the tray.

We carefully set the musical instruments on another picnic table.

I started with three fish, four hush puppies, a mountain of grits, and about a cup of tartar sauce. "What are we drinking?" I called out.

Bill dashed to the back door, disappeared a few minutes, and returned with four beers and, yes, a Coke for me. I didn't protest a word. I was too busy wolfing down my midafternoon lunch. I even stirred some tartar sauce into my grits. The Boys were being polite. Usually when I did this, they moaned and gagged. Today they ignored it.

When everyone was full enough to bust, Frank brought up the subject I'd expected.

"You heard any more about who killed Bobby and June Bug?" he asked.

"Nope. Not a word. John thought June Bug might have killed Bobby Saxon, but June Bug getting shot kinda blew that theory," I said.

"Yeah." Mike smirked. "If what I heard is true, June Bug could have gone after Bobby, but now that I've heard Bobby was about to divorce Bouncy Betty, I think she might have killed him." He grinned. "You still reading all those mystery books, Callie?"

"Sure do, and sometimes I figure out who's guilty before I get to the end of the book."

"If this story was in a book, who'd you think was guilty?" Daddy asked.

"Probably Betty. First suspect is the next of kin and Betty sure has motive," I said.

Bill popped a whole hush puppy into his mouth, talked around it. "Why would Betty kill June Bug, though?"

"Don't talk with your mouth full!" Daddy snapped.

"Anybody would think you younguns didn't get any home learnin' at all, the way you eat and act sometimes."

"Sorry," Bill mumbled through the remainder of his mouthful.

Frank looked up and said, "It's possible that the killer isn't a local person. Maybe some transient going through town."

"Could be," I said, "but then there's Cowboy."

"The one who does those Truck Corral commercials?" Daddy asked.

"Yeah," Mike said. "Peavy. He's had a case of the hips at Bobby Saxon for years, especially since Bobby started working in Beaufort at the same car lot where Cowboy thought he was a star."

"Aww, that boy ain't nothing but talk," Daddy growled. "He'd run off hollering and screaming if a Chihuahua puppy barked in his direction."

"Speaking of dogs," I said, "are you gonna let me take one?"

"I already told you, Calamine," Daddy said, "if you're going hunting, you don't need to take a hound or a gun to your place. Just pick them up on your way to the field."

"Actually, Daddy, that's not what I'm going to do. I want a house dog to keep me company and a gun for target practice."

"Ain't none of my animals house pets, and you'll ruin 'em for hunting if you try to turn 'em into lap dogs." Daddy frowned.

"Yes, sir," I said, trying to hide the disappointment. I should have known he wouldn't let me take a trained hunter to my apartment. "But how about a gun? Will you lend me a gun?"

"Take two or three. Don't matter to me, long as you don't take that Sweet Sixteen." I knew better than to even think about borrowing the sixteen-gauge shotgun. She was my dad's favorite, and as long as I could remember, he'd never let anyone else shoot her.

"Well, I guess I'll go get one and head on home," I said as I stood.

"Not so fast," Mike said. "Bill and I cooked while you guys played. Let's do a few tunes before you leave." Frank took the leftover tartar sauce and butter to the kitchen while Bill and Mike got their guitars. We all met at the front porch, where Daddy and Frank sat on the steps and the rest of us stood in a half circle facing them.

Harmony is a big part of bluegrass vocals, and a lot of the best groups are brothers or family members because relatives' voices harmonize together best. The six of us have that advantage, and once we start picking and singing, it sounds so good and is so much fun that we don't want to stop. The only way the afternoon would have been better was if Jim were home instead of somewhere in the Mideast. By the time we'd done about a dozen songs, shadows had lengthened over the porch.

I confess, for just a few moments, I considered telling Daddy about the night before and asking if I could stay until tomorrow, but The Boys, Daddy, and I only enjoy each other's company for limited periods of time. Before bedtime, Daddy would have been quizzing me about every aspect of my life and nagging me to move back home like my brothers do periodically. We'd had that argument constantly since my divorce, and I wasn't up to it again.

For a refrigerator with no beer, the one in Daddy's kitchen magically produced Coors every time one of my brothers went to the kitchen. It had always done that, except years ago, the magic cooler produced Pabst Blue Ribbon. Somehow, when I asked for something to drink, the can turned to Coke on its way from the fridge to the porch. Oh, well, as Chuck Berry and Emmylou Harris say, *c'est la vie*.

"I need to get home," I said.

"Gotta clean house?" asked Frank, apparently remembering that Saturday was my chores day.

I nodded an affirmative although I'd scoured my apartment before everything happened the night before.

"Do I get a revolver or a shotgun?" I asked Daddy.

"Frank, take her in there to the gun safe and let her have whatever she wants except my sixteen-gauge." Daddy stood. "This has been fun, but I think I'm ready for a nap."

By the time Frank and I came away from the safe, Daddy was stretched out on his living room recliner snoring. According to Jane, I sound just like him. Disgusting!

As Frank put the weapons in the backseat, Bill came over to the car.

"Sis, I got a girlfriend who'll give you a dog," he said.

"What kind?" I asked.

"It ain't a hunting dog. Molly breeds and sells pets."

"How much will it cost me?"

Bill grinned. "That gal will give me anything I want. I'll be over to your place tonight with your new dog."

I drove away with a .22 rifle, a double-barrel shotgun, a .38 revolver, ammunition for everything, and promises to go hunting with Daddy and The Boys sometime soon. Oh, goody.

# Chapter Sixteen

**J**ean Harlow. Marilyn Monroe. Jayne Mansfield. These were the names Dr. Melvin, the pharmacist, mentioned when I paid for my box of beauty at the checkout counter in the drugstore. "Box of beauty" is a joke. That's what my cosmetology instructor sarcastically called prepackaged hair dye. She stressed that beauticians should always buy color from beauty supply shops; however, the nearest professional supply house was in Beaufort. I didn't want to drive that far, and besides, the store closed at noon on Saturdays.

Daddy and The Boys drive me crazy sometimes, but the fine food and music with them that afternoon had lifted my spirits. The guns I'd borrowed had eased some of the fear I'd been feeling.

Women change hair colors at two times: when they're very depressed and when they're very happy. I wasn't at either extreme, but remembering the shine of Betty's almost white hair in the sun that morning made me want to lift my strawberry shade. Maybe not as light as hers, but to a truer blonde. A quick stop at the drugstore on the way home would make that possible.

I carried a package of Tawny Sunlight to the register and discovered Melvin Dawkins there instead of the lady clerk. He's not a doctor, but I've called him Dr. Melvin since I was little. Kinda like kindergarten teachers being Miss First Name.

"Hi, Callie, what can I help you with today?" Dr. Melvin has been a friend of mine for years. He's the pharmacist who sold me all the things Daddy and The Boys called "girly stuff" and wouldn't buy for me when I hit adolescence. In some ways, Dr. Melvin took the place of my mother at a critical time of my life without ever letting me feel embarrassed about anything.

"How are you doing, Dr. Melvin?"

"I've been better, but today's good. Are you planning to change your hair or is this for somebody at Middleton's?" He laughed, then said slowly, "Some body?"

Ignoring his lame joke, I said, "It's for me. I want my hair lighter."

He picked up the box, turned it in his hand, and pointed to the chart that showed results on varying shades of hair. "Looks to me like this will dull your hair, turn it kind of a tan shade. I've never seen you as a beige person. You might want to look at some others."

Since the store was empty except for the two of us, Dr. Melvin followed me to the hair care section and selected another box. "This will look great on you," he said and headed toward the register without even showing me the package.

Dr. Melvin bagged my purchase and handed me my change before I actually saw the name on the box—True Platinum.

"This is going to be very light," I commented and realized immediately that Bouncy Betty's hair was actually that shade.

"It's a great color," Dr. Melvin said, winked, and added, "Jean Harlow, Marilyn Monroe, and Jayne Mansfield."

As I started the Mustang, I knew he was right. The color I'd bought was close to the tint of Marilyn Monroe's in pictures I'd seen of her. Jayne Mansfield's, too. I couldn't remember Jean Harlow, but since Dr. Melvin was Daddy's age, she was probably before my time. Bet the color didn't make me look like any of them.

Going into my apartment and finding it so clean was wonderful. I didn't have to worry about straightening up before the doctor came Sunday night. Good grief, if I was going to date him, I should call him by name instead of "the doctor."

I headed for the bathroom, where I mixed the color and applied it to my hair. Set the timer on the kitchen range and settled on the couch with an old towel wrapped around my shoulders and my face in what I call a recipe mystery. Books about chefs or bed-and-breakfast owners who solve crimes and include recipes for foods mentioned in the stories.

Thirty minutes later, I shampooed and discovered that the label hadn't lied. In books I read, any trip a woman makes to a hair salon turns into a fiasco. Not me. Maybe because I'm a registered cosmetologist, but all I did was follow the directions. I loved the new color. Blow-dried it and admired myself in the mirror before returning to my mystery.

The book wasn't long, and I'd almost finished when I realized my tummy was no longer full of fish. I hadn't shopped for groceries yet, and I didn't want to mess up my immaculate kitchen anyway. Besides, the recipes in the book didn't inspire me enough to want to cook. They just made me hungry. Thank heaven for Domino's.

Right as the delivery man turned away after handing me my deluxe pizza, Bill wheeled his pickup truck into the drive of the next-door apartment. He got out, waved, and walked around to the passenger side. When he opened the door, a spotted gray dog jumped out. Its body was bigger than an adult cocker spaniel's, and it had longer, gangly legs. Bill attached a leash to the dog's collar and walked him to the front door. Like one of my favorite mystery characters, I got some exercise by jumping to a conclusion: This was a grown dog Molly had been unable to sell.

When Bill and his companion entered, Bill disconnected the leash from the dog's collar, hung it over the front doorknob, and sat on the sofa. Bill looked at my hair but didn't say a word about it. The dog climbed up on his lap. "You're in time for pizza," I said and glanced down at the dog. "What's his name?" I asked.

"You can name him," Bill said.

"What name has he been called? You can't just change a grown dog's name."

I brought out paper plates, napkins, and those last two beers from my fridge while we talked. I made it a point to drink from one bottle immediately so Bill would know they weren't both for him.

"Grown dog? He's just a puppy," Bill said.

Ex-cuuze me. This lap full of canine was too big to be a puppy, though he did look like he hadn't yet grown into his legs, and his face had that little boy, I mean little puppy, immature look. When Bill moved from the sofa to the table, he slid the dog onto the floor, where the puppy curled up against Bill's legs. We began eating and Bill hand-fed the edges of his pizza crust to the animal.

"If you plan to leave him here, you'd better stop feeding

him pizza," I said. "You'll upset his stomach and he'll be sick on the carpet."

"But he loves pizza," Bill protested.

"How do you know?"

"I play with him at Molly's house." The puppy rolled over, and Bill rubbed the side of its belly, scratching the spot that makes an animal's leg jerk. The Boys used to do that to Daddy's hounds when I was little. I could never find the right spot. I'd scratch and the hounds would just look at me with moon eyes.

"Stop that." I pulled Bill's hand away from the dog's tummy. Being forced into a reflex action couldn't be pleasant for the puppy.

"Bossy ole Callie," Bill said and nodded toward the last piece of pizza. "You gonna eat that?" he asked.

"Nope," I answered, thinking he wanted it for himself. Instead, he fed it to the dog.

"What breed is he?" I asked. The puppy finished the pizza and ventured over to me. I scratched behind those gray floppy ears.

"He's a Great Dane. Molly raises miniature poodles, and another breeder traded her this puppy for one of her poodles to give to his mother. Molly thought it would be easy to make a profit on him, but he's a merle and she hasn't been able to sell him."

"What's a merle? You mean like a mule, can't breed?" I asked.

"No, it's his color. Danes are usually solid or harlequin. Harlequin is white with black spots like a dalmatian. A merle is gray with black spots."

"If he's so great, why doesn't Molly just keep him?" I slipped my shoe off and scratched his belly with my toes. The dog's belly, not Bill's.

"Molly doesn't like big dogs."

"What's it gonna cost me?" I knew he'd said no charge,

but my brothers don't always shoot absolutely straight with me.

"No charge. Of course, you'll have to feed him and get more shots later. He's had his puppy immunizations. Unless you're going to breed him, you can take him to the SPCA and have him neutered." Bill's voice dropped and he mumbled, "And you'll need to have his ears cropped."

The dog crawled up onto my lap and rolled over on his back with legs jutting out like pickup sticks. His obsidian eyes looked up into mine, silently begging, "Please keep me."

"What did you say about his ears?" I asked.

"He needs to have his ears cropped so they'll stand up. It's just a minor surgical procedure that a vet can do for you."

"If you like him so much, why don't you keep him?"

"Molly's my main squeeze right now, and she doesn't like big dogs. If I keep him and move in with Molly, I'll have a problem."

I laughed. "What's the matter? Daddy getting on your nerves?"

"Yeah, sometimes. You know how he can be."

Buh-leeve me, I know.

"Great Danes are large dogs. How big will he get?" I asked.

"Oh, I don't know, sis. Probably won't grow a whole lot. Do you have any more beer?"

"Nope, those two were the last of the six-pack."

Bill stood. "You can keep the collar and leash. I've got a bag of Kibbles 'n Bits out in the truck to hold him until tomorrow." If I'd been paying attention instead of petting the dog, I might have processed what he said: A bag of dog food would last one day. Bill went out, returned with the sack, and placed it by the front door. He turned to leave, but I stopped him.

"Bill, do you know a dude called Cowboy who works at the GMC Corral in Beaufort?"

"Sure do. We talked about him at lunch. You said he hated Bobby Saxon. What about him?"

"Well, what do you think of him? Is he an okay fellow?"

Bill gave me his "What now?" big brother look. "Nope," he said. "He's not. Stay away from him."

"Why . . . ," I began, but Bill stepped out and closed the door behind himself. In a hurry. Probably had a date with Molly. His warning to stay away from Cowboy didn't mean much. My brothers have never wanted me to talk to any men who weren't in the family.

I filled a Rubbermaid bowl with water and another with Kibbles 'n Bits, set them on the kitchen floor, and played with my new pet.

The dogs of my childhood were outdoor hunters, but Donnie and I had raised a Pomeranian, so I knew a little about house pets. This animal was large, but he definitely played like a puppy. "Come on," I said to him. "Let's clean up the supper dishes." He followed me to the table and watched with big eyes.

I'd barely stuffed the paper remnants from our pizza dinner into the trash when the dog ran to the door, tugged on the leash hanging across the knob, and barked. He had a big, loud voice. Just what I needed to scare away an intruder. I snapped the leash to his collar and took him out. The minute we stepped off the porch steps, the puppy squatted and wet on the grass like a girl dog.

*Wow!* I thought. *He's already trained. He won't be any trouble at all.*

I went to sleep with my unnamed pet lying on an old folded blanket on the floor beside my bed. I awoke in the middle of the night to find him in bed with me. I'd turned on my side and he'd snuggled between my arms. The back of his head and those floppy ears lay on my left arm and rested against my chest. Note I said chest, not breast. Without the bra, there's not enough there to make a comfortable cushion. He'd spooned his back against me and tucked those spindly legs into a fetal position. My right arm lay across his body, and I was actually holding one of his paws. I noticed the size of his feet for the first time. Tremendous. It clicked. He had a name! Big Foot. I knew I should put him back on his blanket, but a warm body cuddled beside me felt kind of nice. I went back to sleep.

Big Foot's big bark woke me. My first thought was prowler, but the clock flashed 6:00 a.m. Surely, if my intended intruder was going to come back, he would do it before morning. I was getting up to see why the dog was barking when Big Foot came running into the bedroom with his leash in his mouth. "Are you in a hurry, Big Boy?" I quickly pulled on jeans, shirt, and shoes.

The puppy almost knocked me over bounding through the front door and down to the grass. "Big Boy, you gotta learn to do it like a boy." As I said it, I realized that his name had changed itself from Big Foot to Big Boy. Big Boy was a better name anyway. I didn't want folks to think I didn't know the difference between a big dog and a Himalayan yeti.

We walked for a while and I was surprised at the number of folks out walking dogs so early in the morning. A lot of them were good-looking men. And a lot of them looked at me and smiled. I should have gone blonder and gotten a dog when I first moved back to St. Mary.

The crisp fall air nipped at my skin, and nature had painted the changing leaves with vivid reds and yellows. I had the day off and the doctor was due to arrive at six for our date that night. For a moment I thought life couldn't be better. Then I remembered that someone had tried to break into my apartment Friday night. Probably the same someone who'd sent me to the hospital with a concussion.

Perhaps the same someone who had warned me to mind my own business.

Life got worse when Big Boy and I went inside. I remembered that though Bill had brought dog food, I still had no people food in my apartment. Temptation urged me to pile Big Boy into the Mustang and head toward McDonald's drive-through for some pancakes, but I resisted. I needed to go to the grocery store, not a fast-food place. I wanted to have at least a Coke in the house to offer the doctor. Should have bought a six-pack of beer or bottle of wine Saturday. Too late. No beer on Sunday mornings in South Carolina.

When I was young, the state had blue laws that prohibited people from buying things like shoelaces, panty hose, and, of course, alcoholic beverages on Sundays. The laws had changed, but sale of alcohol on Sunday mornings was still illegal. Personally, I think more people have had the blues because they couldn't buy beer on Sunday than they did because they couldn't buy shoelaces.

I refilled Big Boy's dishes, patted him bye-bye, locked the door, and drove over to the Piggly Wiggly grocery store. Bought my usual supplies: eggs, bread, coffee, canned soup, doughnuts, and Moon Pies. Added a carton of Coke. Then another bag of Kibbles 'n Bits. No need to buy frozen pizza since Domino's started delivering to St. Mary. I bought a Sunday newspaper and munched a couple of Moon Pies on the way home. My plans for Sunday were great: lie around, read the paper, and goof off until time to dress for my date.

Dalmatian! I dropped the bag of groceries when I opened the front door of my apartment. The living room drapes hung in tatters. Couch cushions gushed stuffing out of holes chewed into their covers. My prized pink Depression glass bowl, which I'd displayed on a brass holder on the coffee table, lay in smithereens on the carpet. The door to the junk room apparently hadn't been closed tightly enough because torn books lay scattered around the room, some of them still slobber shiny.

"Bill can come take you back today!" I screeched at the gawky, gray-spotted creature staring at me with solemn eyes.

I tried. I promise I tried, but I couldn't help what I did next. I sat down amid the broken eggs, shards of glass, and pillow stuffing. Tears gushed from my eyes and my shoulders shook as I sobbed. I squeezed my eyes closed trying to stop the tears. Something warm, wet, and rough brushed my cheek.

Big Boy was kissing my tears away.

# Chapter Seventeen

**G**rrrrufffff! *Grrrrufffff!*

Big Boy sat in front of the door growling and barking though the bell had stopped ringing. "Who is it?" I called. Six o'clock. Sunday night. I knew who should be on my porch, but Friday night's attempted intrusion had made me cautious.

"Donald Walters," the doctor answered.

I peered through the peephole. When I reached for the knob to open the door, Big Boy tucked his tail between his legs. His deep, serious bark changed to a puppy *yip, yip, yip*, and he scrambled to the bedroom.

Roses! The doctor was holding a dozen long-stemmed American Beauties surrounded by fern and baby's breath. No man had bought me roses since my wedding bouquet. Come to think of it, I paid the florist bill for the wedding.

The doctor looked even better than he had in scrubs at the hospital or in a suit at the mortuary. He had on gray slacks and a muted gray silk V-neck pullover under his dark charcoal blazer. The V-neck revealed just a tease of sandy brown chest hair. I swear that if I'd touched him, my fingers would have sizzled. Not that I planned to touch him on the first date, mind you.

I froze, feasting on his looks while he stood in the doorway holding the bouquet. After I recovered from the thrill of the roses and the pleasure of his appearance, I gushed, "Are those for me?" in that whispery Southern Belle voice that I'd always sworn would make me barf if I ever used it.

"For you, pretty lady," the doctor answered with a grin.

I motioned him to a seat on the couch and went to the kitchen for a vase and water. After the door closed behind me, I danced a little jig, pumped my right arm into the air, and mouthed a tremendous, though silent, *Yes!*

When I calmly strolled out of the kitchen and placed the vase on the table beside the couch, Big Boy was lying on his back, legs splayed, at the doctor's feet. The doctor leaned forward, scratching the dog's tummy.

"Quite a puppy you've got here, Callie," the doctor said. "He's going to be a big one."

"My brother Bill gave him to me yesterday. He's a Great Dane, but Bill says he won't be really huge."

The doctor laughed. "This dog will probably be over thirty-three inches tall and weigh about a hundred and twenty-five pounds when he's grown. He's going to be gigantic even for a Great Dane." As if to show his size, Big Boy rolled over and stood.

"Do you know a lot about dogs?" I asked. I sat down and tucked my short skirt around my knees. Actually, around my thighs. I'd changed clothes four times before I settled on a soft, deep maroon blouse, a summer white skirt that didn't quite reach my knees, and pearl chandelier earrings. I love red shoes, and I'd put on heels that matched my shirt, but after thinking about Bouncy Betty Boobs swinging her red-clad feet, I'd changed to low-heeled taupe leather pumps. I'd probably never wear sling-backs or red heels again.

The doctor had predicted height and weight for a specific breed of dog, so I'd asked him if he knew about dogs. Duhhh. He smiled. "I considered vet school before I decided to be a physician."

He leaned back a bit, and the stuffing I'd shoved into the hole came puffing out of the couch cushion. The doctor looked at and tried to pat it back into the pillow. "Excuse that," I said. "Big Boy needs to learn how to respect furniture or I'll have to hire sitters for him." I frowned in the direction of the puppy. His tail and ears drooped.

"And I thought that was just the newest style in curtains." The doctor gestured toward the ragged cloth and strings hanging at my windows.

"I left him for a short time this morning."

"What do you plan to do with him while we're out to dinner?" The doctor rubbed Big Boy's head.

"I really don't know."

"Until you work something out or train him, you might want to leave him in the bathroom while you're gone."

"Good idea. I'll move his dishes in there."

"Give me his food and water. I'll puppy proof the room for you." The doctor followed me into the kitchen, topped off Big Boy's bowls, and carried them to the bathroom. He motioned me to wait in the hall while he gathered the towels and rug. He folded them neatly and put them on a hall table. He removed the toilet tissue from its holder, unhooked the shower curtain, and collected all soaps and items from the counter and around the tub. "Does he have a toy?" the doctor asked as he stacked everything beside the towels.

"Not yet," I answered, kindergarten-cussing myself for not thinking of that when I'd gone to the store.

"Why don't you take him out while I get something

from my car," the doctor said. I snapped on Big Boy's leash and followed him out to water the front yard. The doctor opened the trunk of his BMW and brought out a new chew toy still sealed in cellophane. When we went back inside, he unwrapped it and led Big Boy into the empty bathroom. Big Boy sat on the floor gnawing the toy the doctor had probably bought for his own pet. The doctor pulled the door closed and, at his suggestion, I turned on the radio.

The doctor nodded and smiled. "And now," he said, "what do you plan to call me?"

"What do you mean?"

"I've noticed you don't call me any name."

"It seems awkward to call you Dr. Walters if we're going out. What do you want me to call you?"

"You can call me Donnie. That's the name my family and friends use."

Dalmatian! I was afraid he'd say that. "I'd rather call you Donald or Don."

"All right, *Miss* Callie, let's make it Don. Do you have somewhere special you'd like to go for dinner? I was hoping we could go to Andre's."

"I'd love to go to Andre's," I gushed. What was wrong with me? Surely that silly voice didn't live inside me. I live on Moon Pies, doughnuts, pizza, and an occasional Happy Meal. I'll take seafood, steak, or Italian anytime. I'd even be pleased for him to treat me to a Burger King Whopper. Never in my dreams did I imagine going to Andre's on our first date. Located off Highway 21, between St. Mary and Beaufort, Andre's is a high-dollar, swanky restaurant. I'd never been there before.

**Spanish moss draped** the trees around the parking lot and framed the white stucco building. A forest green canvas canopy over the door was discreetly labeled "Andre's" in white cursive. We'd barely reached the portico when the maitre d' opened the door and greeted us. "Good evening, madam." A polite bow toward me. "Your table is ready, Dr. Walters." Another polite bow.

The maitre d' led us through a long hall with several closed doors on each side. Massive gold-framed impressionistic oil paintings hung on the pale peach walls. Slate floors edged around plush area rugs in shades of green and peach. Don paused before a door, and the maitre d' motioned us into a private dining room.

Smaller oil paintings adorned the dark green silk-covered walls. A round table covered with a floor-length peach linen cloth centered the area. Don held one of the two ornate French chairs with peach and green needlepoint cushions for me. As I was seated, I noticed that the peach roses on the table were fresh, not silk, and the vase and candleholders appeared to be lead crystal.

"Is the light suitable, sir?" asked the maitre d'.

"Just a tad bright," Don answered. The attendant touched a switch beside the door, and the tiny recessed spotlights shining on the oil paintings dimmed so that most of the brightness remaining came from candles on the table.

No sooner had the maitre d' bowed out of the room than a server entered carrying a silver ice bucket with a bottle of wine in it. "Will you be having your usual, Dr. Walters, or would you care to see the wine list?"

Don turned to me. "Do you have a wine preference, Callie?"

"Not really," I answered and heard, to my distress, that my voice had once again changed to that false southern whisper that isn't me at all.

"We'll begin with my usual," Don said. He and the server went through the ritual tasting before the wine was poured. When I lifted my glass, I didn't have to tap the rim to know we were drinking from fine crystal.

I'm not a hick, and I don't want anyone to misunderstand. I'd been to exclusive dining places before. My wedding reception in Columbia was at the Carolina Club, which is far from cheap. But Andre's was a new experience for me.

"My favorite appetizer is Andre's escargot with chardonnay sauce," Don said when the server arrived. "Let's start with those." My face must have reflected that snails weren't my favorite anything. I don't know why a woman who chows down on catfish and crawdads would feel queasy thinking about eating snails, but I did. With or without Andre's wine sauce.

"The Burgundy mushrooms are also spectacular," Don said. "We'll have an order of those, too." He nodded toward me. "That is, if you eat mushrooms." Of course I agreed to try them. Mushrooms don't turn me on, either, but I'll take them over snails or slugs any day.

The server brought the appetizers in oval silver dishes with two delicate china plates. Though we each had a full setting of silverware, the waiter added two sterling silver appetizer forks. We didn't need two. Don fed me mushrooms from his fork. They were delicious, but then I realized he'd just eaten escargot from the same fork. I began sipping wine and quickly assured him I wanted to save room for the main course. When the server removed the dishes, Don held my hand and, at one point, actually nibbled at my fingertips as he told me how beautiful my hair and eyes were by candlelight.

The doctor, without a doubt, was the smoothest man I'd ever dated. Probably the most debonair male I'd ever even met. If a female friend had told me her date nibbled her fingers, I'd have laughed like I do at women who bat their eyelashes and ooze, "You're my hero," to their men.

Somehow, it was different when I was the one receiving all the attention.

I tried to get Don to tell me how he knew Bobby Saxon, but he said, "Tonight is *our* night, Callie. Let's just talk about *us*." Since I didn't see how there was any *us* when we were on our first date, I did the ladylike thing and asked about him. His response was primarily about med school and dedication to his chosen profession. By the time we'd finished our crème brûlée, once again served with two plates, but fed to me from Don's dessert spoon, I was running out of questions.

For years, I teased Jane that the good Lord put men on Earth for two reasons, and one of them was to keep my car running. My thoughts kept going to the other reason. Jane would have called Don a hottie under my living room lights, but he was molten lava by candlelight.

Between being fed and nibbled, I wondered if he could see in the dim light that my face was on fire. My thoughts kept leaping to when we got back to my place. I grew up with five older brothers, and I've heard them exchange score reports after dates. I refuse to be a notch on any man's bedpost. At least not a first-date notch.

We walked into my apartment at five minutes before 8:00 p.m. After we'd taken Big Boy outside, Don asked, "Do you get HBO? If you do, there's a hilarious show you might enjoy. It's called *Six Feet Under*, and it's about a family that runs a funeral home."

I couldn't believe it. He'd suggested we watch my favorite television program! I turned on the TV and sat on the couch. He sat beside me. This was a man after my own heart, though the way he snuggled up to me on the couch made me think of other body parts.

Don laughed as much as I did at the show, and when it was over, he turned the television off and did what I knew he would. He kissed me. I kissed back even though I remembered he'd eaten the snails. He moved his arms and hands from my back around to my sides, pulling me tighter against him. Women learn that hold in their teens. The one where the thumbs actually press into the sides of the bosom. In my case, into inflation. That familiar fire flamed in the bottom of my stomach.

"Are you thinking what I'm thinking?" Don whispered as he nipped at my ear.

"I've been thinking what you're thinking since you arrived tonight," I said and pulled back. "That's why you have to leave now."

He protested, but politely. "My next night off is Wednesday. May I see you again then?" Buh-leeve me. He didn't have to ask twice.

**"You did *what*?"** Jane was so loud over the phone that she hurt my ear.

"I sent him home."

*"Why?"*

"Because it was the right thing to do."

"Girlfriend, playing hard to get is old-fashioned. What are you waiting for?"

"When the time is right, I'll know it."

# Chapter Eighteen

**P**uppy breath. Buh-leeve me. I needed no encouragement to get up when the alarm sounded Monday
morning. Big Boy lay beside me with his head on my pillow. Definitely needed to buy him some of those chewy
teeth-cleaning bones. I shook him awake, pulled on my
robe, and took him outside. Then we had breakfast together. Coffee and a doughnut for me, Kibbles 'n Bits for
Big Boy.

A quick shower and I grabbed the first black dress on
my left. Put it on. Took it off and inflated my bra just a
touch more. Put the dress back on, and sure enough, it
looked better. Wearing funeral home dresses is like wearing uniforms. Takes no time to think what to wear. I keep
them in a row in the closet and just pull out the first one
on the left each day. When I do laundry, I put the clean
ones at the end of the row on the right. Keeps me from
wearing the same dress too often.

Ten minutes later I was in the Mustang headed toward
Middleton's.

Odell met me as I entered through the back door. "We picked up June Bug last night. Otis is preparing him now. He'll be ready for you in a couple of hours. As soon as he's casketed, we need to call the Corley family and let them know. Mrs. Corley wants to see him before she makes final plans."

"Sure," I said and headed toward my office.

"There's fresh coffee in the kitchen," Odell said. "I left some papers on your desk," he added. "How about filing them for me? I'm going to Shoney's, but I won't be gone long. Beep me if anything comes in."

If barbecue is ever added to Shoney's breakfast bar, Odell's workday will be shortened considerably. But then, if Krispy Kreme ever opens a franchise in St. Mary, I may never work at all.

Odell left, and I began sorting the papers stacked on my desk. Among them were copies of applications for death certificates, Bobby Saxon's planning forms, a copy of his insurance policy, Betty and Bobby's marriage license, and an assignment of funds to Middleton's. All properly signed by Betty. Until the sheriff officially cleared Betty of any involvement in his death, the insurance company wouldn't pay off based on a death certificate with cause of death, drug overdose; manner of death, homicide. If Bobby's demise had been correctly identified as murder at the beginning, Otis would never have accepted insurance assignment for payment.

When I got up to get a cup of coffee, I went by the preparation room to speak to Otis. June Bug's body lay on the stainless steel table with a towel thrown across his groin. Otis already had embalming pumps running.

I said, "Good morning, Otis."

"Morning, Callie. This one's going to be tough. With his size and the delay for the postmortem exam, he's going to need a lot of spotting and touch-ups under the skin in addition to the arterial embalming. I'll want you to begin the minute I finish. Mrs. Corley's chomping at the bit to see him."

"Yes, Odell told me. Would you like a cup of coffee?"

Otis motioned toward a cup on the counter. "Thanks. Already got one."

I nodded and went to the kitchen. I like what I do, but I don't care to hang around while a body is being embalmed. I got a mug of coffee, returned to my desk, and continued the paperwork.

All of Bobby Saxon's papers went into one folder, then into the cabinet. Otis had probably been scolded, well, more than scolded, by Odell for accepting an insurance assignment for Bobby's services. Otis had been too impressed by a policy worth so much and Betty's constant assurance that she wanted the best. We rarely saw half a million dollars' worth of insurance in St. Mary. I glanced down at the photocopied insurance papers: "Five Hundred Thousand Dollars," to be paid upon the death of Robert Edward Saxon to his legal wife.

There it was again. That strange wording. Usually policies name the beneficiary. Betty's full name should be shown, not "legal wife." Sounded as though Bobby had grown cynical about marriage lasting very long. Not that I could blame him with his track record. I wondered if Bobby had even considered his marriage to Betty lasting 'til death did the parting. I made a mental note to ask Otis if he'd ever seen a policy worded like that before.

Finished with the filing, I went to my workroom and removed June Bug's new clothing from the cabinet. The suit looked fine, but I steamed it again. Mrs. Corley was picky, picky, picky, and I didn't want to disappoint her.

"Callie, I'm bringing him in," Otis called and pushed the gurney into the room and under my work light. June Bug was now wearing his new Skivvies. The bullet wound and

Y incision on his chest, though stitched, were grotesque reminders that he hadn't died a natural death.

"Whew!" Otis said. "Don't try to move him at all. If you need . . ." He looked down at June Bug's head. "Oh, balderdash, let me get some sealer and go over that again."

The head incision from the autopsy seeped blood-tinged fluid. June Bug's hair was tinted pink.

Bodies are my business, and I don't get emotional over my work, but some folks touch my heartstrings more than others, and June Bug was one of them. He looked even fatter lying dead on the gurney than he had in life. He looked even deader almost naked with his autopsy artifacts than he had lying in the dirt in his overalls.

My personal belief is that the person's soul or spirit leaves at the moment of death. I view my work as creating beautiful memory pictures for families and friends, not as cosmetizing the corpse. I work on shells, the remains of someone who once was. I reminded myself that this wasn't really June Bug, not the man who befriended me and danced with me in his own bar. This was canvas for a picture I would create for his wife, a touching memory as close as possible to her Jimmy Lee on their wedding day.

Otis helped me shampoo June Bug's hair again after he resealed the leak. When we finished, the hair was white as pure-driven snow. Like I know anything about snow. I've only seen snow once in my life and that was barely an inch in Columbia when I was in college.

Mrs. Corley had specifically requested that I shave June Bug's beard and cut his hair. She hadn't requested hair color, and I wondered if I should have suggested it. I frequently do color touch-ups, especially on ladies who've been sick before their deaths. If Mrs. Corley had wanted her husband's hair tinted the brown of his youth, I would have done it.

When I'd completed my work, Otis and I used the body lift to help us dress June Bug. Everything fit perfectly, even the shoes. Otis brought in the extra-large-sized wooden casket and we soon had June Bug properly positioned and ready to be wheeled to the slumber room. The corpse looked amazingly like the young man in the photograph of Mr. and Mrs. Corley on their wedding day. A plumper version, but the same man. He didn't, however, bear much resemblance to June Bug. With short hair and no beard, June Bug was just a heavy Jimmy Lee Corley with white hair. I hoped that was what Mrs. Corley wanted.

I was telephoning the Corley home when the poop hit the fan. I laid the receiver back into its cradle before anyone answered. Funeral homes should be quiet and reverent, sort of like churches. The screaming voice outside my office was loud and full of advanced cussing, more than a master's degree, probably a doctorate.

Before I reached the door, it banged open and Bouncy Betty stomped in. "What's the meaning of this?" she screamed, waving papers in my face. "Where's Otis Middleton? He's going to answer to me."

"Okay, okay," I soothed. "I'll get Otis. We'll work out whatever problem there is." I guided Betty toward a consultation room. I didn't have to find Otis. He'd heard Betty and reached us before we entered the room. That's another funeral home rule. If someone is upset, whether it's tears of grief or screams of anger, an attendant shepherds the person into a side room and closes the door.

Betty plopped down onto a chair and crossed her legs. Her short yellow skirt hiked up, exposing far more thigh than was comfortable to Otis. He looked away. I sat in a chair beside Betty, and Otis sat across the table.

"Now, now, Mrs. Saxon, what has you so upset?" Otis said in his best undertaker voice.

Betty leaned toward Otis, and he flinched away from her. Her yellow-flowered knit top was cut so low that her bouncies were clearly visible. I made a mental note to never, ever inflate my bra anywhere near the size of Betty's chest.

"This," Betty yelled and pushed the papers she'd been gripping right into Otis's nose. Otis gently took them and began reading silently. Betty screeched even louder, "You told me that as soon as you got the death certificates, the insurance would pay for Bobby's funeral and I'd get the rest. What's the meaning of this? What are they talking about?"

Otis uses a tanning bed frequently, but no tan could hide the crimson of his face. He looked up from the papers to me and said, "Callie, please bring the Saxon folder, and get Mrs. Saxon something to drink."

"Betty, would you like a cup of coffee or some tea?" I asked.

"No! All I want is my money. It's mine and I want it!" She uncrossed her legs and began jittering them as she tried to light a cigarette. She was shaking so much that the lighter and the Marlboro bounced in opposite directions several times before she managed to make the connection.

I went out and returned with the file and a coffee service with three Wedgwood cups and saucers on a silver tray. I filled the cups and offered Betty cream and sugar.

"Are you people crazy?" Betty exploded. "I'm talking about half a million dollars, and you want to know if I take cream and sugar in my coffee. I don't even want any coffee. I want some answers."

I left her cup on the tray and stirred three spoonfuls of sugar into mine. I needed that coffee.

"When did you receive this?" Otis asked.

"It came in this morning's mail." Betty crumpled into

sobs and dropped the cigarette on the table. I grabbed it and smudged the butt out in the ashtray. A burned spot on the expensive antique table would be a minor disaster to the twins.

"Mrs. Saxon, this letter says that you tried to file your claim for Bobby's insurance without a death certificate and without mentioning or sending a copy of the lien we hold against the policy. Didn't you agree that I would help you file your claim when we received the proper documentation?" Otis asked.

"Yes," Betty snuffled, "but it was taking too long." She must not have ever dealt with claims and legalities. It hadn't been long, not even a reasonable time if there were no complications.

Otis harrumphed. I'd only heard him make that sound a few times, and only when he was totally disgusted.

"Do you know what I think?" Otis asked. "I believe you didn't think we knew what we were doing and that you planned to collect the insurance and make us wait for our money until you got around to it or maybe not pay us at all." To most people, his tone would have sounded disappointed. I heard tightly controlled anger.

Otis maintains a quiet, tranquil demeanor, while his twin brother Odell vents frequently. Otis is slow to explode, but when he reaches his boiling point, he's much worse than Odell. I thought Otis might be at ninety-nine degrees Celsius, so I intervened to give him time to cool off.

"Betty," I said, "didn't I explain that no insurance company will even consider a claim without a death certificate? The problem now is that Bobby's death has been classified as homicide. Even with the death certificate, the insurance company won't pay until Sheriff Harmon notifies them that you aren't a suspect."

"Me? I didn't murder Bobby." She lit another cigarette and swung her crossed legs faster.

"I didn't say you killed him. I meant they have to rule you out. The spouse is always the first suspect," I said. Otis leaned back. Betty's foot hit the table leg. "You had plenty of motive," I continued. "A half million dollars that you'd never get if the two of you divorced. You had opportunity. When Bobby left the AA meeting, he said he was going home. You could have talked him into taking you to dinner at the Sleep Easy's dining room. Lots of locals eat there. If you cut across from the parking lot to the dining room by going through the pool area, you could have stabbed him with the needle, making him fall into the water."

"But I didn't hurt Bobby!" Betty screeched. "I didn't even see him Sunday night."

In for a dime, in for a dollar. I kept right on. "The only thing missing is means, and if Sheriff Harmon checks around, he'll probably be able to tie you to a drug dealer at some time in your past."

"I swear I didn't murder Bobby!" Betty burst into tears. "I was his *wife*."

"Betty, lots of murder victims are killed by their spouses. That makes you more a suspect, not less."

"That's not what she's talking about," Otis said and handed me the papers.

Betty changed her mind about the coffee. She shoveled in two heaping spoonfuls of sugar and poured a giant dollop of cream into her cup. She reached into her yellow tote bag, pulled out a second pack of Marlboros, and lit another cigarette while one already smoldered in the ashtray.

Otis stewed. Betty smoked. I read.

The papers from the insurance company replied to a letter Betty had written the day after Bobby died, asking them to send her the money. She had enclosed a copy of the obituary from the newspaper and a copy of her marriage license. I expected the response to be that the proper forms had to be filed. I was correct about that, but the next paragraph knocked me for a loop.

> *Please be advised that we have received com- munication from George Lawrence Taylor, Es- quire, Attorney at Law, stating that Mrs. Eileen Shealy Saxon is Robert Edward Saxon's legal wife and lawful heir, as their marriage was never legally terminated by divorce or annul- ment. Mr. Taylor intends to file for payment of this policy on behalf of Mrs. Eileen Shealy Saxon as soon as proper documentation is available. We shall withhold all payment on this policy until the matter is officially settled.*

"Dalmatian," I whispered in surprise.

"Bobby's been married four or five times since Eileen. She can't do that, can she?" Betty asked. She sounded more whiney than angry now. She crossed her legs again and began swinging her foot toward Otis while blowing bluish cigarette smoke in his direction. Otis ignored her. He was concentrating on papers from the Saxon file. Every once in a while, he harrumphed again.

"Betty," I said, "we appreciate you bringing this to us, but right now, you need legal counsel. This Taylor attor- ney is out of Beaufort and supposed to be a hotshot legal beagle. You'd better lawyer up with someone good soon."

"Can you recommend anyone?" she gave a half sniffle, half cough through her cigarette smoke.

I shrugged. "Not really. The only lawyer I've ever con- sulted was for my divorce in Columbia."

She turned toward Otis, whose tannish red look now appeared a sickish green. "Otis, can you advise me?" Betty asked.

Otis harrumphed again. "No."

Betty stubbed out her cigarette, stood, and picked up her yellow patent tote bag. I offered the papers back to her, but Otis said, "Make a copy of those, Callie, and put them in Bobby's file." Betty followed me into the office to the copier.

"I didn't kill him," she said, holding her hands out toward me in a pleading gesture.

"I hope not," I answered. I should have left it at that, but I was annoyed that she'd tried to collect the insurance and probably beat the mortuary out of our pay after all that talk about wanting the best for Bobby. "You know, you probably are a suspect," I added. "After all, you lied about Bobby drinking all day Sunday when he was actually at an Alcoholics Anonymous meeting Sunday night."

"Well, he was gone all that day. I didn't want to admit I didn't know where he was. When they said he drowned, I figured he'd started drinking again. He was hardly ever home the last few months and he never wanted to go out to party." She sighed. "I might as well tell you the truth. He was the one who wanted a divorce, not me. We got along fine the first couple of months, but then he completely lost interest in me." She sniffled. "I couldn't tell people he wanted to get rid of me. If what Eileen claims is true, why did Bobby say he was going to divorce me if we weren't even married?"

I didn't bother to try to respond to that. Had no answer anyway. Just handed her the papers I'd photocopied.

The bounce was gone from Betty's step when she walked down the hall toward the front door. I felt sorry for her. Not a lot, but a little. After all, I believed she was trying to skip her bill for the funeral, but if she really didn't kill Bobby, she was getting a raw deal.

I felt even sorrier for Otis. Bobby's funeral had been expensive. Only the best. Lots of chips. Unless Betty was

Bobby's legal wife and innocent of his death, Middleton's might be out a lot of money. If Eileen collected the insurance, Middleton's could enter a claim against the estate, but Bobby lived in a rented house and drove a dealership car. He wouldn't have much of an estate, and the insurance wouldn't be part of it. Otis and Odell could sue Betty, but I wouldn't hold my breath for the money. No claim could be leveled against Eileen. She hadn't authorized anything.

Not a penny's worth.

Not a single chip.

# Chapter Nineteen

A five-year-old in big-time trouble. That's what Otis looked like when I returned from seeing Betty out. He still sat in the conference room. His shoulders sagged, and his expression was pure despair.

"Have you called the Corleys?" he mumbled so low that I could barely hear him.

"I was doing that when Betty came in, but I hung up before anyone answered so no one could hear her."

"Good. Go ahead and schedule the Corley family in to see June Bug. We still need to make arrangements with them. They've only decided about clothing and the casket." He paused. "Beep Odell, too. I may as well face the music and tell him about this mess with Saxon. I should have insisted on money up front." He rose like an old, old man who could barely stand. "I'll be in my office," he said.

Skinny Penny answered the Corley phone and said they could come right then. I beeped Odell and told him the Corley family members were on their way and that

Otis needed to talk to him. I could hear Odell chewing as he talked to me.

When Odell arrived, he and Otis closed themselves in the main office to review the Bobby Saxon folder. They were still there when the front door announced an arrival with "It Is No Secret What God Can Do."

Mrs. Corley wore a black dress and a pillbox hat with a veil. Her children, their spouses, and the grandchildren were all dressed appropriately for church—men in suits, women in dresses, children in dress-up clothes. I would have to admit I thought that showed great respect for June Bug, but I guessed Mrs. Corley had told them what to wear. Most people don't dress up just to come see the body.

"Hello," I greeted Mrs. Corley. "Let me tell Mr. Middleton you're here."

"That's not necessary," she replied. "Just show my family somewhere to wait. I want to see Jimmy Lee alone."

"Yes, ma'am." I ushered the family into the main sitting room.

"Mama, I think you should let one of us go in with you," said Walter. I remembered he was the son she'd slapped at the house.

"No, I want to see Jimmy Lee by myself."

"Mrs. Corley, Otis and Odell prefer that someone accompany you. May I go with you?"

"Yes, that's fine. I just want to spend a minute with my Jimmy Lee before his children see him."

I grabbed a tissue box from the coffee table in front of the couch and guided Mrs. Corley to Slumber Room A. When we reached the door, she inhaled a gigantic, ragged breath and clenched my hand. She had selected a half-lid casket like most folks do. We don't stock a full couch casket with one long lid, and we haven't special-ordered one in over two years. The half-lid style allows the funeral director to close the foot half while leaving the lid open at the top for viewing, and June Bug looked great even if I say so myself. We'd lowered the mattress so that his paunch wasn't sticking up any more than a six-pack of abs would have if he'd been in shape.

Mrs. Corley stood looking at the body for several minutes before she asked, "May I touch him?"

"Yes, ma'am, but please don't try to move him," I answered.

"Callie child, no one has been able to move Jimmy Lee for years. I just want to feel his hand." She released her grip on me, reached out, and stroked the top of June Bug's folded hands with her fingertips. I've seen this many times before, but I'd never seen it done more lovingly than when Mrs. Corley touched her husband.

She whispered, "So much changed. We adored each other in the early years. Before the children were born. Jimmy wasn't out drinking and dancing back then." I realized that she was looking at him, but talking to me. "Soon as Jimmy got off work, he'd hurry right home to be with me."

She paused. I felt I should respond. "Yes, ma'am," I said.

A tear trickled down Mrs. Corley's cheek. I handed her a tissue as she turned toward me. "Callie child, you did a really great job. Aside from his weight and white hair, Jimmy Lee looks just like he did when we were married almost forty years ago. I just wanted to see him like it was back then, before the kids came along." She looked up at me and smiled. "I loved this man," she said. "I loved him before, and I loved him after he started drinking. I loved him even after he built that building so he could do his rattlesnaking right there in our backyard. I loved Jimmy Lee

Corley the day I married him, and I'll love him 'til the day I die."

"Yes, ma'am," I repeated.

"There's one thing I want before we let the family come in." She grinned and her little beady eyes sparkled. "I want to see Jimmy Lee with shoes on his feet. Were you able to get them on him?"

"Yes, ma'am. Mr. Corley is wearing his shoes. I'll be glad to show you." I lifted the foot end lid of the casket so she could see her husband, head to toe. Her eyes warmed like she was seeing a Greek god. "He was a fine-looking man, wasn't he?" she asked me.

I couldn't think of anything else to tell her, so I said "Yes, ma'am" another time.

Just then, Odell came in. He gave me a look that I knew meant *You can go now* and greeted Mrs. Corley.

"This Callie child is a real jewel," Mrs. Corley said to Odell. "Look, she's made my husband back into the man I married."

"We try to please. If there's anything you want changed, all you need to do is let us know."

"No, I'm ready for the children to come see their daddy. Can we leave it open like this so they can see his shoes? I don't think my youngest son ever saw his daddy wear shoes."

"Of course, we can," Odell said in a soothing tone. He looked at me. "Callie, please bring Mrs. Corley's family in, and then see Otis. He needs some office work completed."

When June Bug's relatives filed into Slumber Room A, I wanted to stay, but I followed Odell's instructions and went to Otis's office.

"How are the Corleys doing?" he asked.

"Mrs. Corley seems pleased. How are *you* doing?"

"Better. It's bad enough as it is, but I figured Odell would throw a fit. He didn't scream a single time."

"I know. I expected to hear him."

"He said what's done is done, but we better lawyer up." He handed me the Bobby Saxon folder. "We've made an appointment to meet with our attorney tomorrow morning at nine. Make two copies of this entire folder, including the letter that was sent to Betty Saxon by the insurance company. When you've finished, file the originals back in the cabinet and put one set of copies on Odell's desk."

"What about the other set?" I reached for the folder, expecting him to tell me to put them on his own desk. I was wrong.

"Sheriff Harmon will pick those up shortly." Otis peeked at a mirror on the wall, brushed back his hair plugs, and headed toward the front of the building, but he was back before I had the copier warmed up in the main office. "Callie, I apologize for interrupting your work, but Mrs. Corley wants to see you."

He walked to Slumber Room A with me. Everyone who'd been in the salon was now standing around the coffin. Otis and Odell had moved the casket. We always position bodies against a draped wall with the deceased's right side away from the wall. Now the casket was almost in the center of the room. Mrs. Corley stepped toward me.

"Mrs. Corley, do you want me to adjust something?" I asked.

"Oh, no, I'm very happy with everything Middleton's has done. Callie child, you did such good work for my Jimmy Lee that I want you and Otis and Odell to join my family for a few minutes."

Otis and I stepped into the circle. I stood between Skinny Penny and Otis, holding their hands.

"Let us bow our heads in prayer," Mrs. Corley said. She paused. "Walter, you're not bowed." He bent his head. "That's better."

I'd been listening regularly to eulogies and funeral sermons for several years, but Mrs. Corley's thirty-minute prayer touched me more than most. Tears filled my eyes before the final "Amen." When the circle broke, she told her family to go home, all except Patsy.

"You stay, Patsy," Mrs. Corley said. "I'll need you to drive me home after I talk with the Middletons."

The family filed out like a well-behaved kindergarten line.

Odell escorted Fatsy Patsy and her mother to our main consultation room. I went to the kitchen and returned with a coffee service and five cups in case Otis joined us. I anticipated a long planning session. Instead, I heard Odell ask in disbelief, "Cremation? You want Mr. Corley cremated?"

"Yes, that's what I said," Mrs. Corley answered.

"Why, Mama?" said Fatsy Patsy.

"Because the people who knew that man in there"—she gestured toward the door—"wouldn't be here for a burial anyway. His mama and daddy knew him. His brother knew him. They're all dead. I knew him, but I've said my goodbyes. If we have a wake and funeral, the people who come will be those drunks who ran around with a fat, bearded alcoholic they called June Bug. I wasn't married to June Bug. I was married to James Lee Corley."

"But, Mama," Patsy interrupted, "I want to see Daddy again, and maybe someone else in the family will, too."

"I want Jimmy cremated. Since when do I have to ask children what plans to make for my husband?" Mrs. Corley stopped speaking. Patsy remained silent. Those "children" she spoke of were in their thirties and forties.

"Would you like a memorial service?" Otis asked.

"No, I want you to cremate him and be sure he's wearing exactly the clothes he has on now. I picked a mahogany coffin in case I decided to do this, so it can be cremated with him, can't it?"

"Yes, the casket you selected is suitable for burial or cremation."

"Do you do it here?" Patsy said.

"No," Otis said, "we don't have a crematorium. Our cremations are handled in Charleston. They'll send the cremains to St. Mary in about a week."

"Is the sheriff going to let Daddy be cremated?" Fatsy Patsy asked.

"It's not against the law to cremate someone," Mrs. Corley snapped.

"No, I meant since Daddy died the way he did. What if they wanted to do another autopsy later?"

"That's even more reason to cremate Jimmy. I won't have him buried, then dug up."

"The sheriff has released the body to us and Mrs. Corley," Otis said.

"Can I see him again, Mama?"

"Yes, we'll look at him before they close the casket." Mrs. Corley turned toward Otis. "Please tell anyone who calls about arrangements that Jimmy's service was very private, for family only."

"We certainly will. I'll need you to sign some papers."

"I already signed papers when I picked the casket."

"Yes, but you need to authorize the cremation. Do you wish to select an urn for the cremains?"

"No, just call when the ashes are back. We'll come get them and spread them ourselves." Mrs. Corley signed everywhere Odell showed her without reading a word.

When Otis walked Mrs. Corley and Patsy to Slumber Room A, I returned to the main office. I thought I'd seen everything since I began work at Middleton's, but Mrs. Corley had given me another first, cremating a custom-ordered mahogany casket and the new shoes and clothes that had been so important to her. As I finished photo-copying the Bobby Saxon papers, I realized that most people purchase caskets and dress their dead for other people to see. Mrs. Corley had planned all along that the casket and clothes had been not for her family nor June Bug's friends. They'd been for her and her Jimmy Lee.

I acknowledged another fact to myself. June Bug Cor-ley was no longer a likely suspect in Bobby Saxon's mur-der. Unless someone killed June Bug out of revenge if June Bug killed Bobby. On the same convoluted brain wave, I realized that Mrs. Corley could be considered a person of interest. That skinny birdlike woman ruled the roost. She was a lot stronger than she looked. What if she'd learned Bobby Saxon had taken her grandchild's virginity and fathered her miscarried great-grandchild? Plenty of motive. The same revenge might have made her kill June Bug, since he'd let their granddaughter hang out in the club and be exposed to the town womanizer. Mrs. Corley had motive, and she definitely had opportunity in June Bug's case. Where was she the Sunday night Bobby Saxon died?

**Anne Bailey, an** eighty-four-year-old resident at the St. Mary Agape Nursing Home, died during a nap. The fam-ily couldn't be reached, but Mrs. Bailey's records named Middleton's as the funeral home to call. Otis went to pick up the body. Odell was in his office with the door closed. I posted the private funeral announcement for June Bug on our web page, pulled out a book, and settled in for a short read until Otis returned.

Sheriff Harmon and an instrumental "My Soul Will

Fly Free" interrupted a really good chapter. "What's this about Eileen claiming to be Bobby Saxon's legal heir?" he asked before we even reached each other in the hall.

"That's what it says in these papers." I handed the folder to him. "Are you going to be able to do something about this for Middleton's?"

"Nothing I can do. Not even fraud. Betty Saxon had no idea she wouldn't be the beneficiary. Sounds like it will wind up in court. When Odell called me about it, I told him I wanted copies for my files on Bobby's murder, but there isn't anything I can do to help collect the funeral debt."

"Do you have any good leads yet?"

"We're looking into several avenues." His answer was short and clipped, but he added, "This makes Eileen as much a suspect as Betty."

I smiled at him, trying to give him that little girl look that used to inspire Wayne Harmon to give me a piece of gum while he hung around with my brothers when I was a child.

"Do you think Mrs. Corley, June Bug's wife, might be a person of interest?"

"For which murder?"

"I was thinking both."

"What makes you think the deaths are related?"

"Call it female intuition. Do you think they're connected?"

"Yes, I do," Harmon said, inching away from me. No gum today.

"You got the hinky cop feeling about it?"

"Not exactly. I've got the preliminary toxicology results showing that June Bug had traces of ketamine in his body. The strange thing is that Saxon's ketamine was injected before he went into the pool and appears to be the cause of death. June Bug was shot dead with a bullet before he was shot with Special K."

"What does that indicate?"

"Not sure yet. Doesn't make much sense." Harmon stopped moving away. "You're an amateur sleuth. What do you think?"

"It seems weird to inject Special K into a dead man. I'll have to consider it."

Harmon took another step away. "On second thought, don't waste your time. I don't need your opinion anyway. Don't know why I even discuss cases with you. Stay out of it. I shouldn't have told you anything." He dismissed me with, "Don't you worry about it, Callie. Remember you work for Otis and Odell, not for me. I don't want your daddy and brothers after my hide because you're playing detective." His tone was serious.

"How about where the Special K came from? Have you identified local sources yet?"

"I told you, Callie. You're not a part of the investigation. Just keep your nose clean." He reached for the doorknob and nodded toward the folder in his other hand. "Tell Otis and Odell I've got these. I'm out of here. Busy day."

I tried one more time. "So you do think Bobby and June Bug's deaths were connected?" Harmon waved as he ignored my question and hurried down the steps.


**A member of** the Bailey family called and made an appointment to confirm funeral plans for Mrs. Bailey on Tuesday morning. He said that prearrangements had been made many years ago. Otis embalmed the body while Odell took chairs and a register to the family home. I called Jane.

"Hey, Callie, what ya doing?" she answered.

"Working, but I'll be off at five. Why don't I pick you up and we'll go somewhere for an early supper before you start work?"

"Sure. Have you figured out who the killer is yet?" Jane asked.

"No, but there are some interesting developments. See you at five." I hung up the telephone as Otis rang the buzzer for me to go to the prep room.

Mrs. Bailey lay on the gurney with towels draped over breasts and privates. The lady was as flat-chested as I am. I wondered if inflatable bras had been invented when she was my age. Otis finished setting the embalming fluid pump and said, "Mrs. Bailey made plans with us long before you came to work here. I pulled her file from the pre-arrangement cabinet. It's on my desk. I have a vague memory that this woman wanted to be buried in a pink dress. I can remember her laughing and telling Odell she wasn't to be buried in 'old lady' black, navy, or maroon, but a pretty pink dress. It's driving me crazy trying to prep her and wondering if I'm remembering the right woman. How about checking it for me?"

I found the prearrangement folder and, sure enough, Mrs. Bailey had specified a "pretty, light pink dress." Otis beamed when I went back to the prep room to tell him. He prides himself on his excellent memory.

"No point in your going to shop for a pink dress since her family may be doing that right now," he said.

"How about her?" I nodded toward Mrs. Bailey. "Do you want me to stay over and finish her today?"

"No, wait until tomorrow. The pink shade of the dress will determine the base makeup you use, and we'll need a photograph to know how the family wants her hair done anyway."

Otis stopped and stared at me. "Did you do something different with your own hair? It looks different."

"Do you like it?" I had no problem asking Otis that question. Even if he hated it, Otis would temper his reply.

Odell would have had no problem telling me if he didn't like it.

"Yes." Otis smiled. "It's very complimentary on you."

When Odell returned, I showed him the prearrangement folder with the appointment slip attached for Tuesday's conference. One of the part-time drivers was taking June Bug to the crematorium in Charleston, and bless Odell's heart, he told me I could leave early.

By four thirty, I was in the Mustang headed toward Jane's. By five, we'd put the top down and decided on a ride before dinner. If I were making up this story, I'd say we talked, but in real life, talking while speeding down the highway in an open convertible isn't an option.

I don't know what Jane was thinking about, but I mentally tried to sort out the two murders and wondered which of Bobby's first and last wives was more likely to have murdered him. Why would either have any reason to kill June Bug? Noise from Jane's side of the car made me wonder if she was trying to talk to me, but when I glanced at her, I could tell she was singing.

We drove through Beaufort, stopped and picked up a couple of Cokes, Dr Peppers, and oyster po'boys, then sped down to the beach at Hunting Island. Jane and I slipped off our shoes, and I guided her from the parking lot to the seaside. We sat on the sand, me with the skirt of my black dress wrapped and tucked under my knees. Jane wore a halter and shorts. My daddy and The Boys would call them "cooter-cutters," but I prefer the term "Daisy Dukes."

Watching and listening to the waves slapping the pearly white shore, we talked and ate. I told Jane about the papers Betty had brought in that morning.

"She was trying to stiff Otis and Odell for the bill, wasn't she?" Jane asked before taking another bite of po'boy.

"I think so. You know, she admits that she lied about

Bobby drinking all day Sunday. Now she says he went out and she doesn't know where. She also claims that when she said she was going to divorce him, she was covering up for her embarrassment that he told her he was going to leave. Her lies make me suspect her. Innocent survivors want to know who caused a death. They tell the truth."

"So you think Betty killed Bobby? If she did, why would she shoot June Bug?"

"I don't know, unless June Bug had some way to prove Betty was guilty of Bobby's murder."

The oysters tasted delicious. I squeezed another packet of hot sauce on my sandwich. "I still think the key to the case might be the source of the Special K. Do you know if June Bug was selling?"

"No," Jane answered. "I never told you June Bug was a dealer. I said you could find someone in June Bug's bar who sold pot. Once again, stay out of it. It scares me to think you'll get involved in a murder case, even if you solve it, but it terrifies me that the murderer might think you know more than you do and feel the need to silence you."

I finished my sandwich, wadded up the wrappings, and shoved them into my purse. "Jane," I asked, feeling a bit ridiculous and maybe a little traitorous, "do you think Odell would kill anyone just for business?"

"What? Sometimes you talk plumb crazy. Why do you ask that?"

"Odell said he was in Columbia the morning Bobby was found, but I opened a letter from the undertakers' association that said he didn't attend that meeting. Odell's been extremely distraught about the slump in business and he's been gone a lot when Otis and I don't know where he is."

"Maybe he has a girlfriend," Jane offered.

"I hadn't thought of that." I pondered the thought for a moment. "He hasn't dated that I know of for several years. To be honest, Odell seems more interested in eating than dating."

"Maybe that's why he's gone so much. He sneaks off to eat," Jane said. "Besides, the time he was supposed to be in Columbia was when the body was *found*, not while Bobby was being killed."

"But then, who knows where Odell was Sunday night?" I said.

"I sure don't." Jane laughed. "Unless he was on the phone with Roxanne."

We stayed by the water as the tide rose and waves tickled our toes. When the tide reached where we sat and our derrieres grew sopping wet, Jane suggested we go back to the car.

As we walked, she asked, "Do you think somebody might have hired June Bug to kill Bobby and then shot June Bug?"

"If the murderer was willing to kill June Bug, why *hire* him to get rid of Bobby? Why not just kill Bobby?"

"Whoever hired June Bug could have started worrying about that old drunk talking too much when he got to drinking. Or maybe June Bug started demanding more money."

I tried, I promise I tried not to be rude and crude, but I said it anyway. "Are you saying the murderer *shot* June Bug to keep him from *shooting* off his mouth?"

"It's not funny, Callie," Jane scolded.

"I'm sorry. I guess it's a possibility, but we both said 'he.' Don't you think Betty or Eileen might have hired June Bug? That would put him back on the suspect list."

"I don't know." Jane sighed. "They both claimed to love Bobby, but money is a powerful motive, and each of them expected to collect that insurance payoff."

Talk stopped when we got into the Mustang. The top was still down and conversation would have been difficult. I think we were both lost in our own thoughts anyway.

By the time I dropped off Jane at her apartment, night had fallen. Driving home under the stars with a tummy full of oysters would have been heavenly, except I couldn't get my mind off the two murders.

Big Boy and I went for a long walk and frolicked around the yard. The roughhousing continued inside the house until the puppy gave up and plopped down, exhausted. I was glad. A quick shower for me, a fake bacon treat for him, and we settled in for a sound sleep.

The phone shrilled at two o'clock in the morning. I don't know who was more frightened by the noise, Big Boy or me. He jumped up, pounded his huge paws on the comforter, and began barking. I fumbled for the telephone receiver.

The same electronically distorted voice.

"Calamine Parrish, mind your own business . . . or else!"

# Chapter Twenty

"**G**rim" is the only word I can think of to describe how Otis and Odell looked when they arrived late to work Tuesday morning. They'd gone to see their lawyer before coming to the mortuary, but neither of them volunteered any information, and I suspected the news was bad. They went into Odell's office and closed the door.

Buh-leeve me. My night of trying to read mystery books between panic and anxiety attacks left me tired and irritable. I couldn't get my mind off the telephone call, especially the "or else." When I called the sheriff's department, the officer said he'd make a report and someone would be back in touch with me. So far, I'd heard nothing from the sheriff or any of his deputies. By mid-morning, I felt sleepy, a little angry at the sheriff's apparent lack of concern, and a whole lot scared.

Mrs. Bailey's desire to be buried in a pretty pink dress didn't gain me another day of shopping on Middleton's time with Middleton's Visa. When the family came to make arrangements with Odell, her adult granddaughter brought a pale rose–colored dress and a picture showing Mrs. Bailey's usual hairstyle. Since Otis had completed embalming the body the previous day, my work was all that remained. Mrs. Bailey was almost ready by the time the family left. Odell recommended that they have lunch in town and come back in an hour or so.

"If business doesn't pick up soon, we don't need three slumber rooms," Otis said as we wheeled the bier into Slumber Room A. It had been months since we'd had bodies in B or C. There'd been times in the past when we'd had bodies in all three slumber rooms and had to wait for the funeral of one person in order to schedule viewing for another body we were holding in the back.

"Come now, Otis, we didn't have a funeral for several weeks, but we've had Bobby, June Bug, and Mrs. Bailey in less than two weeks. Business is picking up. Besides, when I think about slow business, I have to realize it's good when people aren't dying off so fast," I said, trying to redirect his thoughts.

"Yeah, but if we go through too many spells like we had before Bobby Saxon, Odell and I might need to get second jobs." Otis laughed at what he considered humor. I didn't. It wasn't funny. There were only three full-time employees, and I had no doubt about who would be the first out of the door if things got too bad.

Odell's first love is barbecue, but Otis loves numbers and statistics. I made a mental note to check the newspapers and Internet to see how many St. Mary residents took their burial needs to Beaufort funeral homes and to find out if business had been off at all funeral homes in the area during our slow spell. Had the other mortuaries been busy while we had fewer and fewer customers? Did I say fewer? Make that no clients at all for a while. Would the Middletons pay me full salary for another three weeks without business if it happened again? I thought not.

Beaufort funeral parlors advertise. I'd mentioned ads to the Middletons when I suggested Internet memorials, but Otis thinks advertising is tacky for lawyers and funeral homes. Maybe I needed to suggest ads again and back up the idea with statistics. Tasteful ads. Dignified commercials, unlike the ambulance-chasing lawyers or Cowboy's shenanigans for the Corral.

Perhaps we needed to modernize. I'd talked Otis and Odell into the web page, and we had special easels and tables for memorial displays, but we didn't offer video memorials. I'd have no problem scanning the photographs into the software to create the DVDs. Otis and I had checked out the cost after we had inquiries about them from a few families who'd seen the videos at funerals in larger cities. Investment in the software would be reimbursed by sale of the DVDs, and we already had a good computer and scanner.

The problem was that neither Odell nor Otis wanted to spring for a large plasma-screen television to show the videos at visitations. Maybe I could convince them. I could gather statistics on how well the videos sold. Even price the TVs at bigger stores in Beaufort and Charleston. That would give me a good excuse to go back to Charleston. An opportunity to visit Victoria's Secret. *Without Jane!*

I stepped away from Mrs. Bailey's coffin to look at the overall picture. She looked like a little old angel in her rose-colored dress and her delicate pink-lined casket with carved roses on each corner. I'd polished her nails and matched her lipstick to the color of her dress. Her son had ordered a white orchid corsage for us to pin to her dress before the visitation.

The door sounded "Just a Closer Walk with Thee," and I went out of Slumber Room A into the front hall, expecting to greet the Bailey family. I sniffed White Diamonds.

Eileen Saxon headed toward me, dressed in her black dress like mine, reaching out with a small gift-wrapped box tied with a silver bow. My first thought was that she wanted something else buried with Bobby, but that was impossible. As the *other* Mrs. Saxon would crudely say, we'd already planted him.

"This is for you, Callie," Eileen said.

I didn't know what to do. My students had brought me presents regularly, everything from a gift certificate for the Parisian department store to a ragweed picked on the way to school. I had enough "For My Teacher" mugs to open a coffee shop. My face flushed. No one had ever brought a present to me at Middleton's. Should I just say thank you, or should I decline the offering?

"A gift for you. Take it. Open it. I wanted to get something for you for your kindness." She winked. "You know, letting me put the picture in with Bobby."

"The picture?" My tone was innocent, but inside I rejoiced that I now knew who put what in Bobby's Exquisite.

"The little memento I put in the coffin with Bobby. It was a picture of Anna Grace, our baby. She died with SIDS before her first birthday. Crib death, they called it back then. Bobby and I were young, and we couldn't handle losing Anna Grace, especially since there was no grief counseling like now. We both tried to drown our sorrow in whiskey, and I moved away, trying to run from my pain."

Tears welled up in Eileen's eyes. "When I came back a few years later, Bobby had remarried. He said he thought I'd divorced him, but there were never any papers or anything. Bobby knew from then on that we were still married. He meant for me to have his insurance money. After all, he put the beneficiary as 'my legal wife.' No particular name." A tear coursed down her cheek. "And he gave me a copy of the policy when we got back together a few months ago. Bobby called it destiny. We were planning to make up for the years apart." She straightened her shoulders and smiled.

"Enough of the past," she said. "Please take the gift. I want you to have it. My little Anna Grace was buried in the last family plot my daddy bought when I was a little girl. Guess he bought it for me. Now Bobby's buried beside his mother, but at least he has his daughter's picture with him."

"I don't think I'm allowed to accept anything for my services here," I stammered.

Eileen winked again. "This has nothing to do with your official duties here. It has to do with an unofficial favor you did for me."

Suddenly the smile that had accompanied Eileen's wink disappeared. Her eyes widened with shock and anger. She pushed past me toward the back of the hall. I turned and saw Bouncy Betty charging from the back door straight toward Eileen. They smacked into each other and tumbled to the floor. The wrapped present dropped from Eileen's hand. The odor of White Diamonds from the smashed box saturated the hall when the package hit the floor.

I'd never seen two women fight like Betty and Eileen. A couple of catfights back in high school may have come close, but only near. Betty's sling-back stiletto heels flew across the floor as she kicked, jabbed, and scratched wife number one. Eileen yanked and pulled wife number five's hair, shook a handful of it onto the carpet, and grabbed for more. Between profanities, she bit any part of Betty that got in her way.

Did I step in and try to stop this fight? Puh-leeze. I know from experience how to pull apart a couple of five-year-olds, but I've got better sense than to get between those two battle-axes. Otis rushed to see what the noise was about. He stepped away from them and plastered his back against the wall, eyes full of horror. Odell hurried out right behind Otis, but he barged into the fray, cussing louder than the women.

Instead of stopping them, Odell caught a fist in his left eye and a knee in his groin. In the middle of flying arms, legs, fists, and teeth, both women pounded and scratched Odell. At least he was bald, so Eileen couldn't pull his hair, but I saw Betty's hand rake across the top of Odell's head, leaving four bloody stripes. She must have gouged his arm with her nails, too, because he was dripping blood. Eileen's nails were gnawed to the quick, but she had a mean right hook and was biting.

The telephone rang. I looked at Otis. He nodded to me. I ran to the office, closed the door, and answered, "Middleton's Mortuary. How may I help you?"

"This is Ed Bailey," a male voice drawled. "We've finished eating and want to know if we can come on back and see Mama now."

"I'm so glad you called," I said in my professional funeral parlor voice. "We're not quite ready. Would it be possible for you to return early this evening instead?"

"Well, Mr. Middleton said . . ."

"I know, but it really will be better if you wait a while."

"We'll be there around five then." He didn't sound happy, but he was off the phone.

Through the closed office door, I still heard screams and thuds. Odell flung the door open. He was wiping blood from his head with a red-soaked handkerchief. One of the women had torn loose the right sleeve of his suit jacket.

I reached for the phone to call the sheriff. Remembered my childhood. Hung up the receiver and hurried to the kitchen. Filled a large coffee decanter with cold water, lugged it back into the hall, and splashed the whole container onto the two women. Water worked when my daddy broke up fighting dogs. It worked on these two . . . well, I'd better not say that word. It's not cussing. Just another word for dog, but it's not exactly nice.

The women stopped yelling and dropped to the floor. They sat in the puddle of water, shaking their heads while examining their battle scars. Blood dripped from both of them, and swatches of orange as well as blonde hair lay scattered over the carpet.

"I'll get the Shop-Vac," Otis said.

"Better get some spot cleaner, too," I said. "The Baileys will be here at five."

Odell moved close to the hall tree mirror and peered at himself. Drops of blood fell from his head and arms. He looked like the arbitrator at a WWE match that had ended with both wrestlers ganging up on the referee. Odell pointed at the front door and shook his finger. "Get these two out of here," he yelled. "Because if they're not outta here right now, I'm pressing charges."

Betty tugged her bra strap off her arm and back onto her shoulder. She picked up her shoes and tote bag. She flounced to the back door, turned toward Eileen, and hissed over her shoulder, "I'll see you in court."

"You'd better believe it, bimbo," Eileen replied. Her dress hung in tatters like my living room curtains after Big Boy got hold of them. She pulled the shredded cloth together and limped to the front door.

Eileen glanced around the hall at Otis busy spraying cleaner on the carpet and Odell staring at himself in the mirror. "Sorry about this," she said and left.

With the two Widows Saxon off the premises, the Middletons and I tried to put things back in order. Otis took care of the hair and water with the Shop-Vac. The smell of White Diamonds overpowered the rooms. I retrieved a spray can of air deodorizer from a supply closet and managed to remove most of the scent, or at least mix it in with the odors of deodorizer and spot remover. Odell had gone to the back bathroom to clean and disinfect his scratches and bites.

"Callie," Odell asked when he finished doctoring his injuries and came back into the hall, "do you think we should dab a bit of makeup over these before the Baileys return?"

"I'd be scared to do that, Odell," I replied as I sniffed to see if I'd succeeded with the spray. "Makeup in those scratches could start an infection. If anyone asks, just tell them you got into an altercation with a sticker vine."

I tried. I promise I tried, but I couldn't hold back a giggle. Odell's scratches on his scalp looked like he'd sprouted four bright red hairs and combed them across his head in a vain attempt to hide his baldness.

"I could seal those scratches for you," Otis teased and laughed, too.

"Thanks, Doofus, but I'll pass." I couldn't believe it. I'd expected Odell to erupt in anger, but he responded to his brother in a pleasant tone. They went into Odell's office together and closed the door.

I read until the Baileys returned. Sometimes I read to keep from being bored, but I'd already had more than enough excitement. This time I hoped reading would calm me.

The Bailey relatives had the sad but relieved demeanor of families who've lost a loved one who'd suffered from a long illness before death. Plenty of tears were shed, but no one became hysterical. They planned visitation for Thursday evening at Middleton's, and the funeral service would be at their church on Saturday. Another overtime grave opening, but one relative couldn't get to South Carolina until Friday night, and Ed, the oldest son and family spokesman, said, "We can't wait until Monday. We need closure as soon as possible."

Just before leaving work, I remembered that I hadn't replaced my driver's license like I promised Sheriff Harmon. Otis gave me permission to take care of that before coming in on Wednesday morning.

On the way home, I drove through the McDonald's pickup lane and purchased a Happy Meal for myself and a Quarter Pounder for Big Boy. Donnie would have thrown fits if I'd fed the Pomeranian any kind of short-order food, but Big Boy was all mine. I still had to call the vet to see about this ear-cropping business, and I planned to ask him if an occasional hamburger would be harmful to my puppy. Until then, I'd treat Big Boy whenever I wanted.

If I'd known how good it feels to be met by a living creature who is totally overjoyed to see me at the end of the day, I'd have gotten myself a pet long ago. Big Boy hadn't even wet the papers I'd left for him, so I knew he really needed to go, but he jumped on me and licked my hands before barreling out the front door to relieve himself.

I followed my puppy out with the leash in one hand and our McDonald's bag in the other. Big Boy sniffed the bag and squatted simultaneously. Still wearing my black dress and heels, I sat on the porch step and tucked my skirt under my legs. I opened up our dinner.

Big Boy's appetite helped my diet. He ate his Quarter Pounder and all of my fries, then begged me out of the last bite of my little cheeseburger. After we finished eating, I unwrapped the toy that came with the Happy Meal. It was a plastic monster. I threw it over Big Boy's head, and he scampered across the lawn, picked it up in his mouth, and brought it back to me. When the toy landed by the tree at the end of the sidewalk, Big Boy spent a little more time nosing around. He appeared to be eating something, but when I called him, he came running.

By the time Big Boy and I went inside, it was after nine o'clock. As much as I wanted to call Jane and tell her about the Widows Saxon fray, I knew that she'd be deep into her Roxanne work and I'd be intruding. After my shower, I pulled on an oversized T-shirt and crawled into bed with an old Sherlock Holmes mystery. If I couldn't talk with one old friend, I could revisit another on paper.

In one of their books, Sherlock Holmes tells Dr. Watson that the way to solve a problem is to eliminate the impossible. What remains after all impossibilities are gone is the solution. Without the results of the sheriff's investigation into alibis and forensics, this didn't help me with my desire to know who killed Bobby Saxon and June Bug. I couldn't identify the impossibilities. Unfortunately, while I was considering the situation, I fell asleep lying on my stomach with the light on and my face against the open book. Drooled on the pages.

Big Boy woke me. Not by barking, not by climbing into bed with me. He'd crawled into bed the same time I did. He woke me by whimpering. He scrunched close and moaned. I listened hard, but I couldn't hear anything except my puppy crying and the pounding of my own heart. I looked at the clock. Two in the morning. I pulled open the drawer of the bedside table and reached for the .38. I petted Big Boy to calm him, hoping he'd stop his noise so I could hear if anyone was prowling around outside. I was listening so intently for a footstep or a door rattle that I nearly jumped across the bed when the phone rang. I picked it up hesitantly.

The mechanically altered voice again. This time the threat was directed at Big Boy as well as me.

"I saw your puppy eat what I put by the tree for him. This time it will only make him sick, but if you don't back off, your dog will wind up as dead as those corpses you powder and paint at the funeral home. Pumping your stomach won't cure what I'll do to you."

"Who are—"

The disconnect sound buzzed in my ear.

I trembled. Where had the caller hidden to watch Big Boy and me in the front yard? Where was he now? With a cell phone, the killer could be on my porch right that minute. My hands shook so that I could hardly zip my jeans. I stuck the .38 in my pocket.

The yellow pages of the phone book showed a twenty-four-hour emergency veterinary service in Beaufort. I called to be sure they were still in business and told the lady who answered that I suspected my puppy had been poisoned. He was whimpering and shaking.

She said, "Bring him in." I led Big Boy to the car with his leash in one hand and my keys in the other. Stars and the moon shone bright and I saw nothing evil in the darkness as we got in the car to head toward Beaufort. Big Boy lay on the passenger seat with his head in my lap. I locked the doors, reached across the dog, and put the .38 in the glove compartment. I bounced the needle on the speedometer, going faster than the dial showed, on Highway 21. Big Boy moaned and shivered like a sick child until we pulled into the vet's parking lot. As I braked the car, Big Boy threw up all over my thighs.

The vet was the middle-aged, gray-haired lady who had answered the phone. She worked alone through the night. I liked her immediately. She directed me toward a bathroom and gave me a towel to wipe my jeans off as well as possible. She checked Big Boy thoroughly and said he'd probably be fine now that he'd thrown up whatever had made him sick. She asked me what I'd fed him. When I told her about his McDonald's supper, she said, "Too much fat. The grease probably upset his stomach."

I explained that I thought he'd been poisoned because I'd had an anonymous phone call from someone who admitted putting something in my yard to harm my dog. The vet offered to call the Beaufort police, but I assured her I'd report it to Sheriff Harmon as soon as I reached home.

"What's this thing about having his ears cropped?" I asked as I wrote the vet a check for almost half of my week's salary.

"Great Dane ears are supposed to stand up, but to achieve that, we have to crop them. It's not a risky surgery, but it is involved and will require several trips to have bandages changed and check the progress. I prefer to do it when the puppy is between eight and twelve weeks old." She leaned over and lifted Big Boy's ears, held them upright.

"Your dog is probably a little old for the procedure already," she continued. "You need to do it before he gets a growth spurt. I'll be glad to take care of it for you." Must be more Great Danes in Beaufort than I ever realized because that spiel sounded rehearsed.

"A growth spurt?"

"Oh, yes, Big Boy is going to be a huge dog." She then told me how much to expect him to eat when he "got his growth." I gulped. Big Boy's weekly grocery bill would be bigger than mine.

"How much will his ears cost?" I asked.

"Unless there are complications, we can usually complete the procedure for three to four hundred dollars." There went my savings toward a real vacation someday.

"Does cropping help the dog hear better?"

The vet laughed. "No, it's strictly for looks."

I told her I'd let her know if I wanted to have Big Boy's ears cropped. She cautioned me again that it needed to be soon.

Big Boy snored all the way home. I kindergarten-cussed Bill for introducing me to this lovable puppy who needed an ear job before he turned into a giant. Cosmetic surgery for my dog while I was wearing an inflatable bra because I wouldn't have cosmetic surgery myself. I wondered if I could coerce Daddy and The Boys into paying for Big Boy's ear cropping. After all, the dog was for my protection. Maybe I could convince them that cropping his ears would make him hear better to listen for intruders. Doubtful, and I didn't want Daddy and The Boys to know anything about my problems anyway.

I maintained my self-control until Big Boy and I were home and I'd looked in every room, in every closet, and under all furniture to be sure no one was hiding in the apartment. Big Boy had climbed into bed and was snoring again with his head on my pillow by the time I put the clothes I'd worn into the washing machine and turned on the shower for myself.

As the warm water splashed over my tense body, tears streamed down my cheeks. I shivered with fear and kept pulling the shower curtain aside to be sure no one had come into the bathroom. I vowed to myself that I'd never watch *Psycho* again. I hadn't been investigating Bobby Saxon's murder and I had no ideas about June Bug's death unless, like Jane suggested, whoever killed June Bug had paid him to get rid of Bobby, so why was I being told to stop what I wasn't even doing?

Why was this happening to me? Maybe Jane was right. Did the murderer think I knew more than I did? How did he even know I was interested in the case? I hadn't gone out asking questions. And who was he? The person on the phone sounded male. How much could the device change a voice? Could my caller be female?

I toweled off, and though it wasn't cold, pulled on a flannel nightgown. A thick red, yellow, and blue plaid gown

I've had since I was thirteen. Some folks have comfort foods. I have them, too. I also have a comfort nightie that soothes me almost as much as Moon Pies with milk and is a whole lot less fattening. I lay down beside my dog and dialed the sheriff's office.

The deputy who answered made me spell almost every word over the telephone. He either needed spell-check on his brain or I was talking too fast. Maybe both. He ticked me off royally. Acted as though he was doing me a favor to write the report and that I was unreasonable to expect anything more than that. Guess he didn't think an incident about a dog was all that important. I had to settle for his assurance that someone would be back in touch with me.

I really wanted to talk to Sheriff Harmon himself. Not just wanted to talk to him, *needed* to talk to him. I felt totally alone, even with Big Boy asleep beside me. I considered, for one brief moment, calling my daddy, but changed my mind. Instead, I covered my head with pillows and hugged my poor brave dog.

# Chapter Twenty-one

"**N**ada," as Jane would say, "a big fat zero." No clues at all.

I'd brought Big Boy out on his leash to do his morning business. He'd been so good about not wandering out of the yard recently that I'd begun sometimes just stepping onto the porch and watching as he sniffed and squatted. No more. I planned to be right by his side anytime he went outdoors.

When Big Boy finished, I cinched the leash in tight so he was close beside me, and we went to investigate the tree where he'd nosed around and eaten something the previous night. I feared he'd strain at the leash to get back to the tree, but he wasn't interested in that spot at all. I saw nothing except the scraggly grass. Whatever had been there was gone. Either Big Boy had eaten all of the poison or whoever put it there had removed the leftovers.

Jane thought the killer believed I knew more than I did. I knew zip. If I were more like the detectives I read about, I wouldn't have washed the clothes I'd worn last night. I could have had Big Boy's throw-up analyzed to see what had made him sick. The thought hadn't occurred to me at the time. All I'd wanted was for Big Boy to be okay.

I know Big Boy needed a long run or walk, but I wouldn't risk something else happening to him. An uneasy feeling kept me glancing over my shoulder to see if anyone was watching as I led my dog into the apartment.

The Beaufort offices of the South Carolina State Department of Transportation, aka the highway department, open at eight thirty. I wanted to be there early to avoid waiting in line to replace my driver's license. I gave Big Boy a superlarge bowl of Kibbles 'n Bits. After all, he'd lost all of his dinner the night before. Hugged him extra big, and I was on the road by seven thirty with plenty of time to drive to Beaufort, pick up breakfast, and be first in line at the transportation center.

On my way into Beaufort, I'd pass right by a Bojangles'. I waited until I got there to stop for a chicken biscuit, coffee, and newspaper. There's not a Bojangles' in St. Mary and buh-leeve me, that Cajun seasoning is a good waker-upper.

I drove to the state office building, parked, and had breakfast in the Mustang while reading the paper. I turned to the obituary page first. Couldn't tell much from one day. I'd need to check daily and record how many funeral services were being handled by each mortuary to see if Middleton's business was indicative of the funeral industry in general or was just us. Maybe I'd hit the Internet and get numbers for the same time last year. Might even record everything on an Excel chart on my computer to impress Otis and Odell.

At precisely eight thirty, I entered the state building and followed the signs to the Driver's License Renewal window. All my real identification had been with my license in the purse that was stolen, so I'd brought a paycheck stub, electric bill, and telephone bill to verify who I am.

Though the state building is fairly new, the room looked almost exactly like the one in the old building where I'd gotten my first driver's license many years ago. A counter with windows labeled for various transactions lined the far wall. Rows for people to stand in line for each window were roped off with green velvet cords attached to brass stanchions.

The designated rows were unnecessary so early. I was the only person there except for one clerk, who hardly appeared out of her teens. She briskly instructed me that the form I needed was on a display to my right and told me to step to the counter on the left side of the room to fill in my paperwork. I found the pale green form and moved dutifully to the counter.

I looked up when the next customer entered. Nick Rivers, looking good in a blue and white striped shirt, jeans, and boots. I glanced up and smiled, but he ignored me. Is it these black dresses? Do they make me invisible?

Nick went to the area labeled "Motor Vehicle Registration." The young lady who'd sent me to the side counter moved down to Nick's window, flashed a sexy smile, and asked, "May I help you?" Her voice was syrupy, not at all like the sharp tone she'd used with me.

"Yeah, I gotta register my new SUV and get a different tag," Nick mumbled.

More syrup. "If you traded in a vehicle, we may be able to transfer the tag."

"Nah, the weight's different."

"Got yourself a bigger one?" she asked.

"Nah," Nick mumbled.

"Oh, I see," she said, looking down at the papers Nick handed her. "You traded a Savana van in on an Envoy

SUV. My brother-in-law has a Savana. Used it to help me move last month. That baby sure held a lot of furniture. Has yours got that OnStar stuff?"

"Huh?"

"My brother-in-law has this thing where any time the air bags inflate, someone notifies the authorities, and if the van is stolen, they can trace it through this computer chip in it. Did it come on your new Envoy, too?"

"Yeah, well, I got that stuff, too. Didn't really want all that, but it was part of the package. First year is free."

"By the way"—the clerk gave Nick a full-toothed Miss Magnolia Mouth smile and dripped Southern Belle molasses—"I'm not married. I mean, I have a brother-in-law, but I'm single. My brother-in-law is married to my sister." Nick ignored her. She forged right on. "Why'd you trade down to something smaller? Gas mileage?"

"What's my gas mileage got to do with you?" The disgust on Nick's face matched the harsh tone of his voice. "None of your business why I traded. Do you want something else or are you just gonna waste my time standing here gibbering away?"

"No, sir." Her tone turned professional, but still dripped syrup. She looked through Nick's papers again. "Everything seems to be in order, sir. You should receive the tag within two weeks."

"I came to pick it up. I want it now."

"Oh, your temporary tag is good for thirty days. We mail most new tags. It's quicker and keeps the lines of waiting customers down."

"How can waiting two weeks for you to mail it be quicker than standing here waiting for you to hand it over to me? And there ain't no line today, is there?"

The clerk glanced at me standing motionless with my paper in hand. She had to see that I was ready, and she knew that I'd been there first, but she didn't ask Nick to wait. "I'll have it in a moment, sir."

Magnolia Mouth went through a door at the back and stayed gone about fifteen minutes. That might have been the perfect opportunity to get to know Nick better, but he stared off toward the opposite side of the room. His rudeness teed me off, so I ignored him while he ignored me.

When the girl came back in and handed Nick his new tag and registration form, she smiled and said, "Thank you." Nick added Magnolia Mouth to his list of women to be ignored and walked out with that long stride I thought was so appealing when we were in high school.

For five dollars and the green form, Miss Magnolia gave me a replacement driver's license. Didn't even have to take my picture. Just printed out a duplicate license with the old photo, laminated it, and handed it over. She wasn't very talkative. I guess she'd been shocked and embarrassed by Nick's coarse lack of manners. I sympathized with her. Rejection is rough, especially so early in the morning.

When I returned to the Mustang in the parking lot, I saw Nick squatting at the back of his new Envoy replacing the temporary dealer license with a new motor vehicle tag. The similarity between the Savana he'd traded and his new Envoy amazed me. Just a couple of feet shorter. The Savana had looked new, so why get rid of it if not because of gas mileage? And why was he so irritable about it? Like Miss Southern Syrup, I wondered what had prompted the trade. He probably took a loss trading down on the Savana while it was still so new.

Nick stood and walked to his driver's door. For such a slim man, he had a really cute behind. I started to speak to him, but his behavior in the highway department discouraged me. I didn't bother. Just drove off. No point in setting myself up for rejection.

I try really hard not to make or take guilt trips, and there was no reason to feel guilty about being late to work, so I took my time and enjoyed the autumn low country on my way back to St. Mary. Not much to do when I got there. A few people came by to see Mrs. Bailey. I greeted them and escorted them into Slumber Room A. Several florists delivered potted plants, but the cut floral arrangements wouldn't come until Thursday morning. It was still a little early to call Jane, but as soon as Otis and Odell left for lunch, I punched in her number.

"What do you mean you've gotten more threatening calls and your dog was poisoned? I want to know what Sheriff Harmon is doing about this!" Jane yelled at me.

"I've reported everything, but I haven't heard back from the sheriff's office."

"If they don't do something, you need to come over and stay with me."

"So you can make more garlic cinnamon toast," I teased.

"I'm worried about you, Callie. I woke up early this morning and called you at the funeral home, but Otis said you'd be late to work."

"I had to go to Beaufort to replace my driver's license. Guess who I saw at the highway department?"

"Elvis?"

"That is *so* lame. I saw Nick Rivers getting a tag for his new SUV. He must've gotten up on the wrong side of the bed because he was grumpy as a grizzly bear."

"That's no surprise. Nick wasn't ever known for his personality. Just the way he could handle a basketball. Did you talk to him?"

"No, he was obnoxious to the clerk, and he ignored me, so I ignored him."

"Wonder why he bothered to go pick up the license himself? If he traded vehicles, doesn't the dealership usually take care of tags and registration?"

"Guess since he traded the van in Charleston, he figured it would be simpler to handle the registration himself in Beaufort."

"How do you know he bought it in Charleston? Did you ask him?"

"I didn't talk to him at all. Told you he ignored me. It was almost like he thought I wouldn't recognize him if he pretended not to recognize me. I saw him at Charleston Charlie's Cars the day you ripped off Victoria's Secret, and the new Envoy had a Charleston Charlie's temporary tag on it until Nick put on the new one."

"I'm surprised you didn't squeal like a teenager when you saw him in Charleston."

"It was after you pulled your stunt in Victoria's Secret. I wasn't talking to you."

"Let's don't go there, girlfriend. You'll only get irritated with me if you start thinking about that. I don't know why Nick Rivers has always fascinated you so much. He's never going to amount to anything. He bought the old Halsey place when they auctioned it for taxes while you were teaching in Columbia, but so far as I've heard, he's never done anything with it. He's bad news, Callie."

"Maybe so, but he's bad news with a cute behind."

Jane ignored my comment and said, "Why don't you come over for supper tonight?"

"I've got another date with the doctor."

"Check to see if he has a cutie booty. I can guarantee you he's got more future in front of him than Nick Rivers." She chuckled and added, "Undoubtedly a better background even if his tush isn't as attractive."

The front door music sounded "Immortal, Invisible."

"Gotta go, Jane. Talk to you tomorrow."

Sheriff Harmon met me in the hall. "Callie, I'm upset about these calls. Especially the one about someone poisoning your dog last night. I didn't know you had a dog, but if someone poisoned it, you should have had the dispatcher notify me immediately."

"I tried. Buh-leeve me, I tried. He didn't seem interested." I smoothed out the skirt of my black dress and added, "I haven't had the dog but a few days."

"A watchdog?"

"He will be, but he's just a puppy now."

The sheriff went over each fact I'd given the deputy who took my report. He repeated the questions and verified my answers. "You know, Callie, we've got two homicides, and apparently the killer has focused on you for some reason. If anything else happens, and I mean *anything*, even a hang-up call, tell the dispatcher that I said to contact me immediately."

"Sure. Thank you, Sheriff Harmon. Are there any new developments in the cases?"

"Now, Callie, you know I can't discuss leads with you." Yes, I knew he wasn't *supposed* to reveal official facts, but when I was a bratty little girl, teenaged Wayne Harmon took time to talk to me when he was at our house with John. Sometimes the grown-up Sheriff Harmon forgot about the rules and told me more than was officially advisable.

I didn't. I promise I didn't do the Magnolia Mouth routine, but I did smile and say, "Pretty please."

It worked. He said, "We're still checking everything that comes in, but we do have a very likely suspect, and we'll be picking him up soon."

"Who?" I asked, expecting him to tell me, but that was all he'd share.

He turned to leave, then smiled at me. "Saw Odell at Shoney's. He looks like a hundred miles of bad road with all those scratches. Said a cat got hold of him. What happened?"

"It was feline all right. A catfight. He got in the middle

of a scrap between two of Bobby Saxon's widows—Betty and Eileen."

"No wonder he didn't want to tell me about it. I wouldn't want to be between those two myself. It's going to be interesting to see who collects Bobby Saxon's insurance."

Ex-cuuze me. I was more interested in the Middletons getting their money than whether Betty or Eileen received anything at all.

# Chapter Twenty-two

**C**oal black. Ebony. Obsidian. Raven. Inky. Perfect terms to describe my black dresses, but standing in front of my closet Wednesday night, I covered all of them with one word—boring. I'd worn my best skirt Sunday night. The rest of my wardrobe was mainly jeans and black dresses. I'd purchased all of my "little black dresses" for work. Some just below the knee, most ankle length. High necked. Unfitted. There was more variety in my new bras than in my outer clothing.

Big Boy sat on the floor staring into the closet with me. He looked so sad that I leaned over and scratched behind his floppy ears. His tail thumped. Sometimes I almost think Big Boy can read my mind, but I didn't really believe a puppy could commiserate with a thirty-something-year-old woman who had nothing to wear for her date.

Saved by the bell. The telephone.

"Callie, this is Donnie." Even though it wasn't my ex, I rolled my eyes when I heard that name. I despise it that much. The voice was just as smooth as the first time I'd heard it when I came to consciousness with Dr. Donald's blue eyes peering into mine.

"I don't want to disappoint you, Callie, but I've had a really hard day." Dalmatian! Don was calling to cancel our date. "I wondered," he continued, "if we could have a quiet night at your place. I'll pick up dinner on the way and bring a movie. You have a DVD or VCR, don't you?"

"I have both, and that sounds good to me."

"Do you eat Chinese food?"

I almost said yes, just to be agreeable, but I explained, "I love the taste of Chinese food, but the carryout here still uses MSG. It makes me sick."

"Oh." Don paused. "May I surprise you so long as there's no MSG?"

"Surprise me." I paused, then giggled. "So long as you don't bring snails even without MSG."

"See you at seven." He hesitated before adding, "Is it okay if I come casual?"

"Sure," I agreed. Problem solved. Jeans and a tube top pulled over just a touch more inflation. A dark tube top. One that would contrast with my really blonde hair.


**Several hours later,** Big Boy was shut in the bathroom again. Don had shown up carrying a colorful Mexican blanket and an expensive wicker picnic basket. Instead of a movie, he'd picked up a DVD of the first three episodes of *Six Feet Under*.

"I hope you don't mind watching these," he said. "I could see these shows over and over."

He handed me the disc and spread the blanket on my living room floor in front of the television. "Now, you just sit here and relax," he said, unpacking the basket onto the coffee table. No potato salad. No deviled eggs. And, to my sorrow, no fried chicken. He pulled out cheese, crusty French bread, caviar, lemon wedges, and lots of different spreads with fancy little crackers. I slid the DVD into the player and pushed, "Play."

This was not the doctor's first picnic. The basket was too well equipped. Instead of plastic cups, Don's picnic carrier yielded silver flutes for champagne. Plates and utensils were also silver. Linen napkins.

The doctor must have a fetish for feeding women. He smoothed different-colored gourmet foods onto crackers, preparing them two at a time. Slid one into my mouth and popped the other into his as he reached for another container. While we ate, I questioned him about some things that puzzled me.

"How could someone pass an insurance physical if he had advanced cirrhosis of the liver?" I asked.

He almost choked on his spread-covered cracker, then laughed. "That's what makes you so special, Callie. You're the only one I know who'd ask about cirrhosis of the liver while eating goose liver paté."

Oops! I hadn't realized the spread was paté. I put mine on my little silver plate.

I promise I didn't mean to do it, but I looked at him and said in that Southern Belle whisper, "But you're the only person I know who can answer my questions." If I'd fluttered my eyelashes, I might have barfed all over the paté.

He leaned back and put his hands behind his head. Let me say this: In addition to being handsome, Don has a manly chest. That bit of hair peeking from under his shirt didn't hurt, either. Donnie had worked out regularly, and like a lot of bodybuilders, he'd shaved his chest. I like chest hair. I like to look at it, and I love the way it feels.

"You want to know how a person with cirrhosis of the liver could pass an insurance physical? He couldn't pass a physical in the early stages because the blood tests would show irregular liver enzymes and the exam would reveal an enlarged liver. If he had advanced cirrhosis of the liver, it wouldn't be so difficult. As the condition worsens, the liver changes from being enlarged to decreasing in size."

"It shrivels?" I asked as I popped an oil-cured olive into my mouth.

"You might describe it that way. Once the liver has atrophied, it no longer produces the liver enzymes that would show a liver problem in blood tests. It's also no longer an obvious problem when palpated, but the patient would be aware of his condition. To pass a physical, he'd have to lie about symptoms." He stared at me for a moment. "Callie, you don't think you have cirrhosis of the liver, do you?"

"Oh, no. I'm just curious." I wondered if anything he'd spread on the crackers was snail meat. "What about drugs? Do you know a lot about drugs?"

"I know as much as any other doctor, but I didn't come over to talk about drugs."

"Do you know much about a drug called ketamine?" I pronounced the word "cat-ah-mine," like Sheriff Harmon had said it, with a long *i* sound in the last syllable so that it rhymed with my name, Calamine.

"Yes, I'm familiar with it. Formerly an anesthetic. Hardly ever used medically anymore except by veterinarians. By the way, it's pronounced 'ket-ah-mean.' But let's don't talk about medicine or drugs. Unless you're talking about the effect you have on me. Callie, you're more intoxicating than the champagne. Do you know how hard it is to keep my hands off you?"

As expected, this line led to touching. Not crudely and not intimately. He simply ran his fingers down my blue-jeaned leg. I lifted his hand and moved it. Not that it didn't feel good, but I wanted to see what was happening on *Six Feet Under* without being distracted. At least, that's what I told myself.

Before the end of the first episode, we'd emptied the bottle of champagne. Let me say that we were not downing the same amount. He seemed to be filling up my silver flute more often than his own, and I told myself to slow down. I had no interest in losing self-control nor in winding up with another hangover. Don went to his car and came back with another chilled bottle of champagne. I wondered if he had a little fridge in the trunk of his car along with a bag full of animal toys.

I would like to say that after we finished eating, I sat on the couch, behaved, and watched the video. Problem is, we never finished eating. He kept pulling more things from the basket. He fed me delicious juicy fresh strawberries and little green seedless grapes. All the time pouring more champagne.

Being human, the champagne got to me. Before long, we were lying on the blanket making out like a couple of high school kids. Not really like today's high school kids. We moved a bit slower than they do these days. We were still fully clothed, but I was tempted not to move his hand the next time he reached for buttons or a zipper.

Being *very* human, the champagne got to me in more ways than one. I had to excuse myself to the restroom for a few minutes. Big Boy was so glad to see me that he tried to climb into my lap and knocked over his water bowl. I petted him, dried the floor, and refilled the bowl. He whimpered and scratched the bathroom door when I closed it to return to Mr. Champagne Seducer.

Don tried to begin again exactly where we'd left off. Didn't work. The dog now howled. Not a Scooby-Doo howl, but long, sad wailing. Don asked if we could tie Big Boy on the front porch because it sounded as though he was demolishing the bathroom door. I hadn't told Don about my recent problems, but I wasn't about to put Big Boy out where the caller could reach him. I sensed a bit of tension or anger from Don about my refusal.

As though Don had waved a magic wand, the sounds of scratching and canine lamentations stopped. A little more champagne. A few more kisses. A touch on the mute button of the remote control, and Don was in control again. Buh-leeve me. I was weakening. I looked up into those blue eyes and along that aquiline nose. I tasted his sculptured lips and thought, *Yes!*

Then it happened. I looked beyond Don. There sat Big Boy on the edge of the blanket. He'd managed to escape from the bathroom. Though there was still food on the coffee table, my puppy ignored it. He sat looking at me with dark, solemn eyes filled with accusation and disappointment.

"I'm not ready," I said.

"What?"

"I'm not ready," I repeated. "You're moving too fast for me."


**"You did *what*?"** Jane screeched through the phone in a rerun of our conversation after my Sunday night date with Don.

"I sent him home again."

"Why, just tell me *why*. Are you playing games? No action until some randomly designated number of dates?" Jane scolded. "You claim you really like this doctor and he's all kinds of nice, but you're going to run him off. You're not pushing him away because of this fascination you have with Nick Rivers, are you?"

"No, I'm not. It's just not right yet. I've told you before. I want a relationship that includes more than physical attraction. I can't know a man well enough in just two dates, but I don't have a magic number." I didn't mention that the dog had been watching us. "And I haven't run him off. He's asked me out again for next Sunday night."

"Calamine Lotion Parrish, you won't do. I've got to get back to work. Go take a shower and sleep alone again."

I took the shower. Not to cool me off as Jane had insinuated, but to feel clean and refreshed. Didn't go to bed by myself. Don had left the DVD and about a third of a bottle of champagne. I zapped some popcorn in the microwave. Daddy would kill me if I gave popcorn to one of his dogs. Big Boy loved it.

Orville Redenbacher. Big Boy. Three hours of *Six Feet Under*.

I thought life didn't get much better.

Had no idea how much worse it would soon be.

# Chapter Twenty-three

**They** weren't the same size. I couldn't believe it. I'd been trying to decide what bra to wear when I noticed they weren't the same size. Oh, the cups matched each other on each bra, but I didn't have the bras inflated equally. Rightie didn't stand taller than leftie. The cups of each bra were equally inflated, but the bras were different. I set them side by side on my breakfast table. I'd definitely be bustier wearing black than white or red. For some unknown reason, I'd pumped up the peach and the purple bras way bigger than the others. I don't mean Pamela Anderson or Dolly Parton size, but definitely too abundant for me.

I got busy with my little pump. Used a ruler to approach the irregular mountain range problem with mathematical precision. By the time all my cups stood the same size, I was late for work. I called the funeral home.

"Middleton's Mortuary. Odell Middleton speaking. How may I help you?"

I never failed to be amazed at how nice Odell can

sound to a potential customer but how obnoxious he frequently is toward Otis. If Odell talked to me like he does to his brother, I'd cry.

"Odell, this is Callie. Is it okay if I get my stitches out before I come to work today?"

"Sure, Callie. Come in when you finish."

A part of me wished that I had something new and exciting to wear in case I saw Don at the ER. The other part won out. It made more sense to dress for work and go straight to Middleton's from the hospital, so I wore the black dress that matched the one Eileen Saxon had worn to Bobby's visitation. The weather was too nice to leave the top up, and I arrived at the hospital with windblown hair. Didn't matter. They'd mess it up removing the stitches anyway.

Since I'd been unconscious the last time I visited the Beaufort County Hospital emergency room, I had no idea how much rigmarole would be involved. Before I could park, I had to explain to the parking attendant why I was there. Before I could enter the building, I had to show my purse and its contents to the security guard. Before I could see a nurse, I had to sign the paperwork for the admissions clerk. But I didn't want to be admitted. I just needed to have my stitches removed.

No offense, but the clerk looked like a schoolteacher. I ought to know. I used to dress like that myself. She wore a white-collared blouse with a brown corduroy jumper embroidered with bright gold and orange leaves at the right shoulder. Her earrings were little yellow porcelain oak leaves. "Admissions doesn't mean you're going to be an inpatient," the teacher look-alike said. "You have to be admitted to the ER to be seen by anyone."

She led me to her office, and, like a little child, I sat where she told me and answered her questions while she typed the info into her computer.

"I wish the doctor had told me I'd have to do all this when he told me to come back to have the stitches taken out," I said, trying not to whine. "I need to go to work."

"Oh"—the clerk looked up at me—"your stitches were out in at the emergency room?"

"That's what I've been trying to tell you."

"I'll pull up your computer records from then. It'll be quicker." In a few minutes, she handed me a stack of papers to sign. One explained the hospital's privacy policy. One authorized treatment. One okayed my insurance to pay for their services, and another guaranteed I'd pay any amount not covered by my policy. She photocopied my insurance card and driver's license, returned them, and told me to sit in the waiting room until someone called me.

I sat in a mauve and turquoise chair and pretended to read a *People* magazine while mothers told toddlers to be still, be quiet, and don't touch. I knew that emergency rooms filled up with adults and teenagers hurt in fights or wrecks on Friday and Saturday nights. I learned that midweek was reserved for illnesses and little folks with earaches. I wondered why the moms didn't take the children to their pediatricians. Then I thought that it made about as much sense for me to be in the ER to have stitches removed as it did for those little ones to be there for non-emergency illnesses.

After an hour in the chair, a nurse led me to a gurney in a curtained-off area. She told me to lie down. I insisted that I could sit, even stand, to have the stitches removed, but hospital rules decree that patients have to lie down once they're assigned to a cubicle. Like having to ride out in a wheelchair when you're dismissed from overnight in the hospital even though you're walking fine. No point in arguing. I lay down on the gurney and she pulled the beige curtains closed around me and left. I shut my eyes and thought, *I should've brought a book.*

I must have dozed off because I don't remember any preface to the conversation I overheard from the cubicle next to me. At first I thought I was dreaming, but I was awake and heard two female voices.

"Let's put his head up a bit. I think he'll be more comfortable," said voice one.

"He's asleep," said voice two.

"We still want him to be comfortable. He's going to be here a couple of hours until all of these IVs are finished. There. He looks better like that."

"Okay. I'll put a pillow here."

"Hey, check out that purple nail polish. Some reason you've gone funky?" voice one teased.

"That's not funky. That's style," said voice two with pretend attitude.

"Don't let Doc Walters see that. He'll be nibbling those nails right off ya."

Laughter. "You must have been to Andre's with him."

"Oh, yes, I had my turn last year when he first started filling in on weekends. The full treatment. Roses. He fed me snails and nibbled my fingers, too."

"What else did he nibble?"

More laughter. "I'm not telling." A moment of silence. "How about you? Have you had your dinner at Andre's yet?" asked voice one.

"No, but he asked me out for this Sunday night. Do you think I'll get roses and Andre's?"

"Everybody else has. I couldn't believe it when the word first started making the rounds, and I found out my wonderful evening with him was a rerun of everyone else he's dated since he came here. Can you believe he keeps a bag of animal toys and children's toys in the trunk of his car? He uses them to impress women by giving something to their kids or pets on the first date."

"Should I let him know I have two cats?"

"No need to. That man is always prepared. Know what else? I heard he's been asking some patients out."

"You don't mean it." Voice two developed a serious tone. "Isn't there some kind of rule against that?"

"Yep. Guess he figures that the doctor-patient relationship doesn't count with ER treatment."

"Doc Walters better be careful. If administration finds out he's dating patients he's met through work here, he'll soon be a doc in a box."

"Let me tell you what to do." A snicker. "Don't let him even get to first base on the first date. Hold out. He'll call right before time to pick you up for the second date. He'll say he's sorry but he doesn't feel like going out. He'll ask if you have a VCR or a DVD and suggest a quiet evening at your place. He'll offer to bring dinner and a movie."

"You're kidding. Why? Does he spend so many coins on the first date that he doesn't want to put any more money on a horse that won't run?"

"I don't think it's that at all. I think he just wants to get to the couch quicker."

Laughter.

"What will he bring for dinner?"

"He'll suggest Chinese, and he'll feed you with his chopsticks. So far, everyone I know who's had the movie on the couch date has had Chinese. I wonder if he ever picks up anything different."

I felt like Pinocchio. Not because I was lying, because I was spying. If I'd been a wooden puppet, my nose would have been sticking through those beige curtains. I felt so naive to have believed that Don's dates with me had been special. I couldn't stand it anymore.

"I'll tell you what he brings if you don't eat Chinese," I said loudly. "A picnic. He'll bring an indoor picnic."

A feminine hand snatched the curtain aside and I caught a

glimpse of a sleeping man as two women wearing nurses' uniforms spilled into my area.

"Oh, ma'am. We didn't know you were in here," voice one said. She was a fortyish blonde with luminous blue eyes, probably colored contact lenses. "I'm so sorry. We had no idea anyone could hear us."

"Don't worry about it. I'm rude to jump into your conversation, but it sounds like you're talking about a man I've been dating," I said.

"What's his name?" asked voice two, a brunette.

"Dr. Donald Walters."

"One and the same," said the blonde. "Did he take you to Andre's?"

"Yes, brought me roses, too. On the second date, he was too tired to go out and arrived at my house with a special picnic."

"Whew!" the blonde exclaimed. "At least you didn't overhear anything you didn't already know. We would never have talked about him if we'd realized you were here."

"Is that why it's taking so long? Nobody knows where I am?" I asked.

The woman I recognized as voice two interrupted, "Did you say picnic? That sounds romantic." She appeared a few years younger than voice one, wore glasses, and yes, her fingernails were polished plum purple.

"Oh, it's romantic." I laughed. "The doctor shows up with a blanket for the floor and a picnic with lots of gourmet finger foods. Grapes. Caviar. And champagne. Let's not forget the champagne."

"Did you first meet him here at the hospital or somewhere else?" the brunette asked.

"I met him here when I spent the night after these stitches were put in, but he didn't ask me out until we ran into each other somewhere else, so I don't know if that's a violation of hospital policy or not."

The blonde lifted my chart from the foot of the bed and read it. "Just here to have your stitches removed?" she asked. I nodded. "I can do that for you and get you on your way." She paused. "And I do apologize for gossiping. That wasn't very professional."

My turn to laugh. "But educational, definitely an eye-opener."

"Are you dating him now?" asked the blonde.

"The picnic was last night, and he asked me out for Sunday evening." I gestured toward the brunette. "Didn't I overhear you say he's taking you out Sunday?"

"Yes, he asked me out last week for this Sunday night."

"Wonder which one of us he plans to stand up."

The blonde excused herself and stepped out of my cubicle.

"Look," I said to the brunette, "if you're really interested in him, I'll cancel. After what I just heard, I don't care about seeing him again."

"Oh, he's gorgeous, but I already know too much about Dr. Donnie Walters to let myself get involved with him." She giggled and touched my arm. "Let's both cancel on him at the last minute."

The blonde nurse returned with a sterile-wrapped tray. "Lie back, and I'll have these out for you in a jiffy," she said.

I thought removing the stitches might hurt, but I only felt three brief tugs, and the nurse was finished.

Before leaving, I almost asked the brunette for her name and number so we could keep up with Don's dating efforts, but the doctor wasn't worth the bother. I didn't need a dog like him. I had my own Big Boy that I liked a whole lot better than that hound.

* * *

**When I'm excited** or disappointed, I call Jane and
tell her what's happening even if it's earlier in the morning than she usually wakes. I had the cell phone with
me, but I didn't call my friend on the way from the hospital to work. I was embarrassed, ashamed actually, that
I'd been duped into beginning to fall for someone like
Dr. Champagne Seducer. Not a sincere bone in his body.
My brothers used to like a song that asked, "Am I fool
number one or am I fool number two?" With Don Walters, I'd been much higher on the number line than two
or three.

By the time I arrived at Middleton's, it was midday.
Otis asked if I'd take care of things while he went to
lunch. Said Odell had gone somewhere and didn't say
where he was going. As always, Otis instructed, "Beep us
if you get an intake call."

Sitting at my desk, feeling too sorry for myself to even
want to read, I jumped when the telephone rang. Good for
Middleton's if it was an intake call, but my heart jumped
into my throat with fear that it was another threatening
message. My hand shook as I lifted the receiver.

"Middleton's Mortuary," I said. "This is Callie. How
may I help you?"

"Sheriff Harmon here. Are you going to be there for a
while? I need to come by and get a statement from you."

"I'll be here until at least seven tonight. I came in late
and need to make up some hours."

"Okay, Callie, I'll be there soon."

"Why . . . ," I said as the sheriff said, "'Bye," and
hung up.

Harmon had asked so many questions about the calls
and Big Boy, I didn't think he needed any additional

information about that. Why was he coming? More questions about when I found the needle in Bobby Saxon's neck? Was Middleton's in trouble for sending June Bug off to be cremated? Shouldn't be. We had an official release of the body.

I hoped the sheriff wasn't headed over to ask me where Odell was the Sunday night Bobby was killed or the Monday morning the body was found. Maybe the sheriff knew that Odell had lied about going to a meeting in Columbia that morning.

Buh-leeve me. By the time "Blessed Assurance" announced someone had entered the front door, I was drenched with nervous sweat even though we keep the thermostat at a cool seventy degrees. I assumed it would be Sheriff Harmon, and I was right. He peeked into Slumber Room A, then up at the sign by the door. "Mrs. Bailey. She was at the nursing home, right?"

"Agape," I said.

"What happened?"

Good grief. Was the sheriff thinking another murder?

"She had a heart attack during her nap," I said.

"I'd like to go that way when my time comes," Harmon answered. "Can we sit somewhere?"

"Sure, come on into the consultation room. Will this take long? Would you like some coffee? Why do you need to talk to me?" I was so nervous that the questions fell out one right after the other without a pause for the man to answer. Sheriff Harmon and I talk to each other a lot, but I wasn't used to giving formal statements.

"Calm down, Callie. You're shaking like I came to arrest you."

*"What?"* I screeched.

He laughed, pulled a miniature recorder from his pocket, and set it on the table. "Settle down, Callie. All I want is for you to answer a few questions about Wilbert Peavy. Do you mind if I record the conversation?"

"I don't know anyone named Wilbert Peavy, so there's nothing to record."

"Sure you do. He was at Bobby Saxon's funeral and I've been told he came here and talked to you the day Saxon's body was found."

I shook my head. Puzzled. Couldn't remember Wilbert Peavy.

"Cowboy," Sheriff Harmon said.

"Cowboy! Why didn't you say so?" I vaguely remembered my brothers calling him Peavy when I was at Daddy's house.

"Because legally, he's Wilbert Peavy, and he seems to have shouted his hatred for Saxon all over town. You know he made a scene at the cemetery."

"Yes, I was there."

Harmon leaned back in his chair. "I need your spoken permission to record what's said. Do I have your permission?"

"Sure. Record all you want."

The sheriff pressed "Play" on the tape recorder and stated the location, date, time, and our names. He asked if I consented to be recorded, and I said, "I do." Whoops! Last time I said "I do," I wound up in a lot of trouble.

"Calamine L. Parrish, I want you to tell me what Wilbert Peavy said about Robert E. Saxon the first time he came to Middleton's Mortuary." Sheriff Harmon.

My turn. "He wanted to see the body, but of course, the body wasn't ready. Said he wanted to pay his 'disrespects' and that Bobby wouldn't be winning any more sales contests at the Corral. How did you know he'd been here?"

"Callie, I'm supposed to ask the questions."

I gave him my most petulant little girl look.

"Okay, I don't guess it will hurt for you to know," Harmon relented. "Peavy told us. Said you could verify that he wasn't making any effort to hide how he felt about Saxon. Claims if he'd killed Saxon, he would have pretended to be grieving. Says if he'd killed Saxon, he'd have known for certain Saxon was dead and wouldn't have wanted to see the body to make sure Saxon's death wasn't a hoax. Swears he thought it was all some kind of publicity stunt." Sheriff Harmon shifted back in his chair. "Is there anything else you can tell me about Peavy?"

"That's about it. Are you going to charge him with anything for acting out at the graveyard? Maybe disturbing the peace or damaging property? You know that casket spray fell all apart when he threw it, and that was a very expensive arrangement."

I was hoping the sheriff's answer would be yes. I didn't care for Cowboy and couldn't like anyone who showed such disrespect for death and the dead.

Sheriff Harmon pressed "Stop" on the recorder before saying, "He's up for a lot more than that. I'm charging him with murdering Bobby Saxon. We picked Peavy up a couple of hours ago."

"What's the motive?"

"The man's gone all over Beaufort and St. Mary telling everyone how much he hated Saxon. Peavy was top salesman as well as the star of GMC Automotive and Truck Corral's advertising until Bobby Saxon went to work there. After that, Saxon won everything. I learned this morning that the boss at the Corral had told Cowboy he planned to change the commercials. Cowboy blamed Saxon for that as well."

"It seems too obvious," I said. "Don't you think Cowboy would be smart enough to keep his mouth shut if he killed Bobby Saxon out of jealousy?"

"Nope, I think he's attracted attention to himself and

his hate for Saxon in order to use that as a defense. He expected us to look over him for just that reason, to think that nobody who killed someone would be foolish enough to go out talking about how much he hated the man. That's why he bragged about what he said to you."

"Sounds reasonable."

"I'm not buying it. Peavy has no alibi for the Sunday night Saxon was murdered, nor for the night June Bug was shot."

"What would be Cowboy's motive for killing June Bug?"

"To throw us off. Cowboy could have murdered Corley to throw suspicion away from himself since he had no known motive to kill Corley."

"Just the fact he bad-mouths Bobby Saxon and doesn't have an alibi doesn't seem like enough to arrest him," I said, voicing my thoughts aloud. Sheriff Harmon must have heard an argumentative tone because he defended his actions.

"We searched his car and found a bag of syringes and a vial of ketamine." The sheriff pronounced the word with a long $i$ in the last syllable.

"Ketamine," I said, pronouncing it the way the doctor did, with the final syllable sounding like "mean." "That's the correct pronunciation," I added.

"Keta-meeean or whatever," the sheriff said. "We found it in his car."

"Could have been a frame-up."

"I think it's his. He was so sure of himself that he felt positive we'd never even see him as a person of interest."

"I guess you checked out Betty and Eileen and Mrs. Corley." The statement ended with an uplifted tone, turning it into a question.

"Callie," the sheriff said as he tucked the recorder into

his pocket, "leave the detecting to us. We know what we're doing, and we've got our man."

After the sheriff left, I couldn't help wondering how Cowboy liked having to trade his fancy cowboy duds for orange jumpsuits with "Jade County Detention Center" printed on the back.

No rhinestones in jail. No glitter at all.

# Chapter Twenty-four

"**What** in dalmatian are you talking about?" I asked when Jane sang the old "Wee Willie Winkie" nursery rhyme to me over my office phone. I'd just told her about the sheriff arresting Cowboy and explained to her that I should be happy because the arrest would end the threatening phone calls. I said all that, but I had this nagging feeling that it wasn't over. Jane singing a nursery rhyme didn't fit my mood at all.

"I *said*, What in dalmatian are you talking about?" I repeated.

"Bobby Saxon used to sing that song to Cowboy when he was still known as Willie Peavy before he went to work at the Corral and started dressing western, calling himself Cowboy," Jane said. "Bobby made up nicknames for everyone. Most folks didn't mind, but Cowboy hated being called Wee Willie Winkie."

"I hadn't even thought about the two of them knowing each other before they started working together."

"Oh, I forgot," Jane continued. "You weren't here then.

Remember? I told you Cowboy hung out at June Bug's before you moved back to St. Mary. He was a show-off even then when he was Willie Peavy. Used to get up and belt out Alan Jackson songs on karaoke nights. Strutted around like a banty rooster, wanting everyone's attention."

"Did Bobby Saxon have a nickname for you?"

"You better believe it."

"What was it?"

"He called me Calamity Jane because when June Bug rearranged everything, I almost killed myself trying to go to the restroom without my cane or a guide. Bumped into a new booth and hit the floor."

"That wasn't very nice of Bobby. Were most of the nicknames ugly like that?"

"Yep, but it didn't bother most of us except Willie. He positively hated that rhyme and Bobby Saxon."

"Do you think Cowboy hated Bobby enough to kill him?"

"Not then, but he did hate Bobby enough to stop hanging out at June Bug's. A lot of the old gang thought Cowboy Willie moved to Beaufort to get away from Saxon picking on him. Bet it was a real bummer when Saxon went to work there after Cowboy blossomed into a star."

I wanted to ask Jane more about Cowboy, but the distant rumble of thunder made me eager to get off the phone. Not that I had to close windows or anything. Windows are never opened in funeral homes. My fear of lightning goes back to when lightning came into our house on a phone line. Since then, I barely take time to say "Goodbye" when I hear thunder.

Short, late afternoon storms are common along the coast at the end of summer, but Odell came in saying that the radio weatherman was calling for bad weather all night.

"Head on home, Callie," Otis said. "The rain will probably keep some people away tonight, and both Odell and I will be here for the Bailey visitation anyway. Drive carefully. We'll see you tomorrow."

"I was gonna stay to make up for being late this morning," I protested, though it was halfhearted.

"Don't worry about that. I don't want you driving through this rain after dark. Go on home."

He didn't have to tell me twice. Okay, I guess he actually did say it twice. Anyway, I grabbed one of Middleton's extra-large umbrellas and scooted out to my car. The sky was as dark as crematorium ashes. Before I started working at Middleton's, I assumed human ashes would be bright white, like Halloween skeletons. They're not. The ashes are gray. That dismal afternoon sky was the same color.

The storm got worse before I was a block away from the mortuary. The wind howled and bounced the Mustang. Lightning flashed, and my windshield wipers must have needed replacing because the rain sluiced over the glass like a waterfall. Buh-leeve me, I have enough sense to stop when there's no visibility. I guess this time I didn't bother to use it. I slowed down to about five miles an hour and continued creeping down the road.

*Thud.*

I hadn't seen the traffic light change from green to red. Problem was that whoever was driving in front of me did see it change and stopped. I reached for the umbrella and opened the driver's door. A sudden vision filled my mind. A picture from a kid's book showing Benjamin Franklin flying his kite in a storm. The oversized ribs and handle of the umbrella would work just like Franklin's kite, just like a lightning rod. I pulled the car door closed.

I could barely hear the pounding on the side window. I rolled the window down only a few inches. It took a minute to recognize the man standing by my car, pointing at the back of the van I'd bumped into. Six feet, six inches of Nick Rivers glared at me.

"I'm sorry," I said. Nick wasn't nearly as good-looking as the doctor, and I could barely see him for the deluge of water pummeling over him, but I shivered. For some reason, I always felt a little quiver when I saw him.

"I'm coming round to the other side. Unlock the door," Nick said.

As a teenager I'd daydreamed about being in a car with Nick Rivers, but it wasn't quite my fantasy to have him sitting beside me dripping water in my car and scowling.

"I can't believe this!" Nick shouted. "Were you following me?"

"Me?" Thank heaven my answer was in my own voice, not that Southern Belle whisper that occasionally crept up on me to impress the doctor. I knew from Magnolia Mouth at the highway department that the sweet, syrupy, southern sweetie act wasn't any more attractive to Nick than it was to me. Besides, Nick couldn't have heard that voice through the oppressive roar of the wind, rain, and thunder surrounding the car.

"Yeah. You," he said.

"I was headed home from work. I'm sorry. I didn't see the light change and I didn't see you."

"Are you blind like your friend?" A smirk and an ugly tone.

"No. It's the storm." Nervous tone. "I hope I didn't damage your Envoy. It's new, isn't it?"

"Are you trying to make something of it?" A frown and even uglier tone.

"Make something of what?" I asked. "I just want to know if it's dented or scratched. I have insurance."

Nick said, "Ain't no way to tell in this downpour, but it looked okay when I passed it walking back to your car."

"Let me give you my card," I said. "If you see damage when you get the van out of the rain, call me, and I'll contact my agent."

"It ain't a van; it's an SUV." He reached for the card and continued, "What if I was to use this to call and ask you for a date?"

"That's the number at the mortuary, not my home number."

"I'll look you up in the phone book. I ain't got a fancy card like this, but I'll write my cell number on the back of yourn, and if you decide you want me to buy you a beer, *you* call *me*." He used a pen from the Mustang's console to write on the back of my card and handed it to me before he opened the passenger door, stepped out, and slammed it.

"Okay," I said, though I knew he couldn't hear me. I wasn't even worried about the Mustang, could have cared less whether Donnie's precious bumper was dented. I'd cranked the engine and almost pulled away when Nick banged on the window again. I rolled the glass about halfway down and said, "I thought we could take care of this business tomorrow or when the weather's not so rough."

"This ain't business." He looked down at the puddle he stood in. Could the aloof Nick Rivers be shy? "I been seeing you around since you came back to St. Mary. I ain't tied up with nobody special. I was serious about buying you that beer. Right now would be okay with me if you wanna go somewhere."

Buh-leeve me, I almost fainted. I had to concentrate to keep from babbling like a preschooler.

"Sounds good to me," I said, "but not tonight. I'm too tired and wet."

"How about tomorrow night?"

"I have to work until eight."

"I'll pick you up at your place at eight thirty."

I stammered, "I'll write my address for you," and reached for a pen and pad of paper from the glove compartment.

"That's okay. I know where you live. In the brick duplex on Oak Street, right?"

"Uh-huh."

"I'll be there at eight thirty."

He turned and walked away in the pouring rain. He didn't run. Just strolled up to the Envoy, climbed in, and sped away. I waited until he was gone, pumped my fist into the air, shouted "Yes!" and drove home slowly through the storm, miraculously somehow oblivious to the scary thunder and lightning.

Big Boy was either happy to see me or dehydrated. He jumped all over me, licking the rain off. I glanced at his water bowl. It was puppy love. His dishes were full.

Jane works until the wee hours of the morning and generally sleeps through early evening unless she's invited someone over. I hadn't called her on my way from the emergency room at lunchtime even though I'd wanted to tell her all I'd heard about Don, but I couldn't wait to tell her about this.

After all my kisses from Big Boy, I went straight to the telephone and punched in Jane's number. Stood there dripping water on the ugly green shag carpet. Not even thinking about the storm outside. Not even scared of the lightning.

"This better be important to wake me this early," she said instead of "Hello." I heard her yawn. How could she sleep through a storm? A low, distant rumble of thunder always wakes me.

"It is! Guess who I'm dating tomorrow night."

"Guess? You wake me up to *guess* that you're seeing the doctor again tomorrow night?"

"Not the doctor. I've got news about him, all right, but Nick Rivers just asked me out."

"You woke me up for *that*? You need your head examined. I told you to forget Nick Rivers. Why would you drop your doctor for Nick?" Jane knows that I tend to be a monogamous dater. It's one of my rules. I explore one relationship at a time.

I quickly summarized my eavesdropping at the ER.

"So?" Jane said. Yawned.

"So I don't want to date Don anymore."

"What's he done to hurt you? He treats you nice. Spends money on you. Hasn't pushed you into anything you're not ready to do. What's so wrong with the man taking women to the same restaurant? Don't you serve the same first meal to every guy you ever invite to your place for dinner?"

I admitted that was true. Whenever I've dated someone enough to make me feel I should invite him over for dinner, I pick up antipasto salad from the Sicilian pizza place in Beaufort and dump it into my bowls. The second course is always homemade lasagna. Homemade by Jane. At her home. Warmed in my oven just before my date arrives. My favorite bakery supplies great bread and tiramisu.

Jane was right. My first dinner was always the same, so why was Don Walters guilty of anything because his first date was always the same?

"I don't know," I admitted. "When you say it like that, it doesn't sound so bad, but I don't want to see Don again anyway. You know I've wanted to go out with Nick Rivers since high school." I laughed, then added, "I ran into him tonight and he asked me out."

"What were you doing out in this kind of weather?"

"I was coming home, and I really did run into him. I bumped into the back of his new SUV in the rainstorm."

"Must not have hurt it if he asked you out. Most men

would rather wring your neck than date you if you hit their new wheels." I didn't answer, so she kept on, "I understand why you'd want to date Nick. You've had this crush on him as long as I can remember. Handsome, plenty of money, and he doesn't look like the loser he is. What I don't understand is why does Nick Rivers want to date you? Even he isn't crazy enough to ask someone on a date after she hits him in a fender bender, especially if he's in a new vehicle."

"What?"

"Why does he want to date you? Nick's a little like Bobby Saxon was. He looks good, but he drinks too much. He's a player and never hurts for female company. Biggest differences between Nick and Bobby are that Bobby worked an honest job and he married some of his women. I haven't been around Nick much the past few years, but when I barhopped after you moved away, Nick was involved in things you hate. Like drugs. He was sentenced to two years in jail, served one, and got out on probation. Don't want to hurt your feelings, Callie, but I don't think you're his type."

I bristled. "And what is his type?"

"He dated Betty Cross before she got with Bobby Saxon. Bouncy Betty is Nick's type. You're not."

"Thanks loads for being excited for me when I finally get asked out by someone I've wanted to date for years." My voice had the supersarcastic tone I only use with Jane when I'm really angry.

"Well, thanks for waking me up." Same sarcastic tone. She paused and giggled. "And be sure to call and tell me all about your big date with Nick Rivers."

Like there was any way I wouldn't call Jane to tell her every detail.

# Chapter Twenty-five

**S**ome women spend way too much time deciding what to wear. I'm one of them. If Otis and Odell didn't dictate my clothing for my job, I'd be late every day or have to work naked. Nick Rivers hadn't tipped his hand on the date agenda for Friday night. Were we going to dinner? To a movie? Dancing? I needed to wear something that would be appealing and appropriate no matter what he planned. I tried on everything in my closet at least twice after I dried off, showered, and toweled off again.

I worried until I got scared I was nearing a panic attack and called Jane once more even though I knew it was after nine o'clock and I was taking her away from her work. Well, Roxanne's work. Jane laughed at me and advised, "Callie, since you're determined to date Nick Rivers, wear something that looks touchable. You know, something soft or fuzzy, maybe silk or cashmere."

"What if I decide I don't want to be touched?" I asked.

"You don't have to let him touch, just make him want to."

"But Jane," I said, "none of my black dresses or jeans and tees look especially touchable."

"Go shop," she answered.

"Will you go with me?" I asked. Well, okay, I didn't ask; I whined.

"I can go with you after lunch."

"Gotta go in the morning. I have to be at work at one tomorrow afternoon."

"I'm working tonight."

"Come on. This is important to me. Be ready when I pick you up at eight. We can be in Beaufort when the stores open."

Jane's turn to whine. "But I need my sleep."

"Shut Roxanne down early and catch a few hours."

"But I need my money, too. Rent and all those other things."

"Okay, Jane, now who has the yeah-buhs?"

Jane has this theory that some people don't want to solve their problems, they just want to complain. She says they have the "yeah-buhs," meaning "yeah, but" this won't work and that won't work no matter what advice they get. In other words, they don't want any solutions. Just like to moan and gripe. Jane argued that she didn't have the yeah-buhs.

She whined. I begged.

She whined some more. I begged some more.

Finally, she gave in. I said, "See you right before eight in the morning."

Big Boy and I rolled all over the bed that night. I'd drift into sleep, then wake up. Over and over. I kept dreaming someone was in the apartment. Standing over my bed. Telling me to mind my own business. I dragged myself out of bed before six. Big Boy followed me, so I took him for his walk. He still hadn't learned to tinkle like a boy. He squatted just as though he were a girl doggie.

He'd also grown shy and wouldn't do his business unless I turned my back. I felt nervous. If Cowboy was
guilty and in jail, why was I still so edgy? I kept glancing
over my shoulder. Big Boy must have thought I was looking at his boy parts because the poor baby turned it off
and on like a spigot.

Some people don't think dogs have facial expressions,
but they do. I've seen Daddy's hunting hounds grin when
he walked up to them carrying his sixteen-gauge shotgun.
Big Boy looks contented when he climbs into the bed and
he looks happy when I feed him. His expression was pure
relief when I turned to go inside.

Big Boy ate Kibbles 'n Bits while I had two Moon Pies,
a glass of milk, and a cup of coffee. I showered, put on a
black work dress, and pulled my hair up on top of my head
with a clip. The lighter blonde definitely worked with the
black dress.

With Big Boy secured in the bathroom for the day, I
headed toward Jane's. The morning was crisp, yet sunny,
and before I reached her house, I stopped and put down
the ragtop.

The first thing Jane said when she sat in the car was,
"Where are we eating breakfast?"

"I ate with Big Boy. Since we're in a rush, I figured
you'd eat before you came."

"Well, I didn't. And I'm hungry." She said the word
"hungry" in a breathless tone and spread it over about five
or six syllables.

"Is that Roxanne talking this morning?"

"Oops, sorry. I got a real spender on the line and stayed
up talking to him all night. I haven't had any sleep."

"Take a little nap on the way to Beaufort, and I'll stop
at Bojangles' when we get there."

"Okay," Jane said, "do you have a scrunchie with you?"

"Yep, there's one in the glove compartment."

Jane fumbled around, then screamed. "Callie, is this what I think it is?"

She pulled out the .38 and waved it toward me.

"Hey, take it easy. That thing's loaded," I cautioned.

"Loaded?" She threw the weapon on the seat. "You let me grab a live pistol without warning me?" She stretched the long vowel in "live" to about four *i*'s.

I pulled over to the shoulder of the road, stopped the vehicle, and fumbled in the glove compartment. "Here," I said as I pulled the scrunchie out and handed it to her. "Sorry about that. Didn't even remember I'd put it there."

As Jane pulled her long hair into a ponytail, I straightened the papers in the glove compartment and slid the gun up under my seat. Jane was snuggled down with her eyes closed by the time we were back on the road.

In a way, I was glad Jane was tired. Maybe she'd be calm and not tempted to pull any of her shenanigans while we shopped. She seemed to be sound asleep, but her head popped up the minute I pulled into the Bojangles' drive-through.

"I want a chicken biscuit, Bo-Taters, two cinnamon biscuits, orange juice, and a large coffee," she said.

Good grief, if I ate like Jane, I'd weigh a ton, but she has this fantastic metabolism. She's pigged out off and on, for as long as I've known her, without ever having an ounce of fat on her body, and I honestly have never had any reason to suspect her of bulimia. Since I'd already had breakfast, I ordered a BoBerry Biscuit and Coke. Breakfast dessert?

"Annie's Boutique opens at nine, so I thought we'd go there first," I said as I drove, but Jane was too busy eating to pay attention to me. "Is that okay?" I asked, trying to force her into acknowledging me.

"Uh-huh," she mumbled around a mouthful of chicken biscuit. "It's really good."

"Annie's is really good?"

"Yes, Annie's is a great place to shop, but I was saying this food's good. I forgot to eat dinner last night."

Jane can outeat me at times, but she also sometimes forgets to eat. I'd have to be unconscious not to remember a mealtime. That took my mind back to my brief stay in the hospital and waking up to Dr. Donald's handsome face. Then again, if my mother had lived, she would probably have taught me, "Pretty is as pretty does."

We sat in the store's parking lot until all the wrappings and napkins were stuffed into a litterbag. As I opened my car door, Jane put on her rose-tinted sunglasses.

"Don't even think about it," I threatened her. She threw the shades back onto the car seat, got out, and slammed the door. *Tap, tap, tapped* her way inside.

I tried on several outfits, but the ones that complimented me were too expensive. The affordable things didn't do a thing for me. The saleslady followed us and held the door open when we left. As I passed her, she leaned toward my ear.

"Don't let anyone know I told you this," she whispered, "but if you want the class of clothes you tried on here at much cheaper prices, go to Secondhand Rose's Clothes. They carry only top quality, and the prices are really reasonable. It's two blocks up"—she pointed north—"on the same side of the street."

"Thank you," I replied.

She looked at Jane. A lot of the time, folks talk about the handicapped or disabled as though they're not even there. The clerk spoke to me, but she said it loud, too loud even though she was actually speaking for Jane. Like being blind stops a person from hearing as well as seeing. "And thank your friend for not falling down and carrying on this morning, because the next time she does that here, I'm calling the police."

As we drove away, Jane called the lady something considerably unladylike, then added, "I can't help it if I've been there too often. I like their merchandise." She paused. "Are we going to Secondhand Rose's?"

"I don't know. I'm not sure I want to wear used clothing."

"They aren't dirty or anything. Everything is laundered or dry-cleaned before being stocked, and I've heard they turn down more consignments than they accept." She yawned. "It's only two blocks. Can't hurt to look."

"Have you ever been here before?" I asked when we parked.

"No," Jane answered before she reached for her sunglasses.

"Don't even think about it," I said again, in an even sharper tone.

The displays inside were comparable to better department stores. Definitely not a thrift shop atmosphere. A young woman seated behind the checkout counter asked if she could help me and I answered, "Not now. I just want to look around."

"Help yourself," she said and stayed on the stool. I liked that. It really gets on my last nerve when salespeople follow me around and tell me how good everything I see would look on me.

I did, however, tell Jane, "She doesn't mean that literally."

After Jane and I gathered an armful of clothes, I left her in a chair outside the fitting area while I tried on several garments in the dressing room. When I put on a pale teal satin blouse with a pair of tailored, cream-colored slacks that were lightweight but felt like cashmere, I knew I'd found my outfit.

"Feels perfect," Jane said when I took the slacks and blouse out to her.

"Looks as good as it feels," I answered.

A tap on my shoulder. I whirled around to face Eileen Saxon. I should have recognized the White Diamonds scent as soon as she approached me. Guess my mind was wrapped too tight around this long-awaited date with Nick Rivers.

I promise, I didn't really mean to, but my arm drew back in anticipation of hitting her if she struck me. Didn't matter that we'd become friends or that I'd let her put something in Bobby's casket. But when I saw her big grin, I lowered my hand and said, "Mornin', Eileen."

"Hey there, what are you two doing here?"

"Looking at clothes. What else?" Jane's tone was a bit snippy.

Eileen reached out and pointed to the cream pants and teal shirt on Jane's lap. I was glad she didn't touch them. I wasn't sure about the freshness of the blood marks on her cuticles. If they weren't dry, her touch could stain the clothes.

"These are really nice. If neither of you is buying, I want them for myself."

"Too late," Jane said. "Callie's taking 'em."

"Do you shop here often?" Eileen asked.

"First time," I said.

"I buy a lot of things at this store. This is where I got my black dress for Bobby's funeral."

Oops! I'd worried about buying used clothes and now Eileen confessed that her dress that matched mine had been secondhand.

"Guess you heard about Cowboy getting arrested for Bobby's murder," she said.

"Yes." I paused. "I just hope the sheriff is right about it."

"You don't think he did it?"

"Just don't know. It doesn't seem to fit with June Bug's

death." I'd had enough talk about killings. Besides, sleuths are supposed to ask questions, not answer them.

She reached toward the clothing in Jane's lap again. I swooped in beneath her hand and picked them up. In truth, I snatched them, but that doesn't sound nice.

"Whatcha doing in Beaufort besides shopping?" I said as I headed toward the cash register with Eileen and Jane following.

"I'm going to the Corral to clean Bobby's personal things out of his desk. Mr. Attie, the boss over there, heard about me being Bobby's next of kin. He called and told me to come over before Bimbo Betty thinks about it." Her expression grew pained. "Would y'all want to go with me? I really don't want to do it alone."

"No, we're in a hur—" Jane started, but she couldn't see the look on Eileen's face. I could.

"Sure," I interrupted, "we'll go."

# Chapter Twenty-six

"**Why** are we doing this?" Jane complained as we headed toward the Truck Corral. "Thought you had to get back to St. Mary and go to work. Besides, I need some sleep."

"You couldn't see the look on Eileen's face," I answered. "I feel sorry for her. That woman's hurting. Besides, she might find something interesting in Bobby's belongings."

"Didn't you say the sheriff has this all wrapped up? Cowboy's in jail."

"If I were a cop, I'd say I've got a hinky feeling about it."

"If you were a cop, I wouldn't hang out with you."

I laughed. Jane joined with a chuckle, then added, "And if you were a cop, there are times you'd arrest me."

"Flippin' A!"

GMC Automotive and Truck Corral had doubled in size since the last time I'd been there. Cowboy's television commercial bragged they had "acres and acres" of cars and trucks. Being originally a farm girl, "acres and acres" meant hundreds to me, so that was an exaggeration in my mind, but there were a lot of vehicles and probably hundreds of those red, white, and blue plastic triangle signs strung around the lot.

I was looking for a parking place, but Eileen pulled right up to the door of the showroom. I stopped the Mustang just behind her. Jane and I followed her in. Jane had added her sunglasses, and I wondered what scheme she could think up in here.

A nice-looking older gentleman met us and presented himself to Eileen with his hand extended.

"I'm Tom Attie," he said. "You're Mrs. Eileen Saxon, aren't you? I believe I saw you at Bobby's visitation."

"Yes, thank you for calling me," the first Widow Saxon answered.

The man glanced at me, and his eyes widened. His face turned as pale as the summer seersucker suit he wore. I could almost see him remembering what had happened between Eileen and me at the visitation.

"I'm Callie Parrish," I said and stuck out my hand. "This is my friend Jane." She didn't offer to shake. "What you saw that night was a mistake. Eileen and I are friends now."

He exhaled and wiped the beads of sweat from his forehead. "I thought that was you, but you're different somehow."

"It's the hair," Jane volunteered. "Callie changes her hair color when she gets stressed."

"Stressed?" Eileen asked.

I didn't want to go there, so I assured her, "Sometimes I just change it for the sake of change."

"You're blonder," Mr. Attie said before turning away from me to address Eileen. "Let me show you Bobby's desk. I've put a box there for you to pack his things. It's in this cubicle right over here. I appreciate your coming. I may as well admit that I'm doing some hiring right now and need the space." No kidding he was—from what I understood, he now had to replace his two top salesmen, what with Bobby dead and Cowboy in jail.

The division panels were neatly labeled. "R. E. Saxon" on the one Mr. Attie and Eileen entered, and right beside it, "W. 'Cowboy' Peavy." Bet next-door cubicles thrilled the two of them when they worked there.

Bobby's cubicle was typical of every other car salesman's space I've ever seen. A desk with a chair behind it and a computer on it. Two straight-back chairs facing the desk. If the salesperson or customer had been the size of June Bug or Fatsy Patsy, Bobby would have had to work out the deal somewhere else.

Eileen gasped, then smiled, as she sat behind the desk in Bobby's place. She picked up a five-by-seven picture frame and turned it toward me. The portrait was an enlargement of the same baby picture she'd slipped into Bobby's Exquisite. She dropped it into the box and opened the top drawer.

I guided Jane into the corner chair facing the desk and stepped to the opening into the walkway between the rows of cubicles. There was no one around. I could hear some of the salesmen joking in the showroom. I stood there watching for a while, and nobody came back to the cubicle area. Eileen was occupied with flipping through papers as she dumped them into the box. Jane had dozed off.

No time like the present.

Even though I didn't see anyone who appeared to be watching, I flattened my back against the wall, sucked in my tummy, and tried to pull in my chest, but my blow-up bra made that impossible. I quick-stepped around the corner and sat in Cowboy's chair at his desk.

The papers filling the top drawer all seemed related to selling cars. Pieces of paper with names, dates, phone numbers, and info like "prefers shades of blue—color more important than optional equipment." Another one read, "killing time, won't buy." Beneath the papers it looked like Cowboy had saved every old pen and pencil stub he'd ever used as well as two miniature keys, smaller than would fit a car or door.

The middle drawer held a thick scrapbook crowded with photographs of Willie Peavy in his cowboy clothes. They went back years. Each neatly labeled with a date and name of the event. There were pictures of Cowboy in ads, ceremonies presenting him with top salesman awards, him accepting prizes in competitions for most overall deals and most closings on designated models. Cowboy's clothes grew flashier with each picture, but the dates became less and less frequent as time passed.

"Where'd Callie go?" I heard Eileen's voice through the partition.

"Oh, she probably went to the restroom," came Jane's sleepy, sluggish reply. "Do you want me to go check on her?"

"No, that's all right. I'm almost done here." I could picture Eileen nibbling on a hangnail as she spoke and almost hear her thoughts. *Now how could a blind person go look for someone?* What Eileen didn't know was that if she sent Jane to find me, Jane would locate me as quickly or faster than a sighted person. Don't ask me how. She just does it.

Nothing of interest in Cowboy's desk yet, and Eileen was almost finished. I started to go back to Bobby's cubicle without checking the bottom drawer, but I'm not only curious, I'm nosy. I pulled out the lower drawer. A metal lockbox about ten by twelve inches and two inches deep. I set it on top of the desk and tried to open it, but no go. What could Cowboy keep locked up so tight? Pornography?

Too much reading detective books and watching Court TV. The only pictures Cowboy would enjoy were the ones of himself. I rummaged under the top-drawer papers and pulled out the little keys, tried them one by one in the little opening. Just as the lock turned, I heard Jane call through the wall, "Callie?"

"Just a minute," I said and yanked open the box.

Newspaper clippings and folded interoffice flyers. I always carry a normal-sized purse, never totes, not even to the beach. If I'd had a big bag like Bouncy Betty usually had swinging from her arm, I could've slipped the entire box into it. Instead, I crammed the papers into my modest handbag, put everything else back in place, and stepped into the hall just before Eileen guided Jane out of Bobby's office with one hand while lugging the cardboard box with her other arm wrapped around it.

"Get everything?" I asked.

"Yes, not much to get," said Eileen as Jane stepped away from her and headed down the hall, using her cane for guidance.

"Don't guess car salesmen keep many valuables in their desks," I said.

"No, but it was worth the trip just to see that picture on his desk. I knew he'd want Anna Grace's picture with him, but I never knew he'd had it enlarged and put where he could look at it every day." She wiped away a tear, then grimaced. "He hadn't totally changed, though. Lots of women's phone numbers in there."

"They were probably customers who were looking to buy cars," I assured her, though I had no intention of telling her that was what I'd found in Cowboy's top drawer.

"You got time for lunch?" Eileen asked.

"No, thanks, I've got to work this afternoon."

"Thanks for coming with me."

"No problem. Sorry that whenever I see you, it's always a sad occasion."

"Not your fault," she said as we headed to the outside door. Mr. Attie approached. I sidestepped him and called Jane. She'd been looking at, well, in her case touching, a new convertible, but she came toward my voice. We left Eileen talking, went out, and climbed into the Mustang.

I must have taken off faster than I realized because Jane said, "You can slow down. I didn't lift anything."

"I didn't really think you'd stolen a truck back there," I apologized.

"Of course not," Jane replied, "I'd be arrested if I stole a vehicle. I don't have a driver's license."

That was when I realized that I, Calamine Lotion Parrish, who absolutely freaks out when my friend shoplifts or scams businesses, had just stolen personal property from Wilbert Peavy.

I wheeled back into the Bojangles' drive-through when we reached it and treated both of us to chicken, dirty rice, and pinto beans. When I pulled away, I parked in their lot.

"Are we going in?" Jane asked.

"Would I order at the to-go window if we were eating inside?" I answered.

I divvied up the food, then asked Jane, "What's the last thing on earth you'd think I would do?"

"Play doctor with Donald Walters?"

"That's not as probable as it used to be. Come on, what won't I do?"

She named about a dozen activities, none of which I would ever consider. She named some vices I'd never heard of.

"Okay, I give up," she said and wiped her mouth and hands on a wet wipe.

"Steal."

"Steal?"

"Yep, I stole something back at the Corral."

I expected her to say something like, "You go, girl!"

Instead her face clouded. "I don't like that, Callie," she said. "I don't like that one bit. Whatever it is, you take it back."

Puh-leeze. This from someone who acquired most of her belongings in devious ways.

"It's papers," I said. "I went through Cowboy's desk while Eileen gathered Bobby's belongings."

"Figured you were up to something. That's why I told Eileen you were in the potty, but nobody spends that much time in the restroom, and the good Lord knows you don't need to be shopping for a new car so long as the Mustang runs. What kinda papers? Is it a written confession?"

"Don't know. Let's see."

Only a few minutes told us that this was Cowboy's Bobby Saxon file. In addition to newspaper clippings about his death, we found a yellowed write-up from the *Beaufort Gazette* announcing Bobby's move from St. Mary Motors to work at the Corral. Office flyers and newspaper clippings bragged about Bobby's sales record and prize winnings. Many pictures had been doctored with black Magic Marker mustaches or scars. Red ink showed that Cowboy could draw bleeding cuts as well. I described each to Jane.

"I guess this backs up the sheriff's belief that Cowboy killed Bobby," I concluded.

"Not in my mind," Jane answered.

"Why?"

"On the assumption that whoever killed Bobby Saxon killed June Bug, why aren't the clippings about his murder in there?"

I thought about that all the way back to St. Mary while

Jane slept. I dropped her off and was at my desk in the mortuary twenty minutes early. I went through the papers again. Nothing about June Bug. Nothing at all.

**No calls. No** new bodies. No bosses. My afternoon was perfect until I started thinking about Nick Rivers. Not about our date that night, but about him and that Envoy I'd hit the night before.

I mentally pictured Nick turning the Savana into the driveway at Charleston Charlie's Cars the day Jane and I went to Victoria's Secret. The van had looked new and big. As long as the hearse, I mean funeral coach, maybe even longer.

Had he traded because of mileage and gas prices? According to Jane, Nick had plenty of money, and he hardly seemed the type to care much about oil and ecology. He hadn't wanted to discuss it with the girl at the highway department. Whenever one of my brothers buys a new vehicle, that's all he'll talk about for a month. Cars are usually a very safe subject to hold a man's attention.

The Savana seemed to match up better with Nick than the Envoy. The Savana was large enough to move just about anything. *Large enough to move Bobby Saxon's first Exquisite.*

"Wow," I thought, "where did that idea come from?"

Could Nick have stolen Bobby's casket, then traded the van for a smaller SUV to divert attention from his hearse-size vehicle? Maybe he watched Court TV and wanted to get rid of some kind of forensic evidence. Cowboy sure couldn't move a casket in that little red sports car.

But if Cowboy killed Bobby, did he kill June Bug? And if Cowboy was the murderer, why would Nick have stolen the casket? What would he need with a casket? Did he have a body to bury? That made no sense at all. Whoever

stole the Exquisite thought Bobby's body was in it. I did
what I always do in times of stress and confusion, as well
as in times of joy or grief. I called Jane.

"What now?" she asked in a sleepy voice. I expected
her to laugh when I told her what I'd been thinking, but
instead she said, "Makes sense. Especially since Nick
went to Charleston to trade when he could have dealt at
the GMC Corral in Beaufort and saved himself a lot of
driving and probably a little money, too."

I said, "It would explain why he picked up his own license tag, too. He wanted it right away. No one was supposed to notice the change."

"Yes," Jane agreed, "and that's why he ignored you. I
bet he was furious to see you there."

"It all fits except for motive."

"Callie, I want you to call the sheriff and then cancel
your date with Nick Rivers. I could name you lots of mo-
tives. Even jealousy. I told you Nick and Betty went way
back."

That didn't work for me because Bobby had been going to leave Betty. Then again, maybe Nick didn't know
that.

"I'll call Sheriff Harmon," I told Jane, "but unless he
picks up Nick, I'm going to date him tonight to investigate our theory."

"*Our* theory doesn't make much sense if Cowboy
killed Bobby and June Bug, and we don't know what kind
of forensics evidence Harmon has against Cowboy." I
heard Jane yawn once more before she continued, "But I
still don't want you going out with Nick Rivers, especially since if your theory is right, it means Nick's already hit you and given you a concussion that put you in
the hospital."

"I still want to talk to him."

"Talk to him? You want to interrogate him." She giggled

her Roxanne laugh. "I think you want to do something else to him, too. Forget Nick and concentrate on the doc."

"I'll be fine," I assured Jane without bothering to deny my attraction to Nick Rivers. I'd always been drawn to him, but just in case my theory about why he'd traded SUVs *was* right, I decided to play it safe. I added, "I'll call you on my cell phone at ten thirty sharp wherever I am and again at midnight from the apartment. I'm sure I'll be home by then. Go back to sleep. I'll talk to you tonight."

The dispatcher surprised me by being courteous and offering to patch me to Sheriff Harmon.

"Hey, Callie," he said, "I was just thinking about you. Actually wishing I had a reason to tell you the new development in the Wilbert Peavy arrest."

"What kind of development?"

"Peavy confessed."

"Confessed? Did he steal the casket, too?"

"Peavy confessed to everything. I'm sure we'll get all the details from him as soon as he settles down. Right now, he seems agitated, but he hasn't lawyered up."

"I called to suggest you check out Nick Rivers for stealing the casket because he's been acting really strange about his van, and it was big enough to hold the casket."

"Callie, as much drugs as Rivers has consumed and sold, it's a wonder there's a brain cell left in his noggin. He always acts strange. We haven't been able to pin dealing on him yet, but he'll get himself caught again soon. The case against Peavy looks solid."

Hindsight is twenty-twenty. I should have spent the afternoon analyzing my theory. Did I do that? Ex-cuuze me. I never claimed to have perfect vision. I should have called Nick and canceled the date. I wasn't interested in getting involved with a druggie no matter how fine his shiny heinie was, but I wanted to go out with him one time, and yes, I confess, I wanted to ask him some questions. Cowboy had confessed? I just couldn't see him as the murderer. An obnoxious little banty rooster, but not a killer.

I spent the rest of the afternoon at my desk reading a Hercule Poirot mystery before dressing for my date at the mortuary on Middleton's time. The snug slacks and blouse really showed off my figure and my inflatables. Definitely touchable. I mean the clothes, not the inflatables. Well, the inflatables probably looked touchable, too, but what I'm trying to say is that my new clothes were soft, and I felt good about myself when I put them on. I put the top up on the Mustang and spun the wheel like a kid when I pulled out of Middleton's parking lot.

# Chapter Twenty-seven

**N**ick Rivers stood by the passenger door of his new gray Envoy parked in my driveway when I arrived. I pulled into the driveway of the vacant apartment next door. Nick dropped his cigarette to the ground and rubbed it out with the toe of his boot. He didn't smile and didn't move toward me. Why, oh why, did Nick's aloofness always fascinate me?

I smoothed the legs of my new slacks and walked toward Nick.

"You ready to go?" he asked. No hello, no how are you. Not only was I not ready to leave, I wasn't so sure I still wanted to date him. My high school fascination waned rapidly. Would I be in danger with Nick? The sheriff claimed Cowboy had confessed, but the pieces of my theory fit too well. If I'd been a cop, I'd have been hinkying all over.

I taught kindergarten, not science, but I remembered from my own student days that sometimes even an unlikely hypothesis proves correct. What if Cowboy murdered Bobby and June Bug, but Nick stole the casket and knocked me out? I wanted to *know*.

"Hello, Nick. I'll be ready in a few minutes. I have a puppy inside. I need to take care of him first."

"Okay. I'll wait here." He opened a fresh pack of cigarettes, dropped the cellophane on the driveway, tapped out a smoke, and lit it. Don would have followed me into the apartment. Nick didn't appear to be in a hurry to get me on the couch like Don had been. I didn't know if this was good or bad. I wanted him to like me, but if he was the bad boy Jane made him out to be and if he was the thief who stole the casket, I'd need to be on guard from the get-go. Besides, the whole point of this was no longer just to go on a date with Nick Rivers. It was to find out why he'd been so cagey with his vehicles.

Big Boy wiggled all around me and jumped up on my legs the minute I opened the door. Ugh. All I needed was wrinkles and paw prints on my new slacks, but thankfully his feet were clean and didn't leave any marks. When I took Big Boy out, Nick still stood by the van, smoking and watching. I thought he might walk over to see Big Boy, but he didn't. I almost wished Nick would leave, but buhleeve me, after waiting fifteen years to date him and waiting all afternoon for an opportunity to question him, I wasn't about to make up an excuse to cancel. The thought crossed my mind that my date with Nick Rivers might be another long-awaited disappointment, like June Bug's bar.

I secured Big Boy inside with fresh supplies of food and water, plastered a smile on my face, and walked out onto the porch. While I locked the dead bolt on my front door, Nick got into the driver's seat. My smile changed from fake to genuine when I thought about how Jane would howl with laughter when I told her about my wonderful date with Mr. Social Graces.

Daddy and The Boys consider me modern and independent, but I still like men to hold doors for me on dates. Since Nick didn't know that, or didn't care, I opened the passenger door for myself and climbed into the seat. Glad I'd worn slacks instead of a short skirt. The open KFC box of chicken bones on the console beside Nick probably meant he'd eaten while waiting for me. No dinner date tonight.

"What do you want to do?" Nick asked as he gunned the motor and backed out of the drive.

I knew better than to say, "What do you want to do?" even if he wasn't as grabby as Don. I reworded the question and asked something just about as bad: "What do you usually do on first dates?"

Nick laughed. "Well, most of my first dates have been taking girls home from June Bug's in the middle of the night. A get-to-know-you date is kinda a first for me. I never seen you at June Bug's before last week. I said I'd buy you a beer and I don't even know whether you drink."

"Not much. A mixed drink occasionally. Beer sometimes."

"Good. I'll stop here and get us a six-pack." He wheeled into a Shop 'n Save and did the redneck gentlemanly thing: He left the radio on for me. He returned with two six-packs of cold Budweisers and a bag of ice, opened the back of the van, and removed a foam ice chest. He packed the beer and ice into the container and set it on the floor in my foot space. He grinned. He was back around to his side and stepping up to the driver's seat when a confused look washed over his face.

"Oh," Nick said, "I forgot to get out the beers. Pull two of those for us."

"Are you going to drink beer while you drive?" I asked.

"Of course," he said, glancing at me with an expression that accused me of being stupid for asking.

I must have moved too slowly. Nick leaned across me, yanked two beers from the cooler, wiped them off on his jeans, handed me one, popped the top on his, and drained about half of his can in one gulp. He backed the Envoy out of the Shop 'n Save lot and pulled onto the road.

"Let's ride and talk," he said.

That suited me. I had lots of questions for him. "Okay," I said, "I like your new wheels. Did you buy this from Charleston Charlie's?"

"Yeah." He grimaced. "You saw me there, didn't you?"

"Jane and I went to Charleston to buy clothes for June Bug. His wife wanted him all dressed up. That's when I spotted you. That big Savana was hard to miss."

Nick chuckled. "You bought clothes for June Bug at Victoria's Secret?"

I laughed. "No, we went there after we finished at the men's shop."

"Did you tell Jane you saw me?"

"No, I was so angry with Jane I didn't tell her anything." I gave him a blow-by-blow description of Jane's scam.

He guffawed. "Sounds like my kind of girl. I think I'll take her out sometime."

Ex-cuuze me. Tacky, tacky, tacky. This wasn't my idea of how this should be going. I wanted answers to my questions. Furthermore, I'd never gone out with a man who mentioned calling another girl while with me.

I realized we were headed toward June Bug's. Surely Nick didn't think the club was open.

"You do know Mrs. Corley burned June Bug's bar, don't you?" I asked.

"Yeah, I heard that. That's why we're going by there. I wanna check it out. We'll drive over and take a look-see." I felt a little better. At least he wasn't headed toward the old Halsey place or some other lovers' lane. My longtime fascination with Nick Rivers was gone. He tossed his beer can out the window, looked down, picked up the KFC box, and threw it out, too. "Give me another one, will ya?" he said and pointed to the ice chest. I handed him another Bud.

"You didn't tell me why you traded your Savana," I tried.

Nick ignored me and said, "Betty said you accused her of murdering Bobby. Did you?"

"Not really." This was a wrong turn of events. I'd wanted to ask the questions, and now he was the nosy one.

"Said you accused her of killing him for the insurance policy because he was gonna leave her and go back to Eileen."

"I didn't accuse her. I explained that investigators have to consider three things for a murder case: motive, opportunity, and means. In her case, Betty would have a motive to get all that money. She had the opportunity because she lived with him. To prove means, law enforcement would only have to show she had access to ketamine." I made a point of pronouncing the word correctly so that it no longer rhymed with my name.

"You know a lot about everything, don't you, Calamine?" I knew I didn't like the tone of his voice.

"I read a lot of mystery books." I hate to admit it, but the next thing I did was break the law. I opened my beer. We were out in the boonies, not likely to be seen by a deputy. Besides, I remembered that Jane said Nick used to date Betty, and Nick seemed angry that he thought I'd accused Betty. I tried to change the subject back to his vehicle.

"I really like this Envoy. What's it got? A six or an eight?" I said.

"You weren't supposed to notice I traded. That's why I bought the same color as the Savana."

Dalmatian! It sounded like my theory was true. I should have kept my mouth shut. I didn't.

"Not notice?" I said it with a combination question mark/exclamation point. "A brand-new ride like this would be hard to miss." Unless, I thought, I really was a brick short of a load, like folks seemed to think Nick was. To be honest, I was beginning to agree with them.

"Not for most women, but definitely for you, Calamine Parrish. How do you know so much about men's things?"

I almost laughed in his face. I don't know as much about "men's things" as many women do, but that wasn't what he was talking about.

"You can't grow up in a house with five older brothers and not learn about cars, trucks, and guns."

"I guess not. That's why I never asked you out back in high school. I didn't want to date a girl who had five older brothers to come looking for me."

"I had a crush on you in school," I confessed, thinking I might be wise to flirt with him. After all, there's much to be said for using feminine wiles. Maybe even feminine wilds. "I thought you just never noticed me."

"Oh, I saw you, all right, but I wasn't about to make your brothers or your daddy mad at me. Your daddy won every turkey shoot for miles around St. Mary."

"Yes, and he still can." I hoped this would be a subconscious threat to him.

"Did you follow me to Beaufort Wednesday morning?" Nick's voice accused.

"Follow *you*? I was there before you. Somebody stole my purse, and I was there to replace my driver's license."

Nick turned off onto the hardscrabble road leading to June Bug's. I couldn't decide if I was more scared or annoyed. One thing I did know. This would be my last date with Nick Rivers. He was creepy.

We drove past at least half a dozen cars parked at the Corley house. Nick slowed and turned onto the drive to the club's parking lot. We pulled up to the soot-blackened concrete block walls of June Bug's bar. "Let's look," he said and parked. No point in waiting for him to open my door. I got out.

The yellow crime scene tape had been removed. The stale smell of smoke and ashes sifted through the air. We walked to the opening where the wooden door had hung. The inside was a charred mess, made worse by the drenching rain the night before. Twisted metal framing projected through the debris. Some of the plastic beer signs lay melted on the rubbish. Black, incinerated wooden beams crumbled when Nick touched them.

"Lotta good times in this place," Nick mumbled. "Don't see why they burned it. Could of turned it over to one of the younguns and still made money. Or even sold it. I wouldn't of minded running this place myself." He looked across the lot and glared at the spot where June Bug's body had been found.

"You were here when they found June Bug, weren't you, Calamine?" Nick asked.

"No, Mrs. Corley found him. I drove the funeral coach here to meet Odell."

"The what?"

"Hearse."

Nick lit another cigarette. "You're a little highfalutin at times."

"No," I assured him. "Otis and Odell have certain words we use in the business. We call a hearse a funeral coach."

Some part of me still wanted to see Nick in a favorable light. Possibly his weird mood was because of his many memories of times he'd spent in this place with Bobby

Saxon and June Bug. Maybe he was mourning in his own way. Perhaps my theory was just a lot of cow poop, male cow poop, but I wanted to know more.

Nick had questioned me. Now I questioned him.

"I heard you could buy drugs here. Do you think the ketamine that killed Bobby Saxon came from here?"

His eyes narrowed. "You heard I bought drugs here?"

"No, no, I didn't mean you, Nick. I meant anyone."

"Frankly, Calamine Parrish, I don't see how that's any of your business." His tone matched the expression on his face—nasty and sarcastic.

"The smoke smelled like pot while the building was burning," I blundered on.

"There was weed hidden all over this place," Nick said. "Maybe the sheriff's men didn't find it all." He cut his eyes at me. Slits. Barely slits.

"How do you know that?"

"That's none of your business, Calamine." He tossed a cigarette butt onto the scorched ruins.

Calamine. He called me Calamine like Betty did. Like the threatening caller.

Thinking before speaking has never been one of my strengths, and I felt mighty weak.

"Frankly, Nick Rivers," I said in the ugliest tone I could muster, "I don't see where this date is going, and I'd appreciate it if you'd take me home."

"Let's go." He grabbed my arm and stomped to the passenger side of the van, dragging me with him. He yanked the door open and shoved me in. I jerked my foot inside just as he slammed the door.

"Gimme another Bud," he said as he climbed into his own seat. Buh-leeve me. I didn't waste any time handing him a beer.

The wheels spun as Nick pushed the accelerator to the floor and tore out of the parking lot. He gulped his beer and darted cold, hateful eyes at me. I could feel his anger in the air almost as strong as my fear. I should have walked from the club down to the Corleys' house when the red flags popped up. Way too late for that now. We were speeding down the road.

"Nick," I began, trying to think of something to defuse him.

"Shut up!" He swung his right arm at me and if I hadn't been cringing against the passenger door, he would've hit me. Dalmatian! I should have listened to Jane.

"You were always too smart for your own good, Calamine Parrish," he said. "And always sticking your nose in other people's business, just like June Bug Corley."

"You threatened me on the telephone, didn't you?" I said, scrunching as close to the door as possible and looking out the window. Even fear couldn't keep my mouth shut. "You poisoned my dog, didn't you?"

"I warned you and you didn't listen, did you?" Nick looked toward me when he spoke, and the Envoy veered off the road. He jerked the steering wheel to the left. "First you find the needle in Bobby," he said as the Envoy screeched back onto the road. "If it hadn't of been for you, Bobby woulda been buried as an accident and Betty would have collected all that money, but no, you gotta find the needle." He hissed the words. His deep, ragged breaths scared me, but I pressed on.

"Betty's not getting the money. Eileen never divorced Bobby. The insurance policy is made to Bobby's 'legal wife.' That's Eileen, not Betty."

"Then I'll court Eileen and get to the money that way. If the whole thing falls apart, it will be your fault. Everywhere I turn, there you are. I figured I better get rid of the Savana, 'cause ever'time I turned around you were staring at me. Got something too small to move the casket just in case you were talking to the sheriff about me. Most women wouldn't of noticed the difference between a Savana and an Envoy if they was the same color, but Calamine Parrish did. I done all I know to keep you outta this, but you're just too nosy. You and June Bug gotta get in everybody's business."

Nick spit out the window. "Everywhere I turn, there you are."

I thought about jumping out of the Envoy while we were speeding down the road. I was that scared of Nick, but my brain told me to keep him talking. My attraction to him had been why I stared at him, but I doubted that would make any difference to him.

"I thought you liked June Bug," I said. "How did he get in your business?"

"Me and him had stayed at the club after everybody else left. Drinking. When I went out, he followed me in the parking lot up to my Savana, talking about how he might buy a new SUV. The fool didn't even know the difference between a full-size van and an SUV. Don't know how I missed locking the back doors, but he opened the back and looked to see how big it was inside. 'Course, once he saw the casket, I had to shoot him. Gave him a hit of K to try to throw the law off. Now I gotta get rid of you, too."

I grabbed my door handle. The door didn't open. I hit my shoulder against it. "Fancy new locks, Calamine," Nick said with a grin. "You can't open that door until I let you out." I needed my .38, but it was at my apartment.

Everyone said Nick wasn't the brightest bulb in the chandelier. I had to outsmart him. Keep him talking. I'd be dead meat if I couldn't think of some way to escape.

"The casket? You're the one who stole the casket?" I tried to put admiration into my voice, but it was wasted effort.

"Yeah. Still got it, too. Unloaded it over at Halsey's

farm after June Bug saw it and made me kill him." I remembered Jane telling me Nick had bought the old deserted Halsey place.

"Fat lotta good it did me." Nick's breath whistled in and out. "I figured if I took the casket with Bobby in it, nobody could prove nothing. I didn't go to steal the box. I was gonna take the body out. But of course, you had it locked when I got there. That was your fault, too. I didn't know he wadn't in it until I busted it open in the Savana."

"And you hit me on the head, too."

"Shoulda hit you harder, then I wouldn't have to deal with you now." His rapid breathing turned into a cackling laugh.

"I saw you at June Bug's with Eileen," I said.

"Nah, I wasn't *with* Eileen. That was just the whole bunch of us who used to party together, but if Eileen collects the insurance money, I'll be dating her soon."

*Keep him talking.* "Betty told me she was leaving Bobby, but now she says separating was his idea. Did she hire you to kill him?"

"Betty was upset 'cause Bobby wanted to divorce her and go back to Eileen. The jerk even told her he wanted his wedding ring back. I told her no way a man's gonna leave her for a woman fifteen years older. Then, when I run into Bobby that Sunday night after he left AA, he said Betty was right. Bobby was kidding me that he was setting my old girlfriend free. Told me I could have Betty back 'cause he'd sobered up and was gonna divorce her and get back with his first wife." Nick's eyes widened and he laughed. The sound was maniacal, like he was coming apart inside.

"Betty already told me about that insurance policy," he continued. "I got to thinking. Wouldn't be nothing to getting back with Betty if she was a rich widow woman. We been on again, off again for years. Only reason she married Bobby was 'cause I wouldn't get hitched."

The van swerved as Nick reached across me and pulled another beer from the cooler. He popped the top, drained it, and tossed the can out the window.

"It was easy." Nick's tone changed to calm explanation. "I tole Bobby I needed to go by the motel to check on something. He made me promise it wasn't a drug deal 'cause he didn't want to get involved in none 'a that. Finally, he rode over there with me. Nothing to it. Popped him in the neck with the K and shoved him in the pool. Wasn't 'til I was gonna throw the syringe away that I saw I'd broke the needle off in him. Everthing woulda still gone right if you hadn't stuck your nose in it."

"Listen, Nick. I won't tell anybody anything you've said. Just take me home, and I'll forget about the whole thing," I begged. "The sheriff arrested Cowboy and a deputy found Special K in his car. Cowboy's confessed to everything. Nobody will ever know you were involved."

Nick roared with laughter. "You think I'm gonna fall for that?" He pulled over to the shoulder of the road, stopped the Envoy, and leaned across me. I thought he was grabbing for another beer, but he reached under the seat. I jerked away. Grabbed the door handle, shook it in desperation. I didn't get away.

Didn't feel the needle.

Didn't feel anything at all.

# Chapter Twenty-eight

**A**bsolute pitch-black darkness. Waking has always been a gradual process for me. Not this time. I was nowhere. Then I was completely awake, but in an obsidian obscurity. Was Jane's world like this?

Arms by my sides, I lay stretched flat on my back on a mattress. My mind felt alert, totally in tune, but with what? Where was I? More important, why? A face floated in my mind. Nick Rivers. He had lunged toward me with a hypodermic. Ketamine? Had he injected me with Special K? Was the total blackout of my world a K-induced hallucination? Or had he injected me with the same dosage he'd given Bobby Saxon? I saw nothing. Heard nothing. But I wasn't dead, was I?

I'm not scared of dying. My work had taken away my childhood fears of corpses, caskets, and graves. Besides, I might not be in church every Sunday, but I've walked that long aisle to the front of the church with my heart so full I thought it would burst. I've been baptized, a real dunking in the edge of the Atlantic Ocean, and I believe in the afterlife. Making beautiful pictures out of human remains after death doesn't bother me because I believe the essence of a person, some folks call it the soul, moves to another living realm before we prepare the body. This nothingness couldn't be the afterlife I believe in.

Not all my senses were gone. I sniffed a faint whisper of my own cologne. I thought I smelled my own fear also. The sense of touch remained, too. I could feel the softness of the sheet I lay on and the pillow beneath my head. I wiggled my fingers and moved my hand to my chest. The cloth I lay upon and the new blouse I wore felt the same. Satin.

Hoping, praying I was wrong, I reached my hands up over my body. Immediately patted the soft, shirred fine cloth of a casket lid. I didn't have to touch the sides of the box to confirm my fear.

I screamed. My muscles tensed. My body quivered and shook. Dizziness and nausea sickened me as bile surged to my throat. I needed to throw up. I pushed it down. Hard. My heart hammered and pain shot through my chest. Blood pounded in my ears. Was I having a heart attack?

Had Nick buried me alive? I'd read about pull ropes that were threaded through coffins in the past so if the deceased woke up, tugging the cord would ring a signal above the grave. Neither emergency ropes, bells, nor whistles are built into modern caskets, but did I have something new and better? Had Nick put my purse in the casket? Did I have my cell phone? I scissored my legs back and forth in the small space but felt only confinement. I patted beside my body. No purse. I felt the innerspring mattress. I knew. I was in Bobby Saxon's original bronze Exquisite casket.

Pain and panic rose. *Think, Callie, think,* I told myself and made a conscious effort to calm down. I'd solved the murders. Well, it would have been better if I'd figured it all out before getting in Nick's Envoy, but I'd pegged the casket theft on Nick. Given a little more time, I would've put it all together. Nick Rivers had confessed to me, but who would ever know about it if I died locked in Bobby Saxon's coffin? Locked in? No, Nick had told me he broke the lock to find that the casket was empty.

Pressing both hands against the top of the casket, I pushed with my whole body. The lid didn't budge. I beat on it. I shouted. I hit it harder with my fists. I kicked. Nothing. Not even a glimmer of light at the edges.

The Exquisite was equipped with a sealer gasket to make it waterproof. Had Nick figured out how to activate the seal after he broke into it? How long before the air ran out? What time was it? When I didn't call at ten thirty, would Jane just think I'd misplaced the cell phone again? If Nick had buried me somewhere, I hoped he'd sealed me in. I'd rather run out of air than suffer a long, starving death underground. *Insects!* I panicked when I thought of bugs in the dirt.

I sobbed with terror and self-pity. I felt wet. Was the casket already leaking or was I sweating that much? My body trembled and shook with fear and cold. An ache in my chest again. Not sharp and stabbing. Crushing agony. I felt for the lid of the casket to see if somehow it had collapsed on me since I'd beaten on it. It was still in place.

I couldn't catch my breath. I panted like Big Boy. Thoughts of my puppy brought a fresh flow of tears. My dog would miss me. I wept for my family. Daddy and The Boys aren't the most refined men in the world, but they love me. I was scared I would suffocate. I tried to figure how much oxygen would be in a casket the size of the Exquisite. How long would it last? How long had I been here?

My breath came faster and faster. I was hyperventilating. I knew that would use the oxygen up even faster, but

I couldn't stop myself. My brain fogged. Tingling in my face and fingertips. I couldn't stay awake. I tried to turn over onto my side, but the top was too close. I saw dots splattered across the darkness in my closed eyes. I gulped for air.

Thought nothing.

I felt myself going.

Nothing.

# Chapter Twenty-nine

oices.

Pounding.

"Get me another crowbar."

My prison rocked and lurched.

My body banged against the walls.

"Hold that flashlight right here. He's nailed it shut."

The voices drifted in and out of my mind. My head slammed against the satin-covered metal. I felt warm slipperiness running across my forehead, puddling at my eyes and spreading over my cheeks.

Blood. I could smell my own blood.

Sirens wailed in the distance.

Light.

Barely a sliver of light.

I moaned.

"She's alive! I hear her."

"We've got it open!"

More light. Movement. A human form over me. Nick

Rivers. I screamed. Only in my mind. My eyes were closed tight.

Hands lifted me from my prison. Pressed me down gently. A stretcher?

Someone held my left arm, extended it, patted the inside of my elbow. "Her veins are rolling like crazy. I can't get the needle in."

I wrenched my arm. Trying to escape the hands. No needles. NO NEEDLES!

"Callie." A familiar voice.

"It's over, Callie. You're okay." Sheriff Harmon.

Hands tugged. Hands probed. Wiped the wetness from my face.

Sirens wailed.

Flying.

I felt like I was flying.

# Chapter Thirty

**S**unlight cascaded through the vertical blinds at the window. I closed my eyes and wondered if it had all been hallucinations. The scary ride in the Envoy. Nick's confession. Bobby Saxon's casket. My rescue. The ambulance ride.

"She's awake." John.

"Are you sure?" Odell.

"Her eyes blinked." John again.

"I'll get the doc." Odell again.

"Little Sister, can you hear me?" John said. He must have been leaning over my hospital bed because I felt his presence. "We love you, Callie. Everything's okay now. Wake up."

Awareness of movement.

The next sound was Dr. Donald Walters. "Callie? I want you to open your eyes."

"I don't want to look at you, Don," I whispered.

He laughed. "I'm not Don right now. I'm your doctor. I need to look into your eyes."

I didn't even try to open my eyes. The doctor put gloved fingers on my face and pried my right eyelid up with his forefinger.

IV lines extended from the arm I raised to block the glare from the window.

"Someone please close those blinds," Don said and released my eyelid. I opened the eye again.

With the room darker, I could see better. Don leaned over me on my right side while John and Jane stood by my left. Jane was patting my hand. Daddy, Odell, and Otis hovered at the foot of the bed.

"You're in the hospital," Don said, "but you're going to be fine."

Sirens wailed. Not real. Memories.

"Did I come in an ambulance?"

"Yes, EMS brought you here from the Halsey farm. Do you remember any of it?"

"It was Bobby Saxon's casket, wasn't it?" I asked.

"Yes," said John, "the one that was stolen."

"Nick did it," I said. "Nick Rivers killed Bobby and June Bug and left me in the casket. I thought he'd buried me." I tried to sit up. Don gently touched my shoulder and I lay back.

"No," John said. "The casket was aboveground in the barn at Halsey's. Sheriff Harmon found you there and called EMS."

"How'd he know to look for me?"

John glanced at Jane. "When you didn't call Jane at ten thirty like you promised, she got worried. When you hadn't called by eleven, she called Sheriff Harmon and told him about your plans to question Nick. Harmon's old buddy Hank LeGrand, Charleston's chief of police, was able to have Nick located at the Halsey place through the OnStar device on the new Envoy."

John patted my cheek. "Little Sister, you weren't buried and Nick denies you were going to be, but when Harmon arrived at the Halsey farm, Nick was digging a hole big enough for the casket. Why'd you go out with him if you thought he was the killer?"

"I didn't suspect Nick at first. I suspected Betty because she lied about Bobby drinking, but she was trying to justify saying she'd planned to leave Bobby when he was the one who wanted a separation. Then I suspected Odell," I said.

"Me?" Odell asked. "Why me?"

"Because you lied. You weren't where you said. You didn't go to your meeting in Columbia that Monday. Where were you?" I said.

Odell blushed bright red all the way to the top of his bald head. "I was driving on I-26 headed to the meeting, listening to Cousin Roger on WXYW on the radio, and he started advertising this new barbecue buffet in Charlotte. It sounded so good, I just drove on up to Charlotte and checked it out."

I laughed. "Wish you'd told me that when you came back." My thoughts turned more serious. "I suspected Nick of stealing the casket and wanted to talk to him. By the time I realized he was the killer, I was there with him. Where's Nick now?" I asked.

"He's in jail," Daddy said and moved around the bed up toward Don. "And I hope he escapes or makes bail because I want to get my hands on him."

"Yeah, me, too," Odell rasped. "But it's not likely Rivers will be out. Harmon told me they found a lot of physical evidence in the Halsey barn, including the gun that killed June Bug as well as a case of ketamine and a humongous stash of street drugs. Once they knew where to look, the evidence ties Rivers straight to the casket and to the deaths of both Bobby and June Bug." He shrugged. "So far nothing points to Betty being a part of the murders. 'Course, she's mighty ticked off that Eileen is probably going to collect Bobby's insurance."

"Nick confessed he killed Bobby thinking Betty would get the insurance money, but he said Betty didn't know it," I said. "He planned to get back with her for the money. When he learned Eileen might be the legal beneficiary, he planned to date her. I would have figured it all out quicker except for Cowboy's confession and that Special K in his car. What does Sheriff Harmon think about that now?"

"Nick probably planted the drug in Cowboy's car," Daddy said.

"What about Cowboy's confession?" I asked.

"Sheriff Harmon will want to talk to you as soon as I tell him you're up to it," Don said. "He'll probably tell you Cowboy's not the first innocent person to confess. He seems to be a classic attention-seeker."

Jane interrupted, "I told you that Wee Willie liked to show off."

"Wee Willie?" Don repeated.

"Don't worry about that. It didn't have anything to do with the killings." I waved my hand in dismissal. "I thought I was having hallucinations." I struggled again to sit forward, but gave up and leaned back against the pillow. "Nick lunged at me with a syringe and needle. I jumped away. The next thing I knew I woke up in the Exquisite. I was sure Nick shot me full of Special K." A tear slipped down my cheek.

"He tried, but very little of the ketamine actually entered your body," Don said.

"Why? What happened?"

"The needle went into your chest."

"My chest?"

Don laughed. "The sheriff has your undergarment. He needs it for evidence."

"My what?"

"Your bra, Callie, your inflatable bra," said Jane.

"Nick pressed the plunger when the needle touched your blouse," Don said. "By the time the needle penetrated skin, most of the drug was in the air space of your special bra."

"Then why am I here in the hospital?"

"You did get a little of the drug, but you're here because you've been unconscious since the sheriff found you. Your only new injury is a gash on your forehead where you apparently hit the side of the casket. Scans haven't shown any new concussion to your brain." Don patted my arm. "You'll probably be able to go home tomorrow. Apparently your mind was protecting you by blanking out. It's not uncommon." He smiled. "By the way, you missed your date with me Sunday night. You owe me one."

"Don't you think dating me and that nurse the same night might have been a bit much?" Buh-leeve me. I wasn't too weak to rev up a nasty tone.

"I'd already decided to cancel my date with the nurse when I asked you out for Sunday night."

"Don't do me any favors, *Dr. Walters*."

"Little Sister, the doc has been here round the clock since they brought you in during the wee hours of Saturday morning," John scolded me, "and it's Monday afternoon."

I ignored John and continued talking to Don. "I know all about your taking every woman to Andre's the first date and bringing Chinese food or a picnic the second," I accused.

"Guilty as charged." Don grinned. "Tell you what. You plan our next date."

"I might just do that."

"And you don't have to wear your special bra, since the sheriff has it."

"Don't worry," I said. "I have a whole drawer full of them. Never know when a blow-up bra might save a life."